THE BROTHERS O'BRIEN
THE KILLING SEASON

THE BROTHERS O'BRIEN
THE KILLING SEASON

WILLIAM W. JOHNSTONE

with J. A. Johnstone

PINNACLE BOOKS
Kensington Publishing Corp.
www.kensingtonbooks.com

PINNACLE BOOKS are published by

Kensington Publishing Corp.
119 West 40th Street
New York, NY 10018

PUBLISHER'S NOTE
Following the death of William W. Johnstone, the Johnstone family is working with a carefully selected writer to organize and complete Mr. Johnstone's outlines and many unfinished manuscripts to create additional novels in all of his series like The Last Gunfighter, Mountain Man, and Eagles, among others. This novel was inspired by Mr. Johnstone's superb storytelling.

All Kensington titles, imprints, and distributed lines are available at special quantity discounts for bulk purchases for sales promotions, premiums, fund-raising, educational, or institutional use. Special book excerpts or customized printings can also be created to fit specific needs. For details, write or phone the office of the Kensington special sales manager: Kensington Publishing Corp., 119 West 40th Street, New York, NY 10018, attn: Special Sales Department; phone 1-800-221-2647.

PINNACLE BOOKS and the Pinnacle logo are Reg. U.S. Pat. & TM Off.
The WWJ steer head logo is a trademark of Kensington Publishing Corp.

ISBN-13: : 978-0-7860-3110-8
ISBN-10: 0-7860-3110-7

First printing: March 2013

10 9 8 7 6 5 4 3 2 1

Printed in the United States of America

Chapter One

Luther Ironside leaned forward in the saddle. "Well, lookee there, Colonel. I ain't seen something like that in a coon's age, with the times a-changing the way they are."

"Stage out of Lordsburg, I'd say." Colonel Shamus O'Brien sat upright on his horse. "Three, no, four holdup men. I missed one."

Ironside nodded. "Any of our business, Colonel?"

Shamus considered that for a spell, then shook his head. "I don't see how it is, us being no part of the law here and with our own pressing business to attend to."

"They're getting the passengers out." Ironside pointed his finger in the direction of the stagecoach. "And the driver's climbing down. Keeping his hand away from his gun. Now that's savvy of him."

"Is there a strongbox on board, you reckon?" Shamus asked.

"I doubt it. They're more likely to be carrying passengers to Recoil or down Sonora way."

"Yes, you're right. The bandits are collecting the folks' valuables, looks like. Well, that's too bad." Shamus glanced at the sky. "Best be on our way, Luther, if we expect to reach Recoil before nightfall."

Ironside frowned. "I wonder if we'll ever see another one, a stage holdup, I mean."

"It's unlikely, Luther. The West is changing fast, but for better or for worse I can't really tell. The sight you see down there is going the way of the Indian and the buffalo."

"It's a pity, Colonel. I sure liked the old way better. Hey look, feller down there looks like he's refusing to hand over his watch or wallet or something. Even from here, I'd say he's real mad."

A revolver shot racketed, drawing Ironside's attention back to the stagecoach. "Aw hell, now why did he have to go and do that?"

One of the outlaws held a smoking Colt in his right fist and watched a man in black broadcloth slide down the side of the stage and collapse against a front wheel, his head hanging. Another man and a couple of women shrank away from the dead man and even from their position on a rise in the foothills of the Little Hatchet Mountains, Shamus and Ironside heard a woman scream.

Ironside looked at his longtime friend. "Now what, Colonel?"

Shamus sighed. "Well, a murder makes it our business, Luther. I can stand aside from an honest robbery, but not a murder."

"There's four of them bandits down there, Colonel. How do we play it?"

"Like we've always played it, Luther." Shamus drew his Colt. "We charge home at the gallop, of course."

"Like I said, four-to-one odds, Colonel," Ironside said, skinning his own revolver.

Shamus smiled that old, reckless grin Ironside remembered from the late war. "We charged Yankees at ten times those odds and scattered them." Shamus stared at his friend. "Unless you're getting too old for this kind of horse cavalry warfare, Luther?"

"Colonel, I'll be charging so fast your buckskin's nose is gonna be stuck up my hoss's ass. Watch this old man and see how it's done." Ironside let rip with a wild rebel yell and charged down the slope, Shamus right after him, hollering just as loudly.

They rode knee to knee as bullets split the air

around them and Ironside grinned and yelled, "Just like the old days, huh, Colonel?"

"Only then I'd have a cavalry brigade behind me," Shamus pointed out.

"You don't need a brigade when you got me, by God," Ironside hollered.

Two of the outlaws ran from the cover of the stagecoach and for a moment watched the oncoming riders. Standing in the open scrub desert, they threw Winchesters to their shoulders.

Ironside fired and one of the bandits went down, his rifle spinning away from him. The other man fired, and Shamus's hat flew off his head. Enraged at getting a bullet hole in a new, four-dollar Stetson, Shamus charged directly at the outlaw, his Colt spitting fire. Hit hard, the surviving robber staggered, then rose on tiptoe and fell on his face.

Events crowding in on him faster than his brain could register, Shamus was vaguely aware of hearing a shot behind the stage, and of Ironside chasing a fleeing man across the brush flat.

As the outlaw ran, dust erupted from his pounding boots and he glanced fearfully over his shoulder at the fast-approaching Ironside and snapped off shots, his arm fully extended.

Finally, realizing he couldn't outrun a horse, the man, a gangly towhead with mean eyes, stopped, tossed away his revolver, and threw up his hands.

But grim old Ironside, a man not much inclined to mercy in the heat of battle, gunned the towhead down right where he stood. He looked around for another enemy, saw none, and trotted back to the stagecoach.

Shamus had dismounted and now, his face troubled, he kneeled beside the shot passenger, who was gasping his last.

Standing over the body of the fourth outlaw was an older, respectable-looking man with iron-gray hair and mustache. His face was ashen and he held a smoking Smith & Wesson .32 caliber sneaky gun in his hand.

Ironside nodded toward the outlaw and said to the gray-haired man, "You do fer him, mister?"

The stage passenger nodded. In a tight voice he said, "I've never killed a man before." Then for some reason he felt the need to add, "My name is Silas Shaw. I am a merchant in Recoil."

"Don't worry, Shaw, your second dead man will be easier." Ironside turned his attention to the two frightened women who looked like mother and daughter, and touched his hat. "Ladies. Where are you headed?"

The stage driver answered for them. "Recoil. That is, if we ever get there."

"You'll get there," Ironside answered. "Me and my boss are headed to the same place our ownselves."

"Then God help you," the driver said. He was a tall, lanky man with sad eyes, as though handling the reins of a stagecoach team made a man downright melancholy.

"Heard you've been having trouble around this neck of the woods." Ironside nodded in the direction of the dead outlaw. "Was this a part of it?"

The driver shook his head. "Hell, no. That there is Jud Slide, and the ranny you gunned was his brother Clay. T'other two I don't know, but a while back Jud and Clay ran with Billy Bonney and that hard crowd over to Lincoln County way. I reckon they was facing hard times and held up my stage on account of how they was trying to make a few dollars without working for it."

"Who shot the passenger?" Ironside asked.

"Jud did that, afore the gent over there put a bullet in him."

"Who was he? The dead passenger, I mean."

"Him?" the driver asked, as though he was surprised at Ironside's question. "His name was Banjo Ben Barker. He did a blackface song-and-dance act and juggled Indian clubs."

"Hell, why did Jud gun him?" Ironside asked.

"Didn't like how Ben played the banjo, I guess."

"The passenger's done for," Shamus said, stepping beside Ironside's horse. "He was still alive when I got to him, but he died pretty quick. Who was he?"

"A banjo player," Ironside replied.

"That's a good enough reason as any to get shot," Shamus said. He looked at the driver. "I didn't get your name."

"Maybe that's because I didn't put it out. It's Tom Gill."

"Well, Tom, let's get the dead man in the stage," Shamus directed.

"What about the rest of them bandits?" Gill said.

"If the law wants 'em, they can come get them. You're responsible only for your passengers, dead or alive."

"All right, folks, back into the stage, and make room for a dead man," Gill called.

The older of the two women, her long, angular face outraged, used her rolled-up parasol like a sword and poked it into the driver's ribs. "Young man, I'm not riding with a corpse, and neither is my daughter."

"Then you'll have to walk to Recoil alongside the stage, ma'am." Gill rubbed his chest.

"Indeed we will not walk, you impertinent thing," the woman snapped. "We paid for our tickets and we'll ride in the stage. And your employers will hear of this."

"The dead man paid for his ticket too, ma'am." Gill's remark brought parasol blows raining down on his shoulders. He backed away, his hands up to defend himself from the woman's attack.

Shamus stepped between them, receiving a few parasol smacks himself before he was able to grab the weapon. "I have a solution."

"You'd better have," the woman said, her parasol poised over Shamus's head. "My late husband wore the blue and I will not be treated in this way."

"Well, that's a pity." Ironside looked at Shamus. "Ain't it, Colonel?"

"What did you say?" the woman demanded, her eyes bright with anger.

"I said it's a pity you're being treated this way," Ironside lied, "and you the widow of a dead Yankee, an all."

The woman stared at him, considering that for a few moments, but his face was empty. Finally she said, "I should think it is a pity . . . and an outrage." She advanced on Gill again, but he backtracked hurriedly away from her.

"I have an answer, Mrs., ah . . . ," Shamus said.

"My name is Mrs. Edith Ludsthorpe, of the Boston Ludsthorpes, and this is my daughter Chastity."

Ironside suddenly had a coughing fit and put his hand over his mouth.

Shamus gave him a look. "We'll put the dead man on the roof and that way, dear lady, you won't be made uncomfortable by his presence."

"And who are you, sir?" Edith Ludsthorpe demanded.

"Colonel Shamus O'Brien of the Dromore O'Briens." He bowed. "At your service, madam."

"You have the lineaments of a gentleman, Colonel." Edith glared at the cringing Tom Gill. "A quality most singularly lacking in this territory, I'll be bound."

"Indeed, madam." Shamus tipped his hat. "Now if you and your daughter can enter the stage, we can be on our way."

"And the deceased gentleman?"

"We'll get him on top of the coach directly, ma'am."

Edith shook her head. "The very idea," she huffed as she shepherded the pretty but silent Chastity into her seat.

Chapter Two

Recoil lay a couple of miles west of Hatchet Gap, surrounded by the Playas Valley, a vast, dry ocean of sand, scrub, cactus, rock, and lava beds. The town seemed to have no reason for being there, as though it had wandered across the Continental Divide from the east and lost its way in that hot, brutal annex of hell. It looked raw and new, a town thrown together from rough-sawn timber and boundless optimism. The settlement's single street was lined on both sides with buildings, some still under construction, but a few of the grander structures boasted false fronts while others were still roofed with canvas.

As Shamus and Ironside escorted the stage into town, its grim burden sprawled on the roof, Shamus saw a couple of saloons, stores, and a livery stable and corrals at the far end of the street. Some shacks and a few grander, gingerbread houses, the residences of the town's merchants, lay scattered around the town's center.

A false-fronted, two-story building, the queen of Recoil, sported a painted canvas banner above the door.

THE REST AND BE THANKFUL HOTEL
We stock only the finest liquors & cigars

The stage, followed by a billowing dust cloud, jolted to a halt outside a narrow shack with a warped roof and rough timber door. But what caught Shamus's eye was the incongruous sight of a polished brass plaque, screwed to the door, that bore the word *SHERIFF* in gold lettering.

After the dust cloud caught up to the stage, sifted over the passengers, and moved on, Tom Gill cupped his gloved hand to his mouth and yelled from the driver's seat, "Hey, Sheriff, we got trouble here."

The few people who'd braved the afternoon heat of the boardwalk stopped and watched as the lawman's door opened and a tall, slender man with the face of a warrior poet and a star on his vest stepped outside. His eyes went directly to the dead man. "What happened, Tom?"

"Four holdup men jumped us south of the dry lake," Gill explained. "They done fer Banjo Ben and then one of the passengers and these

gents"—he jerked a thumb over his shoulder—
"done for them."

Jim Clitherow's stare flicked at Shamus and
Ironside, but showed no sign of recognition.
"Any idea who the holdup men were, Tom?"

"Sure I know. Well, I recognized two of them at
least, Jud Slide and his brother Clay."

"And they're dead? All four of them?" Clitherow asked.

"Dead as they're ever gonna be, Sheriff. Like I
said, a passenger done for one of them and
these gents gunned t'other three, including Jud
and Clay."

The lawman frowned. "I thought the Slide
brothers had headed out Missouri way."

"You thought wrong, Sheriff, and their bodies
are lying out in the desert to prove it," Gill said.

Clitherow nodded. "See to your passengers, Tom."

He looked around at the growing crowd of
gawkers. "One of you men get Elijah Doddle.
Tell him I've got work for him." He waved at
Shamus and Ironside, his eyes neither friendly
nor hostile. "You two come inside, and I want the
passenger who did the shooting."

Ironside angled a glance at Shamus. "I've had
warmer welcomes."

"Me, too. You sure we got the right Clitherow?"

* * *

"You clearly acted in self-defense, Mr. Shaw. I see no need to detain you further."

Shaw stood before the sheriff, looking worried. "I never killed a man before. I'm not a gunman. I own a dry goods store, for God's sake."

"You did well, Silas," Clitherow said. "No one is blaming you for what happened."

"But what will Mrs. Shaw think? I can only imagine—"

"I'm sure she'll be proud of you, as we all are in Recoil."

Shaw looked at Ironside and Shamus sitting in the visitors' chairs in front of the desk. "I had no choice. I mean, no choice at all."

Ironside nodded. "Happens that way sometimes."

"It's a hard, hard thing to kill a man." Shaw shook his head. "Take away his life and his past, present, and future."

"No, it ain't hard," Ironside disagreed. "All you do is point your iron at his belly and squeeze the trigger."

Shaw was aghast. "Have you killed a man like that?"

"Hell, sure I have. But not so many that you'd notice. Call it a baker's dozen."

Shaw took a step back, his hands trembling. "Oh, Lord help me, I've joined the company of gunmen."

"You got that right, Shaw." Ironside smiled. "Now every tinhorn pistolero and wild kid hunting a rep will come lookin' for you. Hell, Shaw, you're the man who shot Jud Slide."

A look of sheer horror crossed Shaw's face. His eyes wild, he stumbled to the door and fumbled with the handle. "Martha!" he hollered.

Ironside rose lazily and stepped to the door, smiling at Shaw as he opened it. "Call it professional courtesy. One gunman to another."

Shaw ran outside and his feet pounded on the boardwalk. "Martha!" he shrieked. "Marthaaa . . ."

Ironside closed the door, his face split in a wide, delighted grin. "Sure spooked ol' Silas, didn't I?"

"You certainly did, you old Johnny Reb." Clitherow said, rose to his feet, and extended his hand. "How are you, Luther?"

"Hell, Jim, so it is you." Ironside shook the lawman's hand. "I thought fer sure you didn't recognize me."

"Well, you've changed some, but I recognized you straight off. You're not a man easily forgotten. And come to that, neither are you, Colonel O'Brien."

Shamus and Clitherow clasped hands. "It's been

long years since the war, Jim. We've grown older, but probably no wiser."

Clitherow nodded. "It's been long for the South, Colonel."

"Amen to that," Shamus agreed. "Long and mighty hard."

"Three old comrades in arms together again. This calls for a drink." The sheriff produced a bottle and glasses from a drawer in his desk and poured whiskey for his guests.

"If you don't mind me saying so, I see you walk with a limp, Colonel. Is that a souvenir of the war?"

Shamus smiled. "No, Captain Clitherow—"

"Call me Jim, please."

"Then you'll call me Shamus."

Clitherow bowed his head. "I am honored."

"The limp is a souvenir all right, but from an Apache war lance. Landed me in a wheelchair for years until a young surgeon operated on me." Shamus tried his Old Crow and nodded. "Now I can get around just fine."

"Riding a long distance pains him some," Ironside put in.

Clitherow smiled. "At our age even riding a short distance pains us some."

"How come you pretended not to know us when we brought the stage in, Cap'n?" Ironside asked.

The sheriff frowned. "The war's over and we lost, Luther. Please call me Jim."

"All right, Jim. Same question. How come?"

"I think it would be safer for both of you if you weren't associated with me. At least for the time being."

"You're talking about the night riders?" Shamus asked.

"Yes. I think I told you in my letter that they shot up the town about two weeks ago and killed a storekeeper named Fred Rawlings, another man who wore the gray."

"Are they targeting only Confederate veterans?" Shamus questioned.

Clitherow shook his head. "No. Hell, they've killed and robbed miners, travelers, and a few days ago a puncher for the D-Bar Ranch over to the Hachita Valley way was murdered and the cattle he was driving were shot. At least some of those dead men were true-blue Yankees and Republicans."

"I don't see a motive, Jim," Shamus said. "There isn't much profit in robbing a tinpan for his poke and a drover for his horse and saddle."

"And why shoot up Recoil, a one-hoss town in the middle of a wilderness that God started and forgot to finish?" Ironside asked. "Beggin' your pardon, Jim, you being the law here an' all."

"No offense taken, Luther. I've asked myself

that same question a thousand times and still haven't come up with an answer." Clitherow refilled the glasses. "Some say the riders are skeleton men. They have skulls for faces."

He read the disbelief on Shamus's face and nodded that he was telling the truth. "That's what they say."

"Skeletons don't ride horses, men do," Shamus pointed out. "They're wearing some kind of masks to frighten folks."

"If that's the case, they're succeeding," Clitherow said.

"You scared, Jim?" Ironside asked.

"Luther! What kind of question is that to ask a man?" Shamus glared at his segundo.

Clitherow smiled. "I don't mind. To answer your question, Luther, yeah, I'm scared. But not just for myself. I'm scared for the whole damned town."

Chapter Three

Ironside sat on the corner of the creaking bed in room 22 of the Rest and Be Thankful Hotel. "The cap'n asked for our help, Colonel, but he doesn't know how we can help him. Now that's confusing for a man."

Shamus laid a folded clean shirt into the dresser drawer, then turned toward his friend. "He may know better when his deputy and the posse get back into town."

"I didn't say nothin' when Jim told us about the posse, but Stutterin' Steve Sparrow is a friend of Jacob's. At least, I've heard Jake talk about him."

"If he's a friend of Jacob's, I shudder to think what kind of deputy sheriff he is," Shamus drawled.

Ironside didn't look up from the cigarette he was building. "Way Jake tells it, ol' Steve rode with Jesse and them for a spell, then went into the bank robbing business for his ownself."

Ironside licked his cigarette closed and lit it. Behind a cloud of blue smoke he said, "But he never made a go of it. See, with the stutter an' all, by the time he could get out, 'This is a holdup,' the law had already arrived. He did two years in Yuma and then took up the lawman's profession."

"Are you sure it's the same ranny?" Shamus asked.

"How many Stutterin' Steve Sparrows could there be, Colonel?"

"Well, if it's the same man, I'm sure Jesse and Frank taught him the outlaw trade well. He could be in cahoots with the Night Riders, or Bone Men, or whatever you want to call them."

"He could be, Colonel. He could be at that." Ironside thought for a few moments. "Jake said Steve is mighty fast with the iron, faster than Jesse or any of them boys."

"If Jacob says he's fast, then that's bound to be the case. For some reason my son studies on such things."

"Of course, ol' Stutterin' Steve could've got religion and now all he wants is to stay on the right side of the law."

"It's possible," Shamus agreed. "It's not for us to prejudge a man."

"Damn right, Colonel. When you take the

measure of a man, take the whole measure. That's what I say."

"You're a paragon of virtue, Luther."

"Damn right. Whatever the hell *paragon* means."

Shamus settled his hat on his head and buckled on his gun belt. "I've been eating trail grub for a week. Let's go get an early breakfast. I've got a hankering for eggs."

Ironside rose to his feet. "Suits me just fine."

Shamus opened his mouth to say something but never uttered a word. At that moment room 22 exploded.

The shattering, earsplitting blast knocked Shamus off his feet. Ironside landed on the bed and it collapsed under his crashing weight.

Plaster and roof slats showered down and the partition wall separating the room from the hallway was blown clear across the floor. Dust and smoke drifted like a thick gray fog and the acrid smell of gunpowder hung in the air.

Ironside shoved debris off his body, his curses turning the air blue. Somewhere a woman screamed and kept on screaming and a man's voice rose in frightened outrage.

To his surprise, Ironside saw right into the room across the hall. The blast had taken out the wall on that side, too. A naked blond woman sat upright in a brass bed, shrieking in terror, and a gray-haired, potbellied man, just as naked, ran around squawking like a chicken, black powder burns on his jiggling posterior.

Ironside struggled to his feet and touched his hat to the screaming lady. Not seeing his boss, he yelled, "Colonel, are you all right?"

A pile of rubble on the floor moved. "Get me the hell out of here, Luther."

Ironside turned and called, "Are you hurt?"

"How the hell should I know?" Shamus said angrily. "Jesus, Mary, and Joseph, and all the holy saints in heaven, I might already be as dead as Murphy's goose."

"Hold on, Colonel, I'm on my way." It took Ironside three frantic minutes to lift debris off the colonel's body. Fortunately it was just wood and plaster, and fairly light, because the fireplace and brick chimney were not damaged in the blast.

"Are you in pain, Colonel?" Ironside asked, his face concerned as he raised Shamus to a sitting position. "How is your back?"

"My back hurts." Shamus glared at Ironside. "Who did this?"

Ironside shook his head. "I don't know, Colonel."

"Then whoever he is, may he roast in hell

and not have a drop of porter to quench his eternal thirst."

"Can you get to your feet?"

"Take my hand and pull."

Ironside hauled Shamus erect. "You feel all right? How are the legs?"

"I'm fine."

"Are you sure, Colonel?"

"Don't fuss, Luther. I told you I'm fine."

Sheriff Jim Clitherow kicked debris aside and appeared in the hallway, now just a smoky open space. "You boys hurt?"

"We're all right," Shamus said. "But my ears are still ringing."

Ironside nodded to the room across the hall. "The feller over there got his butt burned."

The man and the woman were struggling into their clothes, both of them streaked with black soot from the ruined fireplace, as though they'd been sweeping its chimney.

"That's Higgy Wells, the church deacon," Clitherow said.

"Is he married?" Shamus asked.

"Yes." Clitherow nodded. "He's got a missus who dresses out at around three hundred pounds."

"Then he's got some explaining to do, hasn't he?" Shamus pointed out.

Ironside, his shaggy eyebrows and mustache

covered in white plaster dust, yelled, "Hey, deacon! How's your fanny?"

The man cast Ironside a hurried and worried glance, then stumbled out of the ruined room.

"Hey, Higgy," the blonde yelled. "Where's my money?"

"Later!" Wells called out over his shoulder.

"*Now,* you creep!"

But the deacon was already gone, barefooting it downstairs, his shoes and coat in his hands.

The blonde turned her venom on Ironside. "What the hell are you looking at?"

"I was just wondering if the deacon got his money's worth before his butt got scorched."

"Wouldn't you like to know." The woman grabbed her purse, flounced into the shattered hallway, and followed her paramour downstairs.

"Luther, I wish you wouldn't bandy words with fancy women in my presence," Shamus complained. "Especially when we came so close to meeting our Maker."

"You were lucky, Shamus," Clitherow said. "But I don't think the dynamite was set to kill you. It was a warning."

"Hell, Jim," Ironside sniffed. "Look around you. Half the second floor of the damned hotel blew up. That was some kind of warning."

Shamus nodded. "Jim may be right, Luther. If

whoever it was wanted us dead, he would've used more dynamite."

"And blown up the whole hotel," Clitherow declared.

"With us in it," Shamus added. "I think whoever it was wants us away from Recoil and back in Dromore."

"Was it them skeleton riders?" Ironside asked.

"Could be," Clitherow speculated. "Or someone associated with them."

"Who even knows we're here to help you, Jim?" Ironside asked.

The sheriff shook his head. "Nobody."

"Then it's a mystery," Shamus decided.

"The mystery is how anyone can get a wink of sleep around here."

Shamus turned and saw a tall, handsome young man in an elegant gray suit smiling at him. A large diamond glittered in his cravat and another sparkled from the little finger of his left hand.

The man stared at the destruction. "Someone eat too many refried beans last night?"

"No," Ironside snapped. "Some lowdown snake tried to kill us."

"Or scare us," Shamus added.

"Well, he scared the hell out of me," the young man said. "And just when I was dreaming that Lily

Langtry and I were taking a carriage ride along the Champs-Élysées on our way to breakfast."

Ironside looked baffled. "Mister, I don't know what the hell you're talking about."

The young man looked Ironside over from his scuffed boots to the top of his battered hat. "No, you wouldn't, would you?" He touched the rim of his bowler. "Well, good morning, gentlemen, and please don't play with any more dynamite." He stepped carefully over the mess and made his way down the stairs.

Ironside looked at the sheriff. "Jim, who the hell was the dude?"

"Beats me. Some kind of Yankee drummer maybe."

"Well, I don't like him."

Clitherow opened his mouth to speak, but was interrupted by a small, dark man with the scared, furtive eyes of a henpecked husband. "Sheriff," he wailed, "look what's happened to my hotel."

"I can see it, Orville," Clitherow said.

"What . . . I mean . . . how?" the little man sputtered.

"Dynamite," Ironside pointed out bluntly.

"Dynamite?" Orville Askew repeated.

"Dynamite," Ironside said again.

"These gentlemen were the target of a possible assassination attempt," Clitherow explained.

"In my hotel?"

"Seems like, don't it?" Ironside said.

Askew wrung his hands. "Who's going to pay for this?"

"Talk to the ranny who planted the dynamite, Orville," Ironside said dryly.

"Someone has to pay," Askew said. Getting no response, he pointed to Ironside and Shamus. "You two must leave my hotel at once. Another attempt on your lives and I'll have no hotel left."

"I don't think it will happen again," Shamus said calmly. "At least, not with dynamite or giant powder."

Orville Askew was unconvinced. "Sheriff, I want these men out of my hotel now. I mean this very minute. My God, we're all going to be murdered in our beds. Think of my poor wife."

Shamus's face turned red. "We'll leave. I will not dwell under a man's roof who doesn't want me there."

"Then see that you do." Askew pointed to the stairway. "I don't want troublemakers here, especially damned micks."

Ironside grabbed him by the shirtfront and hoisted him until the toes of the man's boots were not touching the ground.

"Luther, put him down," Shamus cried.

"Can I shake him a little, Colonel?"

"No. Put him down. The poor man is distraught over his hotel and he speaks out of ignorance."

Ironside pulled Askew so close, their noses touched. "Orville, I'm not a mick, though I am closely associated with such."

"I-I'm sorry," Askew stuttered.

"Don't apologize to me, Orville. Apologize to Colonel O'Brien."

Askew turned his head, his eyes frightened. "I'm sorry."

"Your apology is accepted." Shamus looked at Ironside. "Put him down now, Luther."

Ironside opened his hand and let Askew drop. He patted the little man on the head, smiled, and whispered, "If you ever insult the colonel again, Orville, I'll kill you."

Thoroughly frightened, the owner stumbled along the rubble-strewn hallway, stopped at the top of the stairs, and yelled, "I want you two hoodlums out of my hotel."

Then he fled.

Clitherow crossed his arms. "Luther, you're not a forgiving man, are you?"

"Damn right I'm not."

Chapter Four

"Damn it, Luther, we're too old to sleep in a livery stable," Shamus complained. "And too old to be spreading our blankets on the ground, come to that. Somehow I always manage to bed down on a rock."

"I have a couple of empty cells, Shamus," Clitherow offered. "Iron cots and straw mattresses, I'm afraid, but I can supply clean blankets."

"Hell, Jim, anything's better than lying on horse dung," Ironside said.

"You're very kind," Shamus said. "But I don't want you to go to any trouble for us."

"It's no problem. I have a cabin at the edge of town," the sheriff said. "It's about the size of a closet, but it's enough for my needs. I sent the orphan kid who slept in the jailhouse to Dromore with my message and he never came back."

"Jacob takes all kinds of waifs and strays under

his wing and he gave the kid a job at Dromore," Ironside explained.

Exhausted, Shamus quickly put an end to the conversation. "We gratefully accept the hospitality of your jail."

The pretty young Ma's Kitchen waitress refilled coffee cups and smiled, revealing good teeth. "How were your steak and eggs, gentlemen?"

"Just fine, Molly." Clitherow help up his cup.

Ironside looked up at the girl as she filled his cup. "Molly, who is the dude in the gray suit sitting with his back to the wall?"

The girl smiled again. "Ooh, he's very handsome, isn't he?"

"I didn't notice," Ironside said sarcastically. "But who is he?"

"I don't know. I expect he's just passing through, unfortunately." Molly refilled Shamus's cup and turned her attention to the next table.

Shamus took a sip. "Luther, if you're so all-fired determined to know the man's name, why don't you ask him?"

"Hell, no, I'm not doing that. He might be on the scout and I'd embarrass him."

"He troubles you, Luther?" Clitherow asked. "You think he may have planted the dynamite?"

"Nah, I don't think that. Dudes like that just grate on me, is all."

Shamus coughed. "To change the subject, Jim, when do you expect your deputy to return to Recoil?"

"He sent a rider to tell me he'd be back today."

"I hope he's got some news for us. We can't fight an invisible enemy."

Ironside eyed the door. "Uh-oh, I see gun trouble coming down."

A tall, gaunt man had just stepped inside. Dressed in the black broadcloth pants, boiled white shirt, and string tie of the frontier gunman-gambler, he wore an ivory-handled Colt yellowed with age on his right hip. His eyes were almost hidden in the shadows cast by his shaggy black eyebrows.

Silence fell on the crowded restaurant.

A chair scraped. The man in the expensive gray suit tensed.

Jim Clitherow stood, but the gaunt man nailed him with eyes the color of green ice. "Sit down, lawman. This is none of your concern."

Ironside, familiar with the codes and manners of gun fighting men, whispered, "Stay out of it, Jim. He'll kill you."

A look of puzzlement came over Clitherow's face.

"He'll kill you, Jim," Ironside whispered again.

Shamus studied the tall man who had stopped in the middle of the floor. "Sit down, Jim," he said, his voice low and urgent.

Confused, Clitherow still heeded the colonel's warning and sat.

"Some men are better left alone," Shamus said. "That is one of them."

The tall man spoke, his lips barely moving under his mustache. "You know why I'm here, Dallas Steele. I'm calling you out."

"I reckoned on this happening, Seth." The man in the gray suit showed no sign of a weapon. "I thought you might come after me."

"Calvin Downs was just twenty-three years old."

"Your brother was old enough to kill three men in Horse Neck, working for a rich man who wanted to get richer at the expense of everybody else."

"Downs was all right." Seth shrugged his shoulders.

"He was a snake, Seth. You knew it then and you know it now."

"Damn you, he was my brother, and you killed him. I can't let that pass."

"I guess you can't, Seth. You know I'll kill you, don't you?"

"I have to try."

"Walk away from it, Seth. Downs made his

reputation killing old men and farm boys. A tinhorn like that isn't worth dying for."

"I'm faster than Downs, Dallas," Seth said.

"Downs wasn't fast. He didn't come close to being fast."

"I have to try."

Dallas nodded, but said nothing. He looked pained, like a man recalling old, unhappy memories of similar situations that had gone before.

Clitherow tried to rise to his feet, but Ironside held him down. "You're outclassed here, Jim. You stay put."

But Clitherow pulled out of Ironside's grasp and stood, his hand dropping for his gun.

"Damn you, Steele!" Seth yelled.

And he drew.

He was fast. Lightning fast. His gun had even cleared leather when Dallas Steele's bullet crashed between his eyes.

For a single, horrified moment before the darkness took him, Seth Benson, gunman, gambler, man killer, learned what a fast draw really meant.

Jim Clitherow pulled free of Ironside as scared patrons stampeded for the door. "It's over," he yelled. "Go back to your seats and finish breakfast."

"Damn you, Clitherow," a miner in a plaid shirt

and lace-up boots said. "You served us up a dead man for breakfast."

Another male voice claimed that his wife was "all a-tremble" over the killing and other diners muttered their sympathy.

Ironside rose to his feet and in a voice like a thunderclap roared, "The sheriff didn't kill that man."

People looked at each other in puzzlement, then at Ironside.

"I killed him." Dallas Steele walked into the middle of the floor and looked down at the body. "His name was Seth Benson and he called me out."

"Sheriff"—a matronly woman pointed at Steele—"arrest that man."

"For what? It was a fair fight." Ironside was irritated. "Benson went for his gun first and Steele fired in self-defense."

Shamus stood up at the table. "I second that. The gentleman here"—he motioned to Steele—"tried to make it go away. You all heard him."

Several diners muttered agreement and Steele said, "Seth was informed, but he couldn't let it go. It was his way."

Sheriff Clitherow had been silent, but now he looked up at the shooter and said, "You're Dallas Steele, the one they call the Fighting Pink."

"Yes, I believe that's what they call me." Steel gave a little bow. "At your service, Sheriff."

"Are you here in Recoil on official business?" Clitherow asked.

"You could say that. I was asked to assess the situation and report my findings to Washington. This affair with Seth was a complication I neither anticipated nor sought."

Ironside had been the first to declare that Steele had acted in self-defense, but he hadn't warmed to the man. "Where's your gun, mister? The sheriff may want to take it."

Steele pulled back his coat and revealed a short-barreled blue Colt in a shoulder holster. "Do you want my gun, Sheriff?"

"No, I guess not." Clitherow looked around the room. "Somebody get Elijah Doddle. We're sure keeping him busy."

Chapter Five

"First my sleep was interrupted and then my morning coffee. May I join you gentleman and share another pot?" Steele saw the surprise in Shamus's face and added, "I believe we may have a friend in common, Colonel."

"Sit here." The sheriff stood and offered his chair. "I'm going back to my office. Colonel, Luther, I'll see you later." He turned and left the restaurant.

Steele waited to sit down until the sheriff left.

Shamus offered his hand to the young man. "I don't think I've had the pleasure."

"Oh, we haven't met before," Steele said, shaking the colonel's hand. "But I overheard you addressed as Colonel, and you called this gentleman Luther, therefore I assume you are Colonel Shamus O'Brien of Dromore."

Ironside frowned. "Here, have we had gun trouble with you afore?"

Steele smiled. "No, my friend Jacob O'Brien has told me all about you."

Surprised, Ironside asked, "You're a friend of Jake's?"

"Indeed I am. I have him play the piano for me whenever we meet. He's a fine classical musician. And a very complex man."

"It seems that just about everybody knows Jacob," Shamus noted. "He's my son."

"That was my impression, Colonel."

It came grudgingly, but Ironside managed, "Any friend of Jake's is a friend of mine."

"Did you teach Jacob to play the piano, Luther?" Steele asked.

"My sainted wife Saraid taught him how to play," Shamus answered before Ironside could speak. "Luther taught Jacob and my three other sons riding, gun fighting, profanity, whoring, and whiskey drinking. You will notice a notable lack of instruction on Holy Scripture and nothing at all about attendance at church and the partaking of the holy sacraments."

"Damned popery," Ironside growled.

Shamus gave Ironside a sharp look. "What did you say?"

"Nothing, Colonel. I didn't say nothing."

"I should hope not." Shamus peered hard at

his segundo. "Are you sure you didn't mutter something derogatory about the Holy Mother Church?"

Ironside shook his head. "Not a word, Colonel."

Steele saved Ironside from further embarrassment. "Colonel O'Brien, what do you make of this night rider business?"

Before Shamus could answer, the waitress laid a pot of coffee on the table. She looked at Steele. "I know what they are, those night riders."

"Really? Can you enlighten us?"

The girl's brown eyes widened as she leaned forward and whispered, "They're skeleton riders, the living dead come from hell to punish us for our sins."

Shamus crossed himself. "Jesus, Mary, and Joseph and all the saints in heaven preserve and protect us."

"And how do you know this?" Steele asked the waitress.

"I'm walking out with the son of preacher Hall and he says that's what his pa says."

Steele smiled. "Maybe he's right."

The girl glanced over her shoulders, then leaned down closer to Steele. "The night riders carry torches that Preacher Hall says were lit from the very fires of hell."

"Well, we'll be careful we don't get burned." Steele smiled.

"Oh, sir, please don't make a joke, or the demons will ride into town and kill you like they did poor Mr. Rawlings." As though scared by her own talk, the waitress hurried away, leaving behind a scent of lye soap and lavender water.

"People are scared," Shamus said. "But in answer to the question you asked, I don't know what to make of the whole sorry business."

"By my count, the night riders have killed close to a dozen people," Steele said. "It's getting serious."

"What could be their motive?" Shamus wondered again.

"I don't know," Steele said. "But I intend to find out."

"You're staying around?" Ironside questioned the Pinkerton man.

Steele nodded. "I believe I will. And you?"

"We're here to help Sheriff Clitherow any way we can. He saved my life in the late war and I owe him," Ironside declared.

Shamus gave his reason for being in Recoil. "Luther is my friend. So we both owe Jim Clitherow."

"Any chance of Jacob coming here?" Steele asked.

"No. I asked him to stay at Dromore for the spring gather," Shamus answered.

Steele took a drink of his coffee. "Pity. We could sure use his gun."

"Dallas, from what I saw this morning, you don't need anybody's gun but your own." Luther smiled. "Who gave you the handle *Dallas*?"

"My parents are both physicians," Steele said. "They were in Dallas to attend a medical conference when Mother gave birth prematurely."

Shamus nodded. "And she called you after the city."

"Exactly. I've never been real fond of the name, but it's the one my folks gave me so I've kept it."

"They still alive?" Shamus asked, making conversation.

"Yes, but they're both retired. They moved to England and bought a corner of an estate from Lord somebody or other. Father grows roses and mother volunteers at a local hospital for the poor. They seem to be happy enough, especially since father is invited onto the estate for the grouse shooting season."

"Did your pa teach you to shoot?" Luther asked, the subject dear to him.

Steele thought about that for a few moments. "Luther, what I do with a gun can't be taught. It's a skill a man is born with, like Jacob's gift for music." He drained his cup and stood. "I'll see you gentlemen later. I have to talk with the undertaker and honor my dead."

* * *

Shamus watched the young man leave the restaurant, then poured himself another cup of coffee. "Well, Luther, where do we go and what do we do?"

"I say we wait and hear what Jim's deputy has to say. He might have something we can go on."

Shamus looked at Ironside over the rim of his cup. "Why are the night riders doing this? I can't wrap my mind around it."

"For money, Colonel. Isn't that the usual reason for such things?"

Shamus frowned. "What is there of value in this wilderness?"

"A gold mine, maybe?"

Shamus shook his head. "You don't ride all over the country killing and burning to get a gold mine. If they want a mine, why not just take it and be done?"

"It beats me, Colonel," Ironside said.

"There's something else, something I just can't figure." Shamus sat in thought for a few moments, then shook his head and sighed. "No, I can come up with nothing."

Ironside stared out the restaurant window. "Riders comin' in. Looks like it's Jim's posse and them boys look pretty beat."

Shamus stood up. "Then let's go and hear what they have to say."

Chapter Six

Stutterin' Steve Sparrow's eyes were frozen in his head, like a man who'd stared too long at a sight that had horrified him. Like the other eight men in his posse he sat his tired horse outside the sheriff's office and made no attempt to dismount.

Shamus and Ironside exchanged glances, trying to make sense of what they were seeing.

Jim Clitherow stepped out of his office and stood on the boardwalk. He was silent for a while, then said one word. "Steve?"

Sparrow's head moved in the sheriff's direction. "G-g-grangers." Then, after a struggle, "All dead. M-m-men . . ."

"Women and children, all murdered." This from a man who rode a dust-covered pony that could've been any color. "Three wagons burned, up by Black Mountain Draw."

"Night riders, Steve?" Clitherow spoke softly, like a man talking to a frightened child.

The deputy nodded.

"How many dead?" Clitherow said.

Sparrow took a deep breath and tried to force out the words as he exhaled. "Th-three men. F-f-four half-grown boys. Six w-w-women and g-g-girls."

"All shot?" Clitherow said.

Sparrow shook his head. "B-b-b-burned."

Clitherow closed his eyes slowly, seeing images in his mind, and when he opened them again they were haunted.

"The s-s-smell . . ." Sparrow said. "I'll never eat m-m-meat again."

Clitherow nodded. He'd already seen and smelled the massacre in his mind. He looked over the tired posse men. They reminded him of soldiers who'd suffered a crushing defeat in the field. "Any of you men see anything, tracks maybe?"

It took a while before the posse reacted, then a rider reached behind his saddle and produced a piece of board. He held it up for Clitherow to see. Two words had been branded into the pine. *Hell Fire.*

"Got a ring to it, don't it," Ironside said, his face grim.

Shamus turned his head and stared at him for a moment, but said nothing.

"Clem, give me that damned thing," Clitherow said. "The rest of you men return to your homes and get some rest. Steve, that goes for you as well."

None of the men made any objection. Clem handed Clitherow the board then rode away with the rest. Only Sparrow still sat his horse and gazed at the sheriff.

"Go home, Steve," Clitherow said. "Get some rest. You're all used up, man."

"Phantoms," the deputy said. Then, with barely a stutter, "W-we can't fight phantoms." He was a compact man of medium height with hard gray eyes and a black, spade-shaped beard. He didn't scare worth a damn.

But he was scared that morning.

He swung his horse away and rode down the street, his chin on his chest, a man who'd caught his own personal glimpse of hell.

"I surely hate to ask you this, Shamus," Jim Clitherow said.

"Ask away. That's why we're here," Shamus said.

"Would you and Luther ride out to the massacre site and look around? Those men in the posse were tired and scared. They could've missed something."

"What's the country like up there?" Ironside said.

"Thorn scrub desert, mostly," Clitherow said. "It's long-riding country, to be sure."

"How far a ride, Jim?" Shamus asked. It was a question a man with a sore back would ask.

"Near thirty miles. Better take supplies. You'll probably want to make camp tonight and head back tomorrow morning."

Shamus rose to his feet. "Then we'd better saddle up."

"I'll arrange for some grub and a coffeepot," Clitherow said. "There are creeks in the area, but they might be dry. Better take your own water."

"Sounds right cozy," Ironside said.

"I know it's a hell of a thing to ask you," Clitherow said, "but I reckon my place is here in town. The night riders have struck here before. They may do it again. Oh, Elijah Doddle pulled out an hour ago with two wagons and a couple helpers. You'll probably catch up with him."

"He bringing in the bodies?" Ironside asked.

Clitherow hesitated, then said, "Yeah, what's left of them. I guess giving those folks a decent burial is the Christian thing to do."

"It is indeed, Jim," Shamus said. "And may God bless you for that."

"You boys take care, huh?" Clitherow said.

Ironside smiled. "Hell, Jim, we're gettin' too old to do anything else."

By noon, Shamus and Ironside were within sight of Turquoise Mountain, known to the Navajo as Tso odzil. The Indians believed the peak was fastened to the earth by a stone knife and covered with a blue-sky blanket decorated with turquoise. But there was little turquoise to be seen, just the grassy slopes of the mountain that ended here and there in stands of piñon, aspen, and up higher, spruce.

The land was vast and empty, hammered by the sun, and the air smelled like newly-sawn timber.

"What the hell were grangers doing in this place?" Ironside said.

"Maybe headed up Silver City way," Shamus said.

Ironside looked around him. "You can run cattle on this land, but it ain't fit for sodbusters. I swear maybe two inches of soil sits on top the bedrock."

Shamus shook his head. "Luther, there's just no accounting for folks. They do what they want." He arched his back in the saddle and groaned.

"Hurt some, Colonel, huh?" Ironside said.

"Yes, some. I'm already missing my soft bed at Dromore."

Ironside said. "Well, maybe tonight we'll spread our blankets on some nice rock moss."

Shamus smiled. "Just what I need, Luther."

The south end of Black Mountain Draw lay between Black Mountain and Coyote Peak in a wilderness of thorn scrub, cactus, and piñon. At two in the afternoon, Shamus and Ironside, saddle weary, caught up with Elijah Doddle and his parked wagons. Scared like everyone else in that part of the territory, he and his assistants greeted the two riders with leveled rifles.

Shamus and Ironside drew rein.

"State your intentions." Doddle was a tall skinny man dressed in a black claw-hammer coat, collarless white shirt, and a top hat perched precariously on his bald head.

"My name is Colonel Shamus O'Brien and this is my associate Mr. Luther Ironside."

"Then we'll give you the road," Doddle said. "You may be on your way."

"We're friends of Sheriff Jim Clitherow. We're here at his request to investigate this terrible affair."

Doddle thought that through. Finally he lowered his gun and said, "Well, I didn't take you fer night riders. The burned-out wagons are in the draw."

"And the bodies?" Ironside said.

"In the wagons." Doddle mopped his sweating face with a blue bandana decorated with white spots. "But be warned, it's not a sight any God-fearing man would wish to see." Then, as though he'd just remembered, he said, "These are my assistants, Lem Trace and Patrick McGowan."

Trace was a fat, red-faced man who looked too jolly to be an undertaker. McGowan was younger, a gangling youth with clear blue eyes and fiery hair.

"Mr. McGowan, are you a son of Erin?" Shamus asked.

"I am that, Colonel, like your good self. I hear the music of the glens in your voice."

"And in yours, my boy." Shamus was pleased. "We meet in unfortunate circumstances."

"The Irish are no strangers to those, Colonel," McGowan said.

"Indeed we're not," Shamus sniffed the air. "Is that coffee I smell on yonder fire?"

"It's just on the bile," Doddle said, "but you're welcome to make a trial of it."

Shamus swung stiffly out of the saddle and limped to the fire, Luther close behind him, his eyes everywhere. "No sign of the night riders, Mr. Doddle?"

"Only of their murderous handiwork. Let's hope we don't see them before our task is done and we're well gone from here."

"Where were the wagons ambushed?" Shamus said as he drank coffee and tried to work the kinks from his back.

"In the wash, Colonel," Doddle said. "I assume the poor people had camped there for the night."

"They were grangers, huh?" Ironside said. "That's what the deputy said."

Doddle looked surprised. "No, I would say not. When you inspect the ground you'll see they carried no farm implements of any kind, just picks and shovels."

"If they weren't sodbusters, what were they doing here?" Ironside said.

Doddle shrugged. "Your guess is as good as mine."

Shamus had lit a cigar. He stared at its glowing tip and said, "Men, women, and half-grown children brought three wagons and hard-rock mining tools to this wilderness. Does that suggest they were in search of a gold mine?"

"Maybe," Doddle said. "But my job is to bury them, not inquire why they suddenly changed from folks to customers."

Shamus tossed away the grounds at the bottom of his cup. "Luther, let's go scout around the deceased's wagons. The sheriff's posse has probably tromped all over the place, so I doubt if we'll find anything."

"My men too, Colonel," Doddle said.

Shamus nodded. "Well, we'll take a look anyhow and say a prayer to holy Saint Jude that we find something."

"Who's he, Colonel?" Ironside said.

"The patron saint of lost causes, Luther, and damn ye for a heathen."

Ironside muttered something about Jude in particular and Catholic saints in general, but Shamus had his worried mind on other things and did not take him to task.

Chapter Seven

"I gathered you here today to compliment you on last night's work. You all did a splendid job and the boss will be well pleased."

A murmur of thanks rose from the twelve men gathered in the cabin.

Englishman Nate Condor's next words silenced them. "But we can't rest on our laurels."

They listened as he continued. "There is still much work to be done. We can't sit back until every living soul has been eliminated or driven out of this part of the Playas Valley."

The speech was greeted with cheers and cries of "Damn right!"

"It is the boss's wish and mine!" Condor, a tall, slender man with wavy black hair and dark, weathered skin said to more cheers. He knew it was time to dangle the carrot again. "I confidently predict that a month from now every man jack of ye will be rich beyond your imaginings."

"Spoke like the old pirate you are, Nate," a man yelled.

"Not *are*, Joe, *was*. I've turned my back on the sea and I'm well content to undertake my piracy on dry land."

This brought laughter and Condor yelled, "Splice the main brace! Now there's a pirate's order for you, lads."

The men cheered again as a couple of pretty young Mexican girls circulated and poured raw whiskey from earthenware jugs.

Condor took advantage of the din to signal his second in command should step outside.

The two men left the cabin and walked into lilac light as the day shaded into evening. A few sentinel stars hung in a jade sky and fragrance of the surrounding pines was tangled in a web of stillness.

Condor led the way to a tall limestone rock that jutted out of the ground like a flatiron. When he stopped, he lit a cigar. "Barney, I'm concerned we may be moving too quickly."

"Bless you, Cap'n, why would you say that?" Barney Merden said. "I reckon it's all going according to the boss's plan, lay to that."

"Maybe the wagons were a step too far. I mean,

too many dead all at once. It's the kind of thing that could get the army involved."

"And who's to tell them, Cap'n? Hell, that sheriff in Recoil can't even get a United States marshal to ride down here. Once the word gets out that this part of the country ain't healthy for rubes, we'll see no more of them."

Merden, the former first mate of Condor's ship the *Sea Raven*, grinned, showing few teeth and those black. "After that, all we need is a few days to get the job done, then we'll all be riding carriages in Boston town, or London town come to that."

"There are men at the wagons now, poking round," Condor said. "John Landers says he saw at least five of them."

"Then the skull riders will take care of them tonight."

"No, let them be. Wait, I have a better idea. Scare them, Barney. Scare the hell out of them, that's all. But no killing. When I want more killing done, I'll give the word."

"Whatever you say, Cap'n," Merden said. "But I tell ye this, we'll have no peace until that pestilence they call Recoil is wiped off the map."

"That will be the last act, Barney. Then, by God, the winner takes all."

* * *

The hooded, robed riders stood by their horses in the gathering night, waiting the command to ride out.

Barney Merden, dressed like the rest, was already mounted. "Ye know what to do, lads. We stand off and hoot and holler and scare the living daylights out them. Shoot your rifles, but no killing."

"Hey, Barney, can't we plug a few of them?" The man's voice sounded hollow behind his carved skull mask.

"No, Landers. Cap'n Condor says we scare 'em, but there will be no killings. He reckons they'll scamper back to Recoil and spread the word that the night riders are out, and we'll see a skedaddle from the Playas, lay to that."

"Pity," Landers said. "I'd like to bed down another rube or two."

This drew laughter from the waiting riders.

Merden said above the noise, "You'll have your chance soon enough, Landers. The killing isn't over just yet." He raised his Winchester above his head. "Mount up, mates! We'll give them interlopers a taste of hell's fire."

One by one the riders rode past the campfire, leaned from the saddle, and lit their torches. Flames reflected scarlet on bone white masks and Nate Condor, watching from the shadows, thought they truly looked like riders from the lowest pit of Hades.

Among them were some of the West's most notorious gunmen, killers, rapists—all slaughterers of men, women, and children. Condor had commanded many a crew of bloodthirsty pirate rogues, but none like these . . . the most dangerous men on earth.

Even he, accustomed to violent death in all its forms, felt a shiver of fear run down his spine as he watched the riders vanish into the night, their bobbing torches winking like scarlet fireflies. He shook his pigtailed head. The sooner this endeavor was accomplished and the hired gunmen paid off, the better.

Chapter Eight

The Doodle bodies were blackened by fire, frozen in the stiff postures of death. A few had their arms extended, as though begging for mercy or pity from men who had neither.

There was no dignity in death for the thirteen people, an unlucky number. Their bodies were thrown into the backs of the wagons, and the ground around them had soon been littered with rags of burned skin.

Shamus fingered his rosary beads, his lips moving as the evening darkness closed around him. Filled with darkness inside, too, he was saying prayers for the dead. After the last amen, he gave an Irish blessing.

"May God grant you always . . .
A sunbeam to warm you,
A moonbeam to charm you,
A sheltering angel, so nothing more can
    harm you."

* * *

Ironside was no stranger to violence, but what he witnessed was beyond his understanding. To shoot a man was one thing, but to tie his hands behind his back and set him on fire was another. The same had been done to the women and girls—another of Ironside's lines that had been crossed.

Shamus put his beads in his pocket. "What did we learn, Luther?"

Ironside's bleak eyes roamed over the Doddle wagons. "Not a damned thing, Colonel."

"Not a damned thing," Shamus repeated. He nodded. "Yes, that's what we have learned."

"Colonel, I reckon we should find a place to make camp for the night."

"But well away from this accursed place."

"We can head south, toward Recoil."

"Then that's what we'll do." Shamus turned to Doddle, who looked ashen in the waning light, a man under terrible strain. "We're moving out, Elijah. We'll camp somewhere to the south."

The smell of burned flesh hung in the air like a black mist and the moon had not yet risen, as though it feared what it might see.

Doddle said, "No camp for us, Colonel. We're heading back to Recoil and trusting the trail to our night eyes. I will not camp with hurting dead in my wagons."

"Then good luck to you, Elijah."

"And to you, Colonel."

Shamus and Ironside walked to their horses, then stopped in mid-stride as rifles crashed and torches flared in the gloom.

"Is it the night riders?" Shamus yelled.

"It is, and I see 'em, Colonel," Ironside said. "Damned holy terrors."

Both men had their Colts in hand, but the riders hadn't drawn closer, content to scream and yell from a distance. Bullets cracked over the heads of the Dromore men.

"Jesus, Mary, and Joseph, what are they up to?" Shamus said.

"Testing us, maybe," Ironside said. "Could be they want to count our guns."

Doddle, alarmed, ran from his wagons to Shamus and Ironside. "They're attacking us, Colonel," He threw up his hands. "I'm a dead man."

"I'll be the judge of when you're a dead man, Elijah," Shamus said as a bullet kicked up an exclamation point of dust at his feet. He raised his Colt and cut loose, but the range was too great and shots went wild. "Damn them," he said as he reloaded his revolver. "The black crow's curse on them. Why don't they attack?"

"They're trying to scare us, Colonel. Drive us off," Ironside said.

The riders moved closer and bullets thudded into the wagons. Demonic howls and loud cries of "Kill! Kill! Kill!" filled the night.

"Let's get out of here, Luther," Shamus said. "Elijah, get your wagons started."

"The hell with that," Ironside said. "I don't run from yellow-bellied trash."

Before Shamus could stop him, Ironside sprinted to his horse and swung into the saddle like a man forty years younger. He slid his Winchester from the boot and kicked his mount into a run. A wild Rebel yell spiked into the night as he charged the riders, firing his rifle from the shoulder.

Shamus, horrified and scared for his friend, saw the flaming torches waver and a few trailed sparks as they were thrown to the ground. The remaining torches bunched together as though the night riders had surrounded the man in charge and were asking questions.

They'd expected rubes that would turn and run, not a first-class fighting man who kept on coming. Ironside swung to his right in a flanking movement, and his blazing rifle starred the darkness. Fear didn't enter his thinking. In his years, he'd killed more than his share. He was a man to be reckoned with.

The weird shrieks and yells stopped abruptly.

The pounding of departing hooves was heard as torches were tossed away and died in the gloom.

Again and again, the eerie Rebel yell sounded in the night and a rifle crashed with barely a pause. The sound of running horses gradually died away and then there was one last, triumphant yell.

An eerie, echoing silence descended on the brush country and the smell of dust and powder smoke drifted in the air. A few minutes passed.

Unable to see anything but a wall of darkness, Shamus cupped hands to his mouth and yelled, "Luther, are you all right?"

The night turned back the question and it went unanswered.

"Oh, God," Doddle whispered. "He's not dead, is he?"

"Luther!" Shamus called out again. "Answer me, man."

No answer, only the silence of the night.

Long moments passed. Coyotes again yipped in the hills and closer, an alarmed owl asked his eternal question of the darkness.

"He was a brave man," Doddle said. "I've never seen none braver."

"He's not dead yet," Shamus said. "Luther is a hard man to kill, and if he is killed, he'll refuse to stay that way." He hollered again. "Luther! Damn it, man. Answer me!"

The night gloom parted and Ironside emerged like a gray ghost, his Winchester propped upright on his thigh. A thick dust cloud trailed behind him. He was only a few yards away when Shamus saw that he dragged two dead men behind him.

"Damn it all, Luther. I though for sure you were dead as a wooden Indian."

"That'll be the day, Colonel. It'll take more than scum like these to corral me." Ironside drew rein.

Shamus, Doddle behind him, stepped to the dead men. After a while Shamus said, "They're shot through and through. Good work, Luther."

"I think I might have winged another, but I ain't sure," Luther said.

Shamus turned to Doddle. "Recognize these two, Elijah?"

"Maybe." The undertaker kneeled by the corpses and used his bandana to wipe dust from their faces. After studying the men for a few moments, he rose to his feet. "The one on the left in the cowskin vest I don't know. But t'other is Pete Wilson. He is, or was, a bank robber and all-round ruffian out of the Utah Long Valley country and he was a bad one. A few years back in El Paso I buried a man he'd killed. I'd just got the body planted when Wilson stepped up to the grave and emptied his six-gun into the coffin. 'I wanted to make sure the damn cheat was dead,' he said."

Doddle shook his head. "He had no respect for anything or anybody, not even for the grave."

"All you can do with a man like that is kill him," Shamus said.

"Well, Mr. Ironside did a good job of that. Wilson has three bullets in his chest I could cover with the knave of spades." He looked up at the Dromore foreman. "Good shooting by any standard."

Ironside smiled. "Hell, yeah. An' me only half-trying."

"Luther," Shamus said, his face stern, "only the hollow man boasts of his prowess."

"Sorry, Colonel. I'll be sure to remember that."

Shamus smiled. "Nevertheless, you did well. Splendid behavior, Sergeant Ironside!"

"Indeed, a most singular display of gallantry," Doddle said.

"And of the greatest moment because you saved our lives."

Ironside swung out of the saddle and handed Shamus a carved, painted mask. "Took that off one o' them two."

Shamus examined the mask. "I can understand how this could scare folks, especially at night."

Ironside nodded. "Out there in the darkness

them riders were a sight to see. Enough to scare any normal man out of his drawers."

"Then we're blessed that you're not an ordinary man, Luther," Shamus said.

"Damn right, I ain't."

"Elijah, will you take these dead men back to Recoil?" Shamus said.

"No, Colonel. I will not let them lie beside the people they slaughtered."

"Then we'll leave them for the coyotes. That is if they eat their own kind."

As though he'd suddenly remembered something, Ironside said, "The man there, the one Elijah says is Pete Wilson. He said something real strange before he died."

"Dying men sometimes do, Luther," Shamus said.

"Yeah, but this was real crazy. He said, 'San Pedro en Cadenas.' Now what the hell does that mean?"

"I believe I know," Doddle said. "I've buried a lot of Mexicans in my time, and I'm sure it means St. Peter in Chains."

"Hell, then I'm none the wiser," Ironside said.

"Our Savior told St. Peter he was a rock on whom he'd establish Holy Mother Church," Shamus said. "Peter was the first pope of Rome and passed on his authority in unbroken succession to our present pontiff."

Ironside knew better than to belittle popes and popery in the colonel's presence, so he settled for, "Where do the chains come in?"

"I imagine Peter was placed in chains before he was crucified by the Romans." Shamus glanced at Wilson's ashen face. "Odd thing for a man of his stripe to say."

"I'm afraid I can throw no light on the subject," Elijah Doddle said. "If you'll excuse me, Colonel, I'll be on my way."

Shamus yawned. "And it's me for my blankets."

"St. Shamus in bed," Ironside said, grinning.

Shamus looked horrified. "That, Luther, wasn't funny."

Chapter Nine

"God blind me, he drove you off! You let one man put the crawl on you."

"He wasn't one man, Cap'n," Barney Merden said. "He was a one-man army."

"Get him," Nate Condor said. "Find him and bring me back his head. I want him dead, you understand? Dead, dead, dead!"

"But he might be long gone by now."

"I don't give a damn. Go after him and find him. Take all the men with you." Condor gave his second in command a scathing look. "There's safety in numbers."

Merden knew better than to argue.

The traits that had made English Nate a terror on the high seas—a violent temper and a willingness to kill—he still possessed. Added to those were his speed with a gun and his flashing skill with a knife. He wore two Colts in crossed gun belts, rare at that time in the west, and he badly wanted to use them that night.

Merden read the warning in the man's glittering black eyes. "We'll find him, Cap'n. We'll turn over every damned rock until we do."

"Then go. Get out of my sight. And remember, Barney, I want his head. I'll make a damned soup from his skull and relish every hellish sup."

After he heard his men ride out, Condor unbuckled his guns and tossed them on the table. He poured himself a whiskey, lit a cigar, and threw himself into a chair. Disappointment hung on him like a damp cloak. He'd thought his riders the most dangerous men on earth, yet when they'd come up against a real fighting man instead of a terrified pumpkin roller they'd cut and run.

The boss's concept was a good one—chase every rube out of that part of the territory and complete the job without prying eyes reporting their every move to the army or the law. It was a plan that could work, and work well. But he'd been given cowardly rabble to work with, men he'd have fed to the sharks if they'd been part of his pirate crew.

Condor watched blue smoke curl over his head and reached a decision.

Hellfire was the answer.

Use the men he had and move against Recoil sooner than the boss had planned. Burn the damned town and shoot down the fleeing citizens like rabbits, and the rest of the settler scum would scamper for the hills.

Condor smiled. It was an excellent plan; one the boss would appreciate.

That is, while he remained boss. As things stood, there were too many men expecting a cut of the spoils, and eventually all of them would have to go, especially the boss who wanted the lion's share.

He'd get paid all right, not in double eagles but in hot lead.

"Well?" Barney Merden said. "What's your report, matey?"

The man who'd just walked out of the darkness said, "Two old men drinking coffee by a fire and talking. Nothing else."

"You were with me at the big skedaddle," Merden said. "Is one of them the man who attacked us?"

"Damned right he is. I'd recognize him anywhere."

"Big feller, dressed like a puncher?" John Landers said from the darkness.

"Yeah, that was him."

"Condor wants his head. He wants to make soup from his damned skull." Merden looked around him. "Does everybody understand that? I want no slipups this time."

"Hell, let's go get the head." Landers' teeth gleamed white in the gloom. "Them old coots won't know what hit 'em."

Merden sat his saddle, hesitant. "We'll lose men. The big feller is a demon with a rifle."

"Not if we do it fast, Barney," Landers said. "Ride in and gun 'em down. The job's done real quick and ol' Nate's got his soup for supper."

"Joe?" Merden said to the man who'd scouted the camp. "Let's hear you, damn it."

"Well, near as I can tell, it ain't gonna be that easy." Joe swung into the saddle of his paint. "Them old timers ain't fools. They're camped under a rock ledge with a stand of juniper on one side and a cliff face on t'other."

"So we need to go at them straight on?" Merden said. "And across bare rock, damn their eyes."

"I'd say that's about how it shapes up," Joe said.

"Hell, I don't like it," Merden said. "We'll lose too many men riding into their rifles. Three, maybe four, and that's my low count."

"Some of the boys have torches," Landers said. "We can burn 'em out."

"Come to think on it, they got some dry brush in front of them," Joe said, his face brightening.

"That'll burn with plenty of smoke. We'll be on top of 'em before they know what's hit them."

Landers sought Merden's eyes in the darkness. "Is it a go, Barney?"

"Damn right it's a go. Get the torches lit and we'll smoke 'em."

Shamus O'Brien was stretched out, dozing by the fire, the pain in his lower back allowing no sounder sleep.

A restless and uneasy man, Luther Ironside remained awake and his eyes constantly scanned the darkness. The stars glittered close as they always did in the high country, and the air smelled musky of pine. The night was so quiet he fancied that if he listened hard enough he could hear lime green frogs splash into the mountain rock pools.

He allowed himself to become drowsy, lulled by the crackling fire and the rustle of the breeze, and his head dropped lower until his stubbled chin rested on his chest.

Then Ironside slept . . .

He didn't see the first flaming arc of a torch trail sparks through the air and land on brush. Then a second. And a third.

Thick, acrid smoke woke him. He shook Shamus awake, but no words were needed. Ten men had already emerged through the reeking haze, their rifles trained on Ironside, the man they considered the most dangerous.

"Stay right where you're at," Merden said. "Or by God I'll drop you right where you stand."

Shamus froze in mid-movement as his hand reached for his holstered gun. The Winchester muzzle rammed into his right ear convinced him it wasn't the best time to make a play.

Ironside, his eyes red and smarting, his Colt hanging loose at his side, also decided not to buck the odds. He let the revolver fall from his hand.

"Get their guns, boys," Merden said. "And bring them with us out of this damned smoke."

Shamus and Ironside, prodded with guns, followed Merden out of the acrid murk to a clearing angled by moonlight.

"Hey, Barney," Landers said, grinning, "you gonna cut the big guy's head off, like Condor wants?"

"Hell, no. Let him do his own cuttin'. We'll take them back with us." Merden waved his rifle in Shamus and Ironside's direction. "Rope 'em up good and get 'em on their horses."

Shamus leaned closer to Ironside and whispered, "About now, I wish my sons were here."

Ironside nodded, a ghost of a smile on his lips. "Right now, I'd settle for just Jake."

Chapter Ten

"Hey, Jake, what do you make of this?" Samuel O'Brien looked out the window as the day gathered into dusk.

Jacob O'Brien, a brandy in his hand, stepped beside his brother. After a moment he said, "Well, they're not kin of ours."

Samuel's wife Lorena moved to the window. "By the look of them, I'd say they're Mexicans."

Jacob smiled. "There's no question about that." He looked at Samuel. "Are Shawn and Patrick back from the north range yet?"

"I don't think so, but they should be riding in soon."

Jacob placed his glass on the table in front of the window. "Well, let's go talk to those Mexicans and see what they want."

Samuel's face was troubled. "I don't like the

look of this. Those boys are armed to the teeth and they don't look overly friendly."

"I'm with you on that," Jacob said. "I've seen hanging posses with friendlier intentions."

When the O'Brien brothers stepped outside, the Mexicans had already shaken out into a line, twenty bearded, heavily armed men who looked as though they meant business.

But what business?

Under the shadow of their wide sombreros, the riders' black eyes roamed over the house and horse corrals, Jacob noted. It added to his uneasiness.

"Welcome to Dromore. What can we do for you gentlemen?" Samuel said.

The man who appeared to be their leader rode a magnificent American stud with a Texas ranch brand on its shoulder. The Mexican wore bandoliers across his chest and a broad white smile on his dark face. "*Buenas noches, mis amigos*. My name is Álvaro Castillo and I want to be your very best friend." He waved a hand. "And so do my *compadres*. They said to me just a minute ago, 'Álvaro, let's be friends with those nice people.'"

Jacob, his right thumb tucked into his cartridge belt near his Colt, said, "Well, señor, that's true blue of you, except that right now we've got all the friends we need."

The Mexican's smile stayed in place. "Ah, but is that not always the way? The rich never want to be friends with poor men like ourselves. We wander in the wilderness alone, without friends." He shook his head. "It is so ver' sad."

Lorena, to her husband's obvious irritation, had stepped outside. "Are you men hungry? We have coffee and food inside."

"Ah yes, hungry. Señorita—"

"Señora," Lorena said.

Castillo bowed. "My mistake. Your beauty addled my poor brain."

"Are you hungry?" Lorena said again.

The Mexican shrugged. "We are poor and the poor are always hungry. Alas, my unfortunate *compadres* don't eat pork unless they're sick or the pig is. So you see how it is with us, señora. Hunger is not our friend, but it is a constant companion."

Lorena smiled. "Then I will feed all of you."

Jacob scanned the Mexicans, looking for the one who would be fast with the iron. His eyes settled on a tall, thin man dressed in black, who sat his horse at the end of the line to Castillo's right. The Mexican wore two ivory-handled Remingtons in a fancy rig and carried his handsome head with the arrogance of a man who had faith in his gun skills and had killed before.

He'd be a danger, Jacob decided . . . as if two against twenty wasn't danger enough.

Castillo talked again. "We are hungry, señora, but not for beef and *frijoles*. Our hunger is of a different sort. We hunger for gold and silver."

"Then be off with you," Samuel said. "We have none of that here."

The big Mexican turned to his men. "Do you hear that, *mis amigos*? They have no gold or silver. Is so sad, don't you think?"

Jacob's voice cut like a steel blade through the laughter that followed. "Mister, it would be a real good idea for you to ride on out of here."

"Why, sure I will," Castillo said. "I will leave because we are friends—*amigos*. Is that not right? But spare a little gold to ease our journey."

"All I'm giving you is lead," Jacob said. "Take it or leave it . . . friend."

Castillo, still grinning, turned his head, and yelled, "Eustacio! This man is my friend, but he must be taught manners, I think."

Jacob nodded. It was the man in black, just like he'd figured. He had the look.

"You stay right where you are, Eustacio," Jacob said. "I don't want to kill you."

But some men don't read the warning signs, even when they're plain to see. The Mexican casually walked his horse toward Jacob and drew rein when only a couple of yards separated them.

What he saw was a man dressed in ragged range clothes, his great hawk's beak of a nose overhanging a shaggy mustache that was seldom trimmed. The gringo wore his gun high—too high for a fast draw—and he didn't have the slender, long-fingered hands of a true pistolero, but rather the huge, toughened paws of a working puncher.

The Mexican underestimated Jacob O'Brien, and it was the worst mistake of his life. He should've looked into Jacob's eyes and read the hundred different kinds of hell that glowed like blue fire in their depths. Then maybe he would've backed off. But he didn't.

Jacob would later say that Eustacio was one of the fastest men with the iron he'd ever met. His draw was practiced, smooth, and very sudden.

Just not sudden enough.

Jacob slammed three bullets into the Mexican before he got off a shot that pinged off the weather vane rooster on the Dromore roof and sent it spinning. Jacob swung his Colt on Castillo before Eustacio slid off his horse and hit the ground.

Stunned by his pistolero's death, the bandit leader made no attempt to reach for his gun. He froze when he heard the metallic clatter of Winchesters racking behind him. Slowly, carefully, like a man who was not trying to attract attention, he turned his head. His eyes bugged when he saw Shawn, Patrick, and half-a-dozen vaqueros behind him, their rifles leveled, no give in their weather-beaten faces.

Castillo turned his attention to Jacob again, his eyes gleaming like fire-lit obsidian. "You are no longer my friend." He waved a hand. "None of you are the friends of Álvaro, no more."

"Well, we're surely cut up about that," Jacob said. "Now you and your men vamoose and don't come back." He nodded at Eustacio's body. "And take your dead with you."

Castillo said something to his men and a couple dismounted and threw the dead man over his saddle. As they led Eustacio's horse away, the bandit chief said, "We will be back and when we return you will be glad to pay us gold and silver." He stared hard at Lorena. "Be careful of your woman. She pleases Álvaro." He swung his horse and his men followed him into the blue dusk.

Samuel stepped beside his brother. "Jake, I think we have a problem that's not going to go away of its own accord."

Jacob nodded. "I planned to go after Pa and Luther. I reckon that's going to have to wait."

Shawn and Patrick joined them, leading their mounts, questions on their faces.

"We'll discuss what happened at dinner," Samuel said. "But I'll tell you this. I believe

Dromore is in considerable danger and we could find ourselves fighting for our lives."

Shawn looked at Jacob. "But what about Pa, Jake?"

"I think the colonel and Luther are going to have to look out for themselves. At least for a little longer."

"They'll be just fine." Patrick said it more as a question than a statement. "I mean, Pa and Luther are two tough old buzzards who can look out for themselves." He hesitated and added, "Aren't they, Samuel?"

Samuel smiled. "Sure they are, Pat. And they'll be back home before you know it."

But the worried look on his brother's face brought Patrick little comfort.

Chapter Eleven

"Well this is inconvenient. I told my lads to bring me back your heads." Nate Condor nodded in Ironside's direction. "Well, his head." Then to Shamus, "But yours would also have been welcome."

"Damn you for a sorry scoundrel. My name is Colonel Shamus O'Brien of Dromore, and I warn you, my sons will avenge my death."

Condor smiled. "Colonel? In what army?"

"The Army of the Confederate States of America," Shamus said proudly.

"How wonderful for you," Condor said. "You were quite badly beaten, weren't you?"

"Damn your eyes, you're an Englishman, aren't you?"

"Born and bred in Portsmouth town," Condor said.

"Well, this is not the first time I've been in the cold hands of the English," Shamus said.

"But not for long, Colonel, I assure you." Condor looked at Ironside. "And what is your handle? Or do you have one?"

Ironside frowned. "I have a name, but I won't put it out to you, you fatherless, murdering—" Ironside said.

"I've cut out a man's tongue for less than that." Condor let his anger settle and waved a negligent hand. "But it is of no matter. Your name is Luther Ironside. You were described to me, but I didn't quite make the connection until now."

"Who did the describin'?" Ironside said.

"That is no concern of yours, especially since you'll be dead very soon." Condor waved over Barney Merden. "Take them away and lock them up in the old toolshed." He smiled at Shamus. "As befits a man of your rank, Colonel, through the knotholes you'll have an excellent view of the Pelloncillo Mountains and the outhouse."

"Damn you. May you scratch a beggar man's back one day," Shamus said. "May there be a banshee crying at the moment of your son's birth and may the Lamb of God stir his hoof through the roof of heaven and kick you in the arse down to hell."

Condor grinned. "The Irish are good only for two things, cursing and getting drunk." He waved a hand. "Get them out of my sight."

"What are you planning to do with these two,

Cap'n?" Merden said as he and a couple of other gunmen shoved Shamus and Ironside toward the door.

"I don't know—yet," Condor said. "I may behead them with a cutlass as was my original thought, or hang them, or burn them alive. I'll come up with something grand."

Merden grinned. "You always do, Cap'n Condor. You always do."

"Not much room in here, Colonel," Ironside said. "How's the old back holding up?"

"It's fair, just fair," Shamus said. "All I need is a soft bed to sleep in for a night and I'll be fine."

The two men were jammed into a toolshed so small they could only stand upright and breathe shallow.

"What's that devil's name? Seagull or something?" Shamus said.

"Condor," Ironside said.

"Yes, well whatever it is, he said there were knotholes. I don't see any knotholes, do you?"

"Hell, it's so dark in here I can't see my hand in front of my face."

"Try the door again, Luther."

"Its padlocked, and whoever the sodbuster was who made this shed he built it solid, damn his eyes."

"During the war, do you recollect being in this bad a fix?" Shamus said. "Even during the hard times?"

"Hell no, Colonel. When we got in a scrape, we always had a Nashville Plow Works saber in our hand and a good horse under us. Now we don't have a peashooter between us."

"It was a good saber, the Nashville Plow Works," Shamus said. "I never actually owned one, but I've handled one in the past."

"Yeah, it was a fine saber, until the damned Yankees shut the factory down in the summer o' sixty-two."

"Took an edge, the Nashville Plow Works."

"It did that, Colonel. Good steel, I reckon."

"A fine weapon all round, Luther. In my opinion. Though not as finely made as the British 1853 Light Cavalry Saber. I had one of those when the war started and it was a good weapon."

"Both them swords were a sight better than anything the damned Yankees had."

"Oh, I don't know about that. The Ames saber was pretty good." Shamus' fingers strayed to the old battle scar on his left cheek. "It was an Ames that gave me this."

"I recollect that, Colonel. And I remember that it was swung by the biggest damned Yankee I ever seen in all my born days."

"I wonder what became of that Yankee?" Shamus said. "A sergeant, wasn't he?"

"I don't recollect his rank, but he skedaddled and I never seen him again. I looked for him a few times in the field, though."

"Yes, the Ames could get the job done, and no mistake," Shamus said. "Many a lively Southern lad fell to that damned blade."

He was quiet for a while, and then said, "Jesus, Mary, and Joseph and all the saints in Heaven and the holy souls in Purgatory, Luther, listen to us. We're talking about sabers when we should be making our peace with our Savior."

"I still got the rosary in my pocket that Jake gave me," Ironside said. "Do you want it?"

"It was Saraid's rosary. No, you keep it."

"Colonel, you know I don't hold with beads an' such." The old Dromore segundo reached into the pocket of his mackinaw and pushed the rosary into Shamus's hand.

"Thank you, Luther," Shamus said. "I'll pray for both of us."

"You think they'll do for us come morning?" Ironside said.

"I think you can depend on it. That damned Albatross—"

"Condor," Ironside said.

"Whatever the hell he is, he spelled it out for us, didn't he? I'd say he didn't pull any punches—beheading, the rope, or fire—as I recall. Depending on his whim, like."

"That he did, Colonel. Spell it out. Makes a man a might uneasy."

"To say the least, Luther. Now please leave me to my prayers."

Tap-tap-tap . . .

Someone knocked on the side of the shed and a voice whispered, "Are you two old loons through talking about knives?"

"Who is it?" Ironside said. "Identify yourself and state your intentions."

"Shhh . . . Damn it, Luther, you want us all dead?"

"Identify yourself," Shamus said. "We're men at holy prayer."

"It's Dallas Steele. And I want to get you out of here."

"But how—"

"Later, Colonel. Now just hold on for a minute and be quiet. If that's at all possible."

Ironside leaned closer to Shamus and in a hoarse whisper said, "It's the Fighting Pink."

"Yes, Luther," Shamus said. "I figured that out for myself."

"He's kinda fancy, Colonel. Them clothes he wears and the diamond ring an' such."

"What do his clothes have to do with anything?"

"I'm just sayin'."

"I don't care how fancy he is if he can get us out of here."

"He's a big city dude. Likes the bright lights, you know."

"He's also good with a gun."

"Yeah, but I wonder—"

"Will you two shut the hell up," Steele said. "I declare, you're the most speechifying coots I ever met."

"Steele," Shamus said, "does . . . what's his name . . . have pickets posted?"

"He was a sailor."

"Sailors post watches."

"Well, this one doesn't." A few moments pause, then, "Right, I'm going to try a crowbar on the boards." He wedged the tip of the bar between the timbers and pried them apart—with a shrill, screeching shriek.

"That's it. We're dead men," Ironside said.

A long, dreadful silence followed, then Steele whispered, "Rusty nails. I'll try again."

"What about Condor's men?" Ironside said.

"Sleeping the sleep of the just," Steele said. "Here we go."

The crowbar slipped through the planks again and the timber splintered. Steele pulled the board free and came face to face with Shamus. "A couple more, Colonel, and you're out of there. It helps that you two are kind of scrawny."

With Steele pulling on the boards and Shamus and Ironside pushing, within a couple of minutes there was a big enough opening in the side of the shed for the two men to step through.

Steele put a finger to his lips and then listened into the night. The only sound was the night breeze in the trees and the distant calls of a pair of hunting coyotes.

"Let's get out of here while the gettin' is good," Ironside said.

"Hell, no," Steele said. "We've already bucked the odds, so why don't we go for broke? Just for the hell of it, huh?"

Chapter Twelve

"I thought I heard someone down here in the kitchen," Lorena O'Brien drew her dressing gown closer around her neck. "It's cold, Jacob. Why are you sitting here alone at this time of night?"

"Drinking coffee, smoking, thinking. I couldn't sleep." The hard planes of Jacob's face were deeply shadowed in the dim lamplight.

"Mind if I sit?" Lorena asked.

Jacob rose. "Not at all." He held a chair for her and when she sat, pushed her closer to the table. "You want some coffee, Lorena?"

"No, no thank you." The woman sat in silence for a while, then said, "Will talking about it help?"

Jacob smiled and sat down across from her. "A woman's question."

"And sincerely meant."

"I think you know what troubles me."

"You killed a man today."

"Every time I kill a man something inside me dies, something small but significant. How many more men can I kill before I'm finally used up and all of me dies?"

"You may never have the need to kill a man again."

Jacob's smile was slight under his mustache. "Lorena, the Mexicans will be back. I've seen their kind before. They want to plunder this house and take what they can."

"Is that what they want, Jacob, to steal—"

"Everything we have."

"Should I worry about my husband and my son?"

Jacob shook his head. "Worry is like riding a rocking horse, it never takes you anywhere." He rose to his feet again. "You sure you don't want coffee? It's how Luther taught me to make it. He said—and I beg your pardon, Lorena—it should be stronger than stud hoss piss with the froth farted off."

Lorena smiled. "No, thank you. Now I really do think I'll pass."

"Don't blame you." He poured coffee then sat at the table again. "You should be going back to bed, Lorena. You'll get a chill."

"Will you be all right, Jacob?"

"I don't know. You can't see it, but over there in the dark corner by the door there's a black dog. He just sits there, staring at me, waiting his chance to spring. I've known him for many years and he's attacked me a lot of times."

"I know about all about you and the black dog, Jacob. So many times I've seen you go from light to darkness and nobody knows when it will happen."

"Least of all me."

"Why don't you play the piano, some Chopin or Brahms? It might lift your mood."

"And wake up the whole household. My brothers would love that. I don't know about my mood, but they'd sure lift my hair."

"You're worried about the colonel, aren't you?"

"Yes, him. And Luther. I love that old man. He raised me, you know. Pa was always busy with the business side of Dromore, so he pretty much handed me to Luther and said, 'Here, rear him.'"

"He did just fine with you, Jacob . . . and with your brothers."

"Luther taught me a lot." Jacob smiled. "Much of it to the colonel's dismay."

"I've often heard Shamus say so," Lorena said, smiling. She rose to her feet, a beautiful woman, the lamplight tangled in her unbound hair. "Jacob, I'm going to get a switch and chase that black dog out of the corner."

"It's all right, Lorena," Jacob said. "If I see him ready to pounce, I'll chuck a rock at him."

"Well, that might work."

Lorena stepped to the door, but Jacob's voice stopped her. "Thank you."

"I didn't help much."

"You listened."

"Anytime you want to talk, Jacob . . ."

"I know."

Lorena nodded, smiled, and walked out of the room, and only the memory of her perfume lingered.

Too restless for sleep, Jacob poured himself more coffee, then left the kitchen and stepped outside.

The night was cool, the sky scattered with stars. A hollow moon hung above Glorieta Mesa and bathed its summit in mother-of-pearl light. A breeze rustled in the pines near the house and made the badly wounded rooster weather vane point its beak and creak.

Jacob laid his coffee cup at his feet and built a cigarette, his eyes scanning the darkness. His face glowed scarlet as a match flared for his smoke. He shook out the flame let the spent match drop and said, "You better step out grinning from your butt to your eyebrows."

"It's me, Jake. It's Shawn."

"You could get killed walking up quiet on a man like that."

"But I knew it was you."

"Yeah, but I didn't know who you were."

Shawn stepped beside Jacob and accidentally kicked over the coffee cup.

His brother swore. "Shawn, didn't Luther teach you to walk like an Indian?"

"Hell, Jake, who leaves a cup on the ground?"

"I do."

Shawn looked at his brother in the gloom. "Why aren't you in bed?"

"Can't sleep. And I ask your question right back at you."

"I can't sleep either." Shawn wore his gun, a thing Jacob noticed. His brother seldom went armed around Dromore.

"They're out there somewhere, huh?" Jacob said.

"That's my guess," Shawn said. "When will they hit us, you reckon?"

"Today, tomorrow, who knows? But they will."

"There's a bunch of them."

"And most of the hands are out on the range for the gather, scattered to hell and gone." Jacob smiled without humor. "Great time for an attack by a bunch of Mexican bandits." He drew deep on his cigarette, then said, "You ever hear of Álvaro Castillo before yesterday?"

"Maybe," Shawn said, and then fell silent.

Jacob stared at him. "Well?"

"I was in Santa Fe . . . remember when the

colonel sent Luther and me up there to buy a Studebaker wagon and we came home with a 'Paloos stud instead?"

"Yeah, that was a couple years back. I recollect that the colonel had you and Luther cleaning out stalls for a month."

"Well, anyway, I recall that we spoke to a newspaperman in a saloon and he said a town down Texas way had been wiped off the map by Mexican bandits. By all accounts, it wasn't much of a town, but the bandits plundered the place, burned the buildings, and killed everybody they could catch, and that included women and children."

"You think it was Castillo and his men?"

"I'm pretty sure that was the boss bandit's name."

"How pretty sure?"

"Well, now I study on it, I'm sure, sure. Castillo . . . yes, that was the name all right. Hell, Jake, now I can even remember the town. It was called Two Horses. The newspaper feller said the citizens named it that because they didn't want their burg to be called a one-horse town. I remember we laughed, but it sure doesn't seem so funny now."

Jacob said, "Well, if it's the same man—"

"It is," Shawn said.

"Then we're in for some gun trouble. As Pa

would say, I reckon we can put the kettle on for that." Jacob was silent for a while, thinking, then he said, "Shawn, tell Samuel and Patrick about that Texas town, but don't let Lorena hear you. There's no use getting the womenfolk all worked up, especially if there's the slightest chance Castillo figured he had enough yesterday and moved on."

"Do you think he has?"

"Not a chance in hell." Jacob's voice was flat and lifeless and his soul had grown dark.

The black dog had finally sprung.

Chapter Thirteen

"What do you have in mind, Steele?" Ironside said, talking through the darkness.

"You boys need your horses back, so let's go get them."

"Hell, the corral is right up against the cabin," Ironside said.

"I know." Steele's teeth gleamed white in the gloom. "Makes life interesting, don't it?"

"Well, I say we light a shuck," Ironside said.

"Luther, I can't walk back to Recoil," Shamus said. "We'll do as Dallas says."

"Easy does it, Colonel," Steele said. "Keep to the shadows and walk like an Injun."

Shamus grunted. "Damn it, young feller, I can barely walk like a white man."

The stars and bright moon bladed blue light into the darkness as the three men crept up on the corral. The thirty penned-up horses were uneasy and milled around in a dusty circle, white arcs showing in their eyes.

"Luther, we'll need your saddles and bridles as well," Steele whispered.

"I don't have a gun." Exasperated, Ironside gritted the words through his teeth.

"You don't need a gun," Steele said, and his teeth flashed again. "If it comes down to it, I'll do the shooting for both of us."

Shamus shook his head. "I sure hope those boys of Condor's are taking a night off."

"And so do I." Steele whispered, "This is a Savile Row riding outfit I'm wearing. I'd sure hate to get blood on it." He waved Shamus and Ironside forward. "Let's go."

The cabin remained quiet and dark as Steele, who'd never been a puncher and was wary of horses, stood by with his gun while the two others cut out their mounts. Steele took the reins of Ironside's horse and said, "Luther, get the saddles and bridles and don't forget the blankets."

"Now I ain't likely to forget the saddle blankets," Ironside muttered, irritated.

Steele led Shamus to a patch of shadow and waited for Ironside to catch up.

"Maybe you should go help him, Dallas," Shamus said. "The saddles are a load for one feller."

"He'll manage," Steele said.

"You're not much of a man for hard work, are you?" Shamus said.

"I don't know. I've never tried it."

Disaster hit.

The door of the cabin opened and a man stood in the doorway in his long-handled underwear. "Here, who's out there?" he demanded.

Steele drew his Colt, crouched, and headed toward the cabin, keeping to the shadows. He stopped when the yip of a coyote came from the corral.

"Git the hell out of there," the man at the door yelled. He picked up a split log from near the doorway and tossed it into the darkness.

Another *yip-yip* sounded, then silence.

"Damned coyotes," the man said before he stepped back inside.

A couple of tense minutes passed, then Ironside emerged from the gloom loaded down with a saddle on each shoulder.

"Was that you, Luther?" Steele said.

"Who? The man at the door or the coyote?"

"The coyote, of course."

"Yeah, it was me. A young Kiowa woman teached me that call, among other things."

"You saved our bacon," Steele said. "Three cheers for the man from Dromore."

"Seems like I did, don't it?" Ironside grinned.

Dallas Steele led the way through the rustling

darkness to a shallow dry wash where Shamus and Ironside saddled their mounts. The wind moved across the open brush country and lifted fine veils of yellow sand.

"You'd better mount up, Dallas. Those devils will track us soon as they find our horses missing." Shamus looked around. "Where is your mount?"

"Over there, by the dead juniper," Steele said. "He's kind of hard to see in the dark."

"But that's a burro," Ironside said. "It's not a hoss."

"Yes, I know, but he's a fine animal. His name is Jonesy and he's a well-mannered creature, obviously a burro of good breeding."

"Why are you riding a burro?" Ironside said, his face disbelieving.

"It was the closest thing to a horse I could find in Recoil. I could probably have requisitioned one, since I work for the government through the Pinkertons, but that would have blown my cover." Steele smiled. "The gentleman at the livery said Jonesy will carry me all day and into the next."

Despite the fact that the eastern sky over the Little Hatchet Mountains showed a streak of gray, Ironside wouldn't let it go. "You came all the way from . . ."

"Denver."

". . . without a hoss?"

"Yes. I traveled by train and stage, and I'll return that way."

Ironside shook his head and tried to get to the bottom of the mystery. "You don't own a hoss? I've never heard the like."

"I don't care for them much," Steele said. "I like my women wild, but not my means of transportation."

"And there you are, all dressed up for riding like an English lord," Shamus said.

"I am riding, Colonel," Steele said. "I'm riding a burro. Now we'd better hit the trail for Recoil before Condor comes looking for us."

Ironside ignored that and then, as though he'd just heard the worst heresy ever uttered by a human tongue, he said, "You don't like hosses."

"Not much," Steele agreed. "They're temperamental creatures for the most part, and dangerous."

Ironside's chin hit his chest. Then, at a loss for words, he finally managed, "Colonel, he don't like hosses!"

"Luther, if the man doesn't like horses, he doesn't like horses," Shamus said. "We can't all be old centaurs like you."

"I . . . I . . . I've never heard the like. A man who don't like hosses . . . it just ain't natural. It's like saying you don't like hound dogs."

Suspicion clouded Ironside's face. "Hey, you do like dogs, huh?"

"I just love them to pieces. Now, as fascinating as this discussion is, I suggest we ride. We're already pushing our luck." Steele gathered up the burro's reins and straddled the little animal, his feet trailing on the ground. "Gee-up, Jonesy," He pumped the reins.

Behind him, Ironside groaned in a horseman's pain.

Chapter Fourteen

Shamus O'Brien led the way into Recoil, riding through a thin dawn light. The street was empty. The sporting crowd had just gone to bed and the merchants hadn't yet opened their stores.

But Edith Ludsthorpe and her daughter already sat on the porch in front of the hotel. Edith sipped prune juice and viewed the three riders with obvious distaste, as did the man sitting next to her, a goateed, exotic creature wearing a paint-stained smock and a black beret so large it swept over his left shoulder.

"Halloo there, my good man . . . you riding the donkey," Edith called out.

Steele reined the burro to a stop and touched the rim of his plug hat. "Your servant, ma'am."

"You're too heavy for that poor animal. Is it not so, Chastity?" Without waiting to hear her daughter's comment, Edith said, "That is a most singular act of cruelty and of the greatest moment as far as I'm concerned." She picked up her rolled parasol and shook it at Steele. "Dismount that poor beast this instant!"

"Of course, ma'am." Steele swung off the burro. "His name is Jonesy, by the way."

"I don't care what his name is, young man. If I catch you mistreating him again I'll . . . I'll box your ears."

Steele said nothing, all his attention on the man in the smock who had stepped to the edge of the porch. His glowing eyes were fixed on Ironside and his face bore an expression of wonderment. "Hallelujah!" he yelled. He tilted back his head and called out again, "Thank the gods." He swung his arms wide and then clasped his hands in front of his chest. "You there, the fellow in the blue shirt!"

"You talkin' to me?" Ironside asked.

"Yes, my dear fellow, I'm talking to you. You splendid specimen. I want your head! Oh, I want your head so badly."

"Seems like all of a sudden every jackass in the territory wants my head," Ironside grumbled. "If you want it that bad, mister, you'd better go heel yourself, because I ain't givin' it up easy."

Shamus said, "I swear to God this town has gone crazy since we left, Luther. Let's go get breakfast."

"No, wait, my dear fellow. You don't understand!" the smock said.

Edith rose to her feet and her shoes thumped on the porch as she stepped beside the man and glared at Ironside. "I've already been exposed to your impertinence at that dreadful stage holdup and I'll have no more of it, so keep a civil tongue in your head."

"Talkin' about my head again," Ironside said.

Edith ignored that and waved an imperious hand, like old Queen Vic introducing a favorite courtier. "This is Mr. Maurice Bird, the famous artist. Already he's been compared most favorably to George Catlin and, needless to say, he is streets ahead of those low persons currently masquerading as painters."

Her eyes, hard as steel ball bearings, fixed on Shamus. "You may understand this, Colonel, though your companions won't. I attended an exhibition of Mr. Bird's paintings in Chicago, and right there and then, enthralled, I said to myself, 'Edith, you must travel west so Chastity can study under Mr. Bird's tutelage.'" She angled a look at the artist. "At great expense, may I add."

Bird smiled sweetly and gave a little bow. "Madam is very generous and her daughter is so talented. She's still raw, to be sure, but talented nonetheless."

"Hey, Maurice, if you're so talented how come we've never heard of you?" Ironside said.

"It takes time to build a reputation," Bird said. "I'm working on it, I assure you. My paintings of the Playas Valley will make me famous and, I may add, wealthy."

"How about the exhibition in Chicago?" Dallas Steele said. "I imagine that must have brought in some commissions and offers from galleries."

"Ah, well, you see, I sort of sneaked into that exhibition with a few of my paintings," Bird admitted. "They were not on view for very long."

"Until you and your canvases were thrown out into the street, you mean," Steele said.

"Something like that," Bird said. "I was at the mercy of barbarians."

"The works were on view long enough for me to determine that you are an artist of genius, Mr. Bird," Edith said. "And when I say that someone is an artist of genius, it is so."

"Then you understand why I must have that man's head, Mrs. Ludsthorpe." Bird waved a hand at Ironside.

"No, quite frankly I don't."

"Look at him with the artist's eye, Mrs. Ludsthorpe. See the scowling frontier ruffian in that face. See the savagery, the cruelty, the ignorance and arrogance. Yet your eye will also behold a certain nobility of countenance, the pride of the noble savage, the aspect of a wild Indian chief."

"Oh, yes!" Edith exclaimed. "Mr. Bird, I do! I do! But only a virtuoso like you could have opened my eyes so thoroughly. For the first time in my life the scales have dropped from mine eyes and I can seeee!"

Ironside gave Shamus a sidelong look. "Should I shoot that paint daubing so-called *artist*, Colonel?"

"Give me time, Luther. I'm studying on it."

"Luther, you can't rob the world of such a great artist," Steele said with a straight face.

Ironside ignored that and impatiently said to Shamus, "Well, should I plug him?"

"No. We'll go to breakfast instead."

"Mind if I join you?" Steele asked.

"Buying breakfast is the least I can do for the man who saved my life," Shamus said.

Ironside looked at Steele, then at his burro. "Walk behind us at a distance as though you don't know us." As he and Shamus rode in the direction of the restaurant, Bird ran after them. "Come to my studio," he yelled at Ironside, tugging on his stirrup. "Let me do a quick sketch at least. Damn it all, man. I must have your head!"

Suddenly Bird found the muzzle of Ironside's

Colt in the middle of his forehead and his eyes grew big.

"Mister," Ironside said, "this is your first and last warning. Stay the hell away from me."

The artist trembled, his mouth working. Then he turned and ran back to the hotel where he threw himself, sobbing, into Edith Ludsthorpe's arms.

The woman clutched him to her bosom and yelled over his head, "Philistines!"

"Hey, Luther, she's talking about you again!" Steele yelled, grinning.

Chastity Ludsthorpe wore a flowered dress, a wide straw hat with a pink ribbon tied around the crown. She stopped in front of the table where Ironside, Shamus, and Steele were sitting. "I came to apologize for my mother. There are times when she's a little hard to take."

"Amen to that," Ironside said.

The three men had finished breakfast and were lingering over coffee and cigars. The restaurant's air was thick with the smell of steak, bacon, and grease.

"So you plan on becoming an artist." Steele decided she was as pretty and glowing as a polished pearl.

"I have no talent for painting," Chastity said. "None at all."

"Then why does your mother—"

"Because there's not a thing I can do about it. Mother wants me to be a painter and that's that. I've tried to tell her I've no talent in that direction but she refuses to listen."

"What do you want to do, child?" Shamus asked.

"I'd like to be an actress, like Sarah Bernhardt." Chastity smiled, white teeth in a pink mouth. "She's my hero. Or should that be heroine?"

"Heroine," Steele said, "especially when you talk about the Divine Sarah. She's all female."

"Have you ever met her?" Chastity said, her blue eyes alive.

"I've never met her, but I saw her in New Orleans a few years ago. She's a stunningly beautiful woman. She took my breath away when she smiled at me."

"Unfortunately, I'm not a stunningly beautiful woman who takes men's breath away," Chastity said.

"Oh, I don't know about that," Steele said. "I think you would light up any stage, or parlor, come to that."

"He's right," Ironside said. "Hell, honey, you're so pretty you could make a glass eye wink."

Chastity blushed. "Thank you, Mr. Ironside."

"He does have a way with words, doesn't he?" Steele said dryly. "Quite the rustic bard is Luther."

"Damn right," Ironside said.

"Beggin' your pardon, ma'am, but it seems to me that you should get out from under your mother's thumb and head east," Shamus said. "I expect that's where the acting opportunities lie."

Chastity shook her head. "There are plenty of opportunities right here in the West, Colonel, mostly in the big cities and the mining boom towns. Why, I'm sure a retired actor lives in this very town."

"A he or a she?" Steele said.

"He's a man."

"How can you tell he was an actor?" Steele said.

"Oh, there are lots of ways. The way he holds himself, the way he talks. He's obviously had stage training."

"And who is this paragon?" Steele said.

"Chastity!" Edith Ludsthorpe stood in the restaurant doorway. "Come away from there. I'm surprised to find you in such rough company when poor Mr. Bird needs comforting." She glared at Ironside. "He was assaulted in the street by a rowdy brandishing a murderous revolver, you know."

Chastity rose to her feet. "I must go." Then, in a whisper, "I do apologize."

After Edith took her daughter in tow and swept out of the restaurant, Steele said, "A real pretty girl."

"Pity about the mother," Ironside said.

Shamus drained his cup. "I wonder who the retired actor is?"

"Could be anybody, I guess," Steele said. "Anybody at all."

Chapter Fifteen

Patrick O'Brien was excited. He'd never before seen *Leptotes Cassius,* the very rare Tropical Striped Blue, in this part of the territory. He didn't have one in his collection and he badly coveted the magnificent specimen.

His net poised, Patrick had followed the elusive butterfly from Dromore house to the thick brush at the base of Glorieta Mesa. As though it was aware of being hunted, the Blue would allow him to get tantalizingly close, then flutter away again, leading him deeper and deeper into rough country.

Samuel had warned him to stay close to the house and arm himself, but Patrick had ignored both orders. A vaquero had told him he'd seen a striped blue butterfly near the mesa and it was too golden an opportunity to pass up. He needed that Tropical Blue.

Just before sunup, he'd slipped out of the house with his net and a paper sack containing a roast beef sandwich and a bottle of Bass ale, planning to be gone the whole morning. With his quarry within reach, his entire concentration was fixed on the fluttering Blue, a stray from the south, maybe as far away as Old Mexico.

The butterfly led Patrick a merry chase. It allowed him to get tantalizingly close before flitting away again, outside the range of his net.

He was tired, thirsty, hot, and torn up by cactus, but the Blue was too much a prize to let out of his sight. He'd badly twisted his ankle on a rock and shortly afterword almost walked into a coiled rattler, noisily informing him that it resented his presence so close to the mesa.

The butterfly alighted on a yucca bloom and folded its wings. and Patrick took the opportunity to wipe off his steamed-up glasses.

He settled the round spectacles on his nose again, going from blur to focus—and looked into the cold, black eye of a leveled Colt.

"*Buenos días, mi amigo,*" Álvaro Castillo said, grinning. "It is a fine morning, is it not?"

Patrick dropped his hand to where his holstered revolver should've been and remembered it still hung on the gun rack in his room. It wouldn't have done him much good anyway.

Castillo had three men with him, scar-faced rascals who looked none too friendly.

"So, why do you have a net, amigo?" the Mexican said. "Are you catching little pigs, maybe?"

"Butterflies," Patrick said.

Castillo's eyes widened in amazement, then he flung words over his shoulder to his riders. "*Aggara mariposas!*"

This drew bellows of derisive laughter from the bandit's men and Castillo himself laughed so hard he shed tears. "Aye, aye, aye, the men of Dromore are much to be feared," he said, wiping his eyes with the back of his hand. "They spend their time catching butterflies."

"Why don't you ask Eustacio about that?" Patrick said.

Castillo's face changed from a grin to a scowl. "Now you are not my friend. I was going to make you my friend again because you catch many butterflies, but now I will not." He motioned with his gun. "What do you have in the pack on your back?"

"Just a paper sack with a sandwich and a bottle of beer."

"And a gun, I think."

"I don't need a gun for butterflies."

"Ah, let me see anyway," Castillo said. "I'm a ver' curious hombre."

Patrick removed his pack and threw it on the ground.

Castillo swung off his horse and examined the pack. He found the paper sack and opened it. "Just as you say, beer and bread." He bit into the sandwich and nodded. "Good for a hungry man." Then he opened the beer and swallowed some, his throat working.

He wiped off his mouth, burped noisily, and said, "Ver' good. I think I will make you my friend again because you carry such good beer."

"I don't want to be your friend," Patrick said. "You're a piece of trash, Castillo."

"Ah, then you will be my enemy, I think." He waved a hand to his men. "*Take him!*"

Patrick fought hard and even managed to land a crunching blow on one of the Mexicans' noses, but he was thrown to the ground and kicked almost senseless. His arms were bound to his sides with ropes and a noose was looped around his neck.

Moments later, he was dragged behind a horse through the brush and timber country at the southern end of the mesa. The heat was intense. Torn by cactus and brush, his head was reeling from the beating he'd taken.

He felt a pang of regret that the Tropical Striped Blue was probably long gone. As the rope yanked cruelly at his neck, he was reminded that he faced a much bigger woe.

Two miles north of Barbero Canyon, Castillo swung east through a narrow arroyo that led into an open meadow where the rest of his men were camped.

Exhausted by an hour of dragging through some of the roughest country in the territory, Patrick collapsed onto the grass.

Castillo ignored him. He was suddenly faced with a mutiny and began yelling at his men. "I ordered a watch on the arroyo, yet we rode through unchallenged. Why were my orders not obeyed?"

Patrick lifted his buzzing head. He had been taught Spanish by the Dromore vaqueros and knew enough of the language to catch the drift of what was happening.

"Because you are not the boss anymore, Álvaro." The tall, slim man wore his sombrero tipped back on his head, its leather string dangling under his chin. A black cheroot glowed between his white teeth and his hand was close to his holstered Colt.

"And why is this so, Juan?" Castillo said. "I made you my friend. You and me, we are the very best of *amigos.*"

As Patrick watched from his lowly viewpoint,

men moved away from behind Juan and any possible line of fire.

"You were the death of Eustacio Vasquez, yet you let the gringos drive you away," Juan said. "You are not fit to lead this band."

"Is this what you all think?" Castillo said, spreading his arms wide. "All of you who have been my very good friends for years."

His question was met with a sullen silence and one man spat in Castillo's direction.

The bandit chief nodded. "I see, *compadres*. It is easy to tell that you don't want me anymore. I am no longer your friend. I can see it in your eyes. After all I've done for you, after all the gold and silver I've given you, I see only hatred for poor Álvaro."

He removed his sombrero and after running a trembling hand across his sweaty brow held it in front of him. "And who will be your new leader? Who will lead you and put money in your pockets and beautiful señoritas in your beds?"

"That would be me, Álvaro," Juan said.

"You, Juan Santiago? A filthy pile of dog doo like you?"

Even through his cracked, dirty glasses, Patrick saw that Castillo had already drawn his gun, using his sombrero as a shield. He fired once through the top of the crown.

Stunned, Santiago staggered back a step and

his hand dropped to his Colt, his handsome face suddenly haggard.

Still firing through his hat, Castillo shot three more times. Santiago stood up well to the first couple of rounds, even managing to clear leather, but he rode the third bullet into hell.

Taking his time, his hands remarkably steady again, Castillo punched out the spent rounds from his Colt and reloaded from his gun belt. He let the revolver hang at his side as he said, "Is there anyone else who will be the leader of this band? Who says Álvaro is no longer his friend."

There were no takers.

"Good. Then you are all my friends again." Castillo stared at his shot-up sombrero, shook his head, then stepped to Santiago's body. "Pig!" Slamming kicks into the dead man's ribs, then ripping the sombrero from Santiago's body, the bandit leader examined it closely, then settled it on his own head.

He glanced at the dead man. "Take that carrion away from here and leave it for the coyotes."

Several men rushed to do Castillo's bidding.

Álvaro was the *patrón* again.

Lashed to the trunk of a cottonwood near a sluggish stream buzzing with mosquitoes, Patrick O'Brien watched Castillo's men seek shade to doze through the hottest hours of the day. His tongue stuck to the roof of his mouth and his lips were cracked, thirst raging at him. To his northeast, El Barro Peaks were purple under a cloudless sky and he fancied that if he could reach out and touch them they'd be cool under his fingertips.

To his surprise there were several women in the camp. Two of them were old and slack-breasted, but the third was young and shapely. Her black hair tumbled down on her back in glossy waves and she moved like a panther.

Castillo talked to the young woman, then nodded in Patrick's direction. The girl smiled and stepped to a smoking black cooking pot that hung over the fire.

Patrick wanted to keep looking at the girl, but to his surprise Santiago's body was dragged back into the camp. Castillo kicked the corpse again and then he too found a spot under a piñon, lay on his back, and tipped his hat over his eyes.

Patrick was puzzled. Why did they retrieve Santiago's body? Was it because Castillo wanted to kick it whenever he wanted? He'd no time to ponder the question because the girl, her hips swaying so her bright scarlet skirt swirled around her ankles, walked toward him, bearing a filled plate.

Patrick croaked, "*Agua.*"

"I can speak good English," she said. "I was taught by the holy sisters at the mission of Santa Maria de Cervellione in the city of Cabo San Lucas." She laid the plate beside Patrick and said, "I will bring you water."

When the girl returned she poured water from a jug into a clay cup and held the cup to Patrick's lips. The water was brackish, but it was cool and he drank deep.

"That is all for now," the girl said, taking the cup from Patrick's lips. "I will give you some more later. Now you must eat."

"Can you untie my hands?" Patrick asked.

"No. I will feed you. It is tortillas and antelope stew. It is very good."

"Did you cook it?"

"One of the older women did. The old ones know how to do such things."

"What's your name?"

"Modesta."

"Pretty name."

"The holy sisters gave it to me when I was brought to the mission. Santa Maria de Cervellione protects sailors from shipwreck. Did you know that?"

"I can't say I did,"

"She's a very powerful saint and sits very close to God. Now eat."

Patrick wasn't hungry but he managed to eat a spoonful of stew and few bites of tortilla.

Modesta pouted. "You did not eat much. You didn't like it?"

"I don't have much of an appetite."

The girl settled Patrick's eyeglasses more firmly on the bridge of his nose. "You are not Álvaro's friend, and that is bad for you. It is a very bad thing to be his enemy."

"What does he plan to do with me?"

Modesta shook her head. "I don't know."

"Hold me for ransom, I guess," Patrick said.

"Maybe so."

"Dromore doesn't pay ransoms."

The girl's beautiful black eyes saddened. "Then that is another bad thing for you, I think."

"Modesta, everybody's asleep. Cut these ropes."

"That I cannot do," the girl said, rising to her feet. "Álvaro would kill me. And you."

Chapter Sixteen

"Real nice place you got here, Captain Condor," the man said.

"Well, I guess that goes to show that you're either extremely stupid or that you live in squalor." The escape of O'Brien and Ironside rankled Condor, and the letter he held in his hand promised no good news.

The man laughed. "Ha, very good, Captain. My name is—"

"I don't give a damn what your name is." Condor tapped the unopened letter on the table. "Did the man who gave you this say anything?"

"No, Captain. He told me where to deliver it and said he'd give me five dollars when I got back. He loaned me one of his hosses, that buckskin out there."

Condor's cold eyes assessed the messenger, a

small man wearing a ragged suit that was too big for him and a plug hat that rested on his ears.

The former pirate sighed, opened the letter, and read. There was no salutation.

> *Do not move against Recoil until I give the word, but show yourselves on the hills at night. Maybe we can scare the rubes out of here without an outright attack that could draw unwelcome attention.*
>
> *But a killing or two outside of the town limits would not go amiss.*
>
> *I want two men shot on sight. One is Colonel Shamus O'Brien, the other is named Ironside. I made an attempt on their lives at the hotel, but it did not go as planned. A man called Dallas Steele is in Recoil and I don't yet know why. He is called the Fighting Pinkerton and he's dangerous. We may have to get rid of him, too.*
>
> *Sheriff Clitherow is an idiot, and requires no further action at this time.*
>
> *Have the goods been located yet? Let me know as soon as they're found.*
>
> *The bearer of this note is nothing. Eliminate him and return my buckskin at a later date.*

There was no signature.

"Good news, Captain?" the messenger asked. "I always like to bring good news." The man's face clouded. "But I seldom hear any."

Condor stared at him as though he was studying a strange new humanoid species. "You live in Recoil?"

"Sure do. I swamp the saloons and I do odd jobs around. Do you have any you want done, Captain?"

"You are impertinent." Condor picked up the long-barreled Colt from the table and shot the man between the eyes.

A few moments later, Barney Merden burst inside. "Are you all right, Cap'n?"

"I'm fine." Condor motioned to the dead man on the floor. "Get rid of that and then come back. I need to talk to you. Oh, and take good care of the buckskin out there."

"I think he's making a mistake," Merden said. "I say we burn the place and kill everybody we can find."

"What you say doesn't matter," Condor said. "Tell me about this Dallas Steele."

"The Fighting Pink?"

"I suppose it's the same man."

"It's the same man all right. The sheriff has put his name around town enough."

Condor nodded. "Continue."

"Well, he works for the Pinkertons and sometimes the government. He usually operates only in towns, and the wilder the better. Some say he's killed a dozen men, some say less, but all say he's good with a gun." Merden's slow brain cast back into memory. "Dresses like a dude and I believe he works out of Denver. Some say he a personal friend of the president of these United States, but I don't know about that."

"Some say . . . some say . . . I want facts. Is he as dangerous as the boss thinks he is?"

"I reckon, Cap'n. He was a named gunfighter even before he became a Pinkerton."

"Then we'll get rid of him as a precaution." Condor picked up the Colt and laid the barrel on his shoulder, an aggressive motion not lost on Merden. "Now, tell me about last night."

"Somebody helped them two escape, Cap'n."

"I know, Barney, I know." Condor's voice hardened. "A dozen men bedded down within yards of the toolshed and nobody heard a thing, huh?"

"Jim Hogue said he heard coyotes near the corral and went outside and chunked a rock at them."

"That was the colonel and Ironside stealing their horses back."

Merden had no comment to make and lapsed into silence.

Condor dragged out the silence then said, "Tell Hogue he's lucky, real lucky. I felt like killing a man this morning and I already did."

"I'll let him know, Cap'n."

"Do that. And tell him he should stay away from me for a few days."

"I'll let him know that too, Cap'n."

"And there's another thing, Barney. Tell the boys to ride out during the day and scout the country around Recoil. If we can kill a few travelers or picnickers, it will put the town on edge."

Merden grinned. "Sounds like a lot of fun, Cap'n."

"Shoot and run, Barney. Don't get caught."

Merden nodded. "Just as you say."

Condor laid his revolver on the table. "Now get out of my sight. You're as responsible for the escape as the rest of them."

Merden sprang to his feet, glad to leave with his life. He stepped to the door then turned at the sound of Condor's voice.

"Send me one of the Mexican girls. I always feel the need for a woman after I kill a man."

Chapter Seventeen

Shamus O'Brien was not in favor of Sheriff Clitherow's plan for a direct assault on the lair of the Condor and his night riders. "You'd be attacking across open country and going up against some top-ranked Texas gunfighters. I don't see you winning that battle, Jim."

"There's the three of us, and I might be able to convince Dallas Steele to join us," Sheriff Clitherow said. "That'll give the posse a backbone."

"It's too thin," Luther Ironside said. "Condor won't fight us in brush country. He'll lure us onto open ground of his own choosing and use his numbers to cut us to pieces. I don't think a posse of store owners, miners, and married men will stand against professional gunmen. And I wouldn't blame them."

"Then what do you suggest?" Clitherow said. "I'm open to anything."

"I'll answer that." Shamus lit a cigar, taking his time.

The early afternoon sun slanted through the sheriff office's window and made the dust motes dance. A brewery wagon trundled past on the street and somewhere close by children at play raised a ruckus.

Shamus finally gathered his thoughts. "We're agreed that Condor and his hired guns are here for a reason. Is that not so?"

"That's why they're killing and terrorizing folks, yes," Clitherow said.

"Then what do they want, Jim?"

"I don't know that, Colonel, and neither do you."

"Exactly."

The sheriff shook his head. "I'm not catching your drift."

"We find what Condor and his men want, and take it away from them," Shamus said. "And we mount a search and do it quickly before more innocent people die."

"That would take the wind out of Condor's sails," Ironside said.

"Yes," Shamus said, "and convince him that there's nothing to be gained by hanging around."

"So, how do we find this . . . whatever it is?" Clitherow asked.

Shamus smiled. "I haven't a clue."

"There's another problem," Ironside said. "If we find whatever it is the skull riders want, do we let Condor and his boys just ride away? They're murderers and rapists and if men ever needed killing, they do."

"No, we don't let them ride away," Clitherow said. "I'll bring them all to justice if it's the last thing I ever do as a peace officer."

"It may well be the last thing you ever do, Jim," Ironside said.

"Please, Luther, no more doomsday comments, if you please." Shamus looked away from Ironside to Clitherow. "But you're right. No matter what happens, we can't let Condor and his gang of brigands escape. We must bring them to justice."

The sheriff thought for a few moments, then said, "There's a Navajo lives down to Bar Ridge with his wife and a Negro hired man. His given name is Anaba, but most folks know him as Scout, since he scouted for the army during the Apache troubles."

"You think he could help us find whatever it is that Condor wants?" Ironside said.

"Yeah, that's the general idea," Clitherow said. "There's only one little problem."

"And what's that?" Shamus asked.

"They say he's a skinwalker, a shape-shifter."

"A what?" Shamus was confused.

The lawman looked uncomfortable. "Other Navajo claim Anaba can change from a man to an animal and back again."

Shamus crossed himself. "Jesus, Mary, and Joseph preserve us. I sense the devil's work at play here."

"Colonel, it's what folks say and it isn't necessarily true. People say a lot of things."

"Is the Injun a good tracker?" Ironside said.

"The best there is around."

"Then he could find Condor's . . . whatever it is?"

"He'll have more chance of finding it than we do." Clitherow looked uncomfortable again. "Luther, one thing you don't do is mess with a shape-shifter. The Indians call them *Yee naldlooshi*, and if they get riled at you, they can be real bad news."

"Why are you telling me this?" Ironside asked incredulously.

"Because, Luther, sometimes you talk without thinking," Shamus said.

"And you don't want to get into an argument with a skinwalker," Clitherow said, but he smiled.

"Does this poor, benighted heathen come into Recoil?" Shamus said.

"No," the sheriff said. "Unless he visits as a coyote or a bird."

"Then may holy St. Francis of Assisi help him," Shamus said. "If this shape-shifter talk is true, then the poor man is a sad, unnatural creature."

"Who is she, Colonel?" Ironside said.

"What are you talking about, Luther?"

"The gal who's the patron saint of all the animals."

"She's a him, Luther." Shamus glared at his segundo. "I'm surprised you don't know that, living in a good Catholic household like you do."

"I'm fond of animals," Ironside said. "Hell, I've even petted Jake's mean calico cat a few times and that's like picking up a roll of barbwire."

"Then I'm sure St. Francis is very proud of you," Shamus said.

"Damn right she is," Ironside said.

Clitherow smiled his way back into the conversation. "Now we've got that settled, Colonel, have another favor to ask."

"You want us to talk with the Navajo," Shamus guessed.

"That sums it up," the sheriff said.

Shamus turned to Ironside. "What do you think, Luther?"

"Anything's better than sitting on our butt around town."

"And sleeping in Jim's jail," Shamus said. "All right, we'll do it."

"Just explain to him what the problem is and

let Scout take it from there," Clitherow said. "I'll have to pay him of course."

"How do we get there?" Ironside asked.

"Ride due south and after a couple hours you'll come up on Bar Ridge. Scout's cabin is on the north side of the rise so you can't miss it."

"Jim, we don't have guns," Shamus said. "That damned pirate Condor took them."

Clitherow got to his feet and walked to a cabinet that stood against the wall near his desk. He turned a key in the lock and swung the doors open. "Take your pick. The long guns are in the rack by the door."

The cabinet was stacked with gun belts, all of them with a revolver in the holster.

"I've confiscated these from roosters who got drunk and decided to shoot up the town, or each other," Clitherow said. "Take whatever you like, except for the Remington in the canvas belt and holster. It's rusted out."

Shawn and Ironside examined the guns, all showing neglect and abuse. One beautifully engraved Colt was scarred by some puncher who'd used the barrel to string fence wire.

"Hardly choice weapons, Jim," Ironside said, his face sour.

"Better than nothing," the sheriff said, a shrug in his voice. "The rifles are better."

Finally Shamus and Ironside found a couple of

Colts that worked and strapped the belts on their hips to carry them.

"Both .44s I hope," Clitherow said. "That's the only caliber ammunition I have."

Luckily the revolvers were in .44-40 caliber, as were the two Winchesters Ironside chose from the gun rack.

"Scout might feed you or he might not, so I advise you to take along some grub." The sheriff extended his hand to Shamus and then Ironside. "Good luck."

"Hey, Jim, how do you kill one o' them skin-walkers?" Ironside asked.

"With a silver bullet."

Ironside couldn't decide if Clitherow was joshing him or not.

Chapter Eighteen

"Strip him, *compadres*. I want his shirt, pants, and hat." Álvaro Castillo smiled at Patrick O'Brien. "I hope this will not be an inconvenience. You can get your clothes back later if you don't mind taking them from a dead man who's already beginning to stink."

The Mexican rounded on his men, scowling. "Hey, I made a good joke."

He was rewarded by laughter and if it sounded forced he seemed not to notice.

Patrick's arms and feet were untied and rough hands removed his shirt and pants. "Damn you, Castillo," he said, his eyeglasses askew on his face, "what the hell are you doing with my duds?"

"I will make another good joke," the bandit said. "But since you are no longer my friend, I will not tell you what it is." He turned to his expectant men. "Dress the pig Santiago in the gringo's clothes. Hurry now. And then make me a cross of wood"—Castillo's fingers moved hurriedly over his chest—"the kind they have in church."

"What are you going to do with me?" Patrick asked.

The Mexican pretended to ponder that question, then said, "Are you Álvaro's friend again? You will tell me true."

Patrick realized the man was steeping along the ragged edge of outright insanity. He smiled. "Yes, you are my friend."

"Then we are *amigos* again?"

"Yes, we're *amigos.*"

"Then I will tell you this. I am not going to kill you, at least not yet." Castillo jabbed a forefinger at Patrick. "You are what the gamblers call my ace in the hole. If what I plan fails, then I will use you as barter. Maybe, if you're still alive by then."

He leaned back and slapped his ample belly with both hands. "See, friend helps friend. That is the way of the bandit." His face became solemn. "Now I must tie you up again, and that makes Álvaro ver' sad." He spread his arms. "But what else can I do, amigo? You might try to run away."

"I give you my word I won't try to escape," Patrick said.

The Mexican looked pained. "Unfortunately

mi amigo, the word of a gringo is as worthless as a needle without an eye. I'm sorry, but you must be bound and you must stay that way."

As Castillo's men retied Patrick to the tree, the bandit walked away and said over his shoulder, "Perhaps you will be free soon, amigo, and Álvaro will be a rich man. That night we will all celebrate with mescal."

Samuel O'Brien found his brother Jacob shoeing a horse at the blacksmith's forge. He looked around and said, "He's not here either."

"Who's not here?" Jacob asked.

"Patrick. He didn't come down for breakfast and he's not in his room."

"Is his butterfly net gone?"

"I don't know. I'll go take a look and then come back. Where is Shawn?"

"He's out on the range. We won't see him until tomorrow. Go check on the butterfly net, Sam, while I finish this last shoe."

Samuel left and returned quickly. "It's gone and so is the pack he wears."

Jacob let down the horse's leg and straightened. "We told him to stay close, damn it."

"His gun is still in the rack."

Jacob sighed. "Then we'd better go look for him. Saddle a horse, Sam. I'll ride this paint."

They hadn't reached the forge door when Lorena pushed inside, her face ashen. "Samuel, Jacob, you'd better come quick."

"Lorena, what's happened? Is it Patrick?"

"Come outside. Look at the mesa. Oh, dear lord, look at the mesa."

Jacob brushed past Samuel and sprinted outside. He looked toward the mesa and whispered, "Oh, my God."

Beside him Lorena sobbed and Samuel's face was stricken.

The dead body of Juan Santiago, wearing Patrick's clothes, hung on a rough cross made from pine trunks lashed together. Another rope was looped around the corpse's forehead, hidden by Patrick's hat. Every so often a man hidden in the brush near the edge of the mesa pulled on the end of the rope as though the body was raising its head in spasms of pain.

Before Castillo left the man he grinned and said, "Not too often, Pablo, and only when you see the gringos at the big house look up. Then just once or twice. We don't want them to see that the crucified man is not the butterfly gringo. Understand?"

"Si, patron."

"Manuel Vargas will ride out with a pack horse

to greet the *Americanos* at the house," Castillo said. "And when he returns he will be loaded down with much gold and silver."

"Then we ride away from here, Álvaro," Pablo said. "Is that not so?"

"Pah, what nonsense you speak, Pablo. The gold and silver is only the beginning. Soon I will sit in the big house and look out on my fat cattle and green land. Álvaro Castillo, the spawn of peasants, will live like a king. What do you think of that?"

"It is good for you, Álvaro, but I sense danger here." Pablo shook his head. "Much danger."

The bandit leader was silent for a moment as black flies droned around Santiago's bloody head and insects made their small music in the brush. "Tell me of this danger, Pablo." Castillo had the peon's superstitious respect for those gifted with the second sight. Pablo's mother was a famous witch. She had white, blind eyes but she saw much in dreams and Pablo dreamed, too.

"I can tell you little, Álvaro. But in a dream I saw a man who walks in darkness and he prayed in a church of holy St. Peter. I was much afraid and when I drew closer I asked him his name and he said, 'Death.' Aye, it was a terrible dream."

"Where is this man?"

Pablo pointed. "Down there in the great house. The one who killed Eustacio."

For a moment, Castillo was troubled. Then he smiled and said, "Pah. He can die like any other man."

Pablo nodded. "Perhaps he can. I do not know."

"You are an old woman, Pablo."

"I see what I see."

"Then keep watch and when you see the gringos come out of the house, do what I told you."

"*Sí, patrón.*"

Castillo was silent for a few more moments, then said, "I dream of gold, not death."

"It is good to dream of gold."

"And silver. I dream of silver."

"That too is good."

"Then you have nothing to fear." Castillo turned and walked away

Behind him, Pablo took a small cross from around his neck, kissed it, and put it away again.

"I can't tell you to wait until Shawn and the vaqueros get here," Lorena said. "So I don't know what to tell you."

"We can handle it," Samuel O'Brien said.

"No, you can't. You're just two men against twenty."

"We can't let Patrick die."

"I know that. I don't know what to do or say."

"There's nothing you can say, Lorena," Jacob said. "We've got it to do, Sam and me. There's nobody else."

"The servants . . ."

"They're not fighters, Lorena," Samuel said.

The woman bowed her head, tears falling to the ground at her feet.

"All right. Let's get it done, Jake." Samuel gathered up his horse's reins.

Jacob said nothing, his eyes fixed on the rider who had just emerged from the shimmering heat haze. The man was astride a mustang and he led another, pannier baskets hanging at its sides.

Sam followed Jacob's eyes and said, "A parley, do you think?"

"A demand more like," Jacob said.

Lorena shielded her eyes from the sun. "There's only one."

"Do we listen to what he has to say?" Samuel asked.

"We listen," Jacob said. "For a while at least."

The rider was a plump, jolly looking man with quick, intelligent black eyes. The brass cartridges in the belts that crossed his chest gleamed in the sun. "Greeting, *mis amigos.*" He removed his sombrero and fanned his face. "It is real hot today, is it not?" He smiled, showing the gold in his teeth. "Too hot for the man on top of the mesa. He may die soon, I think."

"What do you want?" Samuel said. "State your case, then beat it."

"Ah, my *patrón* Álvaro Castillo, has a . . . how do you say . . . proposition for you."

"What's he offering?"

"That's easy, señor. You will fill the baskets on my packhorse with gold and silver. Coins would be excellent, but gold and silver vessels and plate from your fine home will also be welcome, for we are very poor men."

"And if we do, what then?"

"Then? Why, we will cut down your . . . brother, is he not? . . . and restore him to you in good health and fine spirits." The Mexican glanced at the washed-out blue sky and replaced his hat. "It is too hot to talk anymore. Let us get our business done and I will be gone from here."

Jacob's gaze moved to the crest of the mesa where Patrick hung on the cross. His brother's head moved now and again, so he was still alive.

Samuel crossed his arms. "We don't pay extortion money or ransoms. So be on your way."

The Mexican looked less jolly. "You will let your brother die?"

"We'll do what we have to do," Samuel said. "Now you git while you can still breathe."

"Álvaro won't like this, *señores.* He won't like this at all. It could be very bad for the man on the cross."

"I told you to git. I won't tell you again."

The Mexican leaned from his horse and spat into the dirt. "Filthy pig gringos. You have refused Álvaro's generous offer and now your brother is a dead man."

"And so are you," Jacob said.

The man's black eyes swung on Jacob. "I came under a flag of truce. You cannot shoot me."

"I don't see a flag." Jacob drew and fired three times, the shots sounding like one. The bullets punched an ace of clubs dead center in the Mexican's chest and the man was dead when he hit the ground.

"Well," Samuel said, "that pretty much rips it."

Jacob nodded. "I know. But Dromore will not be held hostage and threatened by brigands. Now let's go save Patrick."

Chapter Nineteen

"I reckon that's the place," Luther Ironside said.

Shamus O'Brien nodded. "It's the only cabin in sight, so it's got to be." He kneed his horse forward. "We'll go in grinning, Luther, like we're visiting kinfolk."

"If ol' Scout has turned into a dog today, we can pat his head, like," Ironside said, grinning.

"Just so long as he wags his tail," Shamus said.

"Damn right." Ironside smiled. "That was funny, Colonel."

"Good, because I don't much feel like being funny."

They rode closer, their eyes everywhere.

The sun cast a golden hue on the day and birds sang in the trees. There was no suggestion of danger, yet Shamus felt uneasy and Ironside had dropped his right hand closer to his holstered Colt.

The wide arc of Bar Ridge curved around the cabin and tall pines grew close, almost shielding the flat-roofed stone building from view. Smoke from an iron chimney tied bows in the air and a couple of paint horses munched hay in the adjoining corral.

Ten yards from the front door, they drew rein. "Hello, the cabin!" Shamus yelled.

A few moments passed and then a man's voice said, "Mister, I got a Sharps fifty centered on your chest, so don't make any of them fancy gunfighter moves." Another pause then, "What the hell do you want?"

"My name is—"

"What do you want?"

"Jim Clitherow sent us. We're here to ask you to do a job for us."

The lace curtain in the cabin window twitched a little. "What kind of job?"

"We want you to find something. That is, if your name is Scout."

"That ain't my real given name, but it will do for a white man."

Shamus heard the murmur of a woman's voice, then Scout said, "I won't do your killing for you."

"No killing," Shamus said. "Just finding."

The man called Scout appeared at the cabin door, the Sharps still in his hands. "What did you say your name was?"

"You didn't give a chance to say my name, but it's Colonel Shamus O'Brien of Dromore and this is my segundo and friend, Luther Ironside."

"From up Glorieta Mesa way in the cattle country?"

"Indeed I am, and before that Texas and before that the blessed green isle of Ireland."

"How's Jake?"

"If you're talking about my son Jacob, he was doing just fine when I left."

"Jake's a good man, a fighting man," Scout said.

"Damn right he is," Ironside said. "I taught him all he knows."

Scout didn't comment on that. He studied the riders with eyes that missed nothing, and then seemed to make up his mind. "You are Jake's father, Colonel, and therefore a welcome guest in my home. Light and set, both of you. My woman has coffee on the stove."

Shamus and Ironside dismounted and Scout led them inside.

The cabin was neat, the old oak furniture waxed and polished to a honey color, and fine Navajo rugs covered the floor. In all, it was as cozy a home as Shamus had ever entered.

Scout circled the slender waist of a pretty Indian woman with his arm and smiled. "This is my wife, Abequa. She is Chippewa of the Little Shell tribe and she makes good coffee."

"I am honored to enter your home, ma'am," Shamus said, removing his hat before giving the woman a little bow.

"You have a dog, Scout?" Ironside said.

"No dog. Why do you ask?"

"I just wondered."

Ironside quailed under Shamus's blistering look and was glad when Abequa waved him into a chair at the table.

The woman served coffee in blue china cups, placing sugar and a small jug of canned milk within reaching distance.

Shamus produced a cigar. "May I crave your indulgence, ma'am?"

"Please do. My husband often enjoys a pipe."

For a while the three men drank coffee in silence while Abequa sat in a chair by the fireplace and applied flowered beadwork to a pair of buckskin leggings that were much favored by Chippewa women in wintertime.

"You have the manners and style of the old South, Colonel O'Brien," Scout said. "Did you fight in the war?"

"I had that honor. And so did Mr. Ironside."

"You bear a scar on your face. Was that from battle?"

"Indeed it was. A Yankee saber."

"Battle scars are honorable things, like gold medals."

"That is how I think of them, yes," Shamus said.

"What is it you wish me to find, Colonel O'Brien?" Scout said after a silence.

Shamus frowned. "The short answer is that I don't really know."

"To search for an unknown thing is impossible."

"Damn right, Scout," Ironside said. "So iffen you're gonna tree this coon you'd better bring all the dogs."

This brought him another glare from Shamus, who waited until Ironside squirmed, then said, "Scout, perhaps if I tell you what's happening, you can make a decision from there."

The Navajo nodded and the colonel told him about the night riders and their attempt to drive settlers and miners out of the southern Playas Valley.

"The question is why," Shamus said. "I can find no explanation."

After a moment's thought, Scout said, "Gold is usually what men desire and its glister can make them do evil things to acquire it."

"You mean them night riders are after a lost gold mine or some such?" Ironside said.

"It's likely."

"If there is such a mine, can you find it for us?" Shamus asked.

"Perhaps, but not in a day or a week and maybe not in a month."

"Come with us back to Recoil, Scout. Find the gold mine as quickly as you possibly can."

"You wish the gold for yourself?"

"No, I don't. But I believe if we take away what motivates Nate Condor and his men, the killings will stop."

"I have heard the name English Nate Condor," Scout said. "He is a man to be reckoned with."

"So I believe," Shamus said.

Scout was silent for so long that Shamus thought the Navajo's talking was done. But then he said, "I will think on this. Go back to Recoil and if I decide to help you I'll meet you there."

"When might that be?"

"When I think the time is right."

Shamus and Ironside exchanged glances and Abequa smiled at them from her chair as though it was a conversation she'd heard many times before.

"We'll pay you, of course," Shamus said, pushing it.

"Of course." Scout rose to his feet. "You can make Recoil before dark. I have no food to offer you because I have not hunted since the last full moon. My hired man, Mr. Hyde, will hunt tonight. You understand?"

Shamus rose and said he understood, though

he didn't. "We would not care to impose upon your hospitality further." He looked at Abequa and smiled. "You make a fine cup of coffee, ma'am. It was much appreciated."

"Thank you, Colonel. My husband will see you to your horses."

Shamus noticed for the first time that the woman's eyes were green flecked with gold . . . like those of a cougar.

"Well, hell, that didn't help much," Luther Ironside said.

"It wasn't conclusive, Luther, no."

"You think he'll show up in Recoil?"

"I really don't know."

"Why did he tell us he'd no grub? There was something cooking in a pot on the stove."

Shamus turned his head and smiled. "Would you want to eat it, whatever it was?"

"No, I guess not. It was probably something he killed under a full moon, huh?"

"An owl, maybe," Shamus said, grinning.

But Ironside wasn't listening. He rose in the stirrups and pointed east, to the foothills of the Big Hatchet Mountains. "Lookee, Colonel, among the trees. What the hell is that?"

Shamus reached behind him and retrieved a pair of field glasses from his saddlebags. He drew rein and scanned the aspen line for a few moments, then said, "It was there and now it's gone."

"What was it?"

"A cougar," Shamus said. "Small enough to be a hunting female, I reckon. She moved through the aspen like a puff of smoke, then vanished."

Ironside grinned. "Maybe it was ol' Scout."

"Or someone close to him."

Chapter Twenty

"Hell, Jake," Samuel O'Brien said, "how do we play this?"

"We shoot our way up the side of the mesa and free Pat before it's too late for him . . . and for us."

Samuel shook his head. "Thin. Damn, it's thin."

"Any ideas? I mean the kind that come to you real fast?"

"Not a one."

"Then we shoot our way up the mesa like I said."

"Wait!" Lorena yelled. She rushed from the front of the house to where Jacob and Samuel sat their horses. "Look behind you."

Four men rode from the direction of the barn, all carrying rifles except for old Amos the butler who toted a massive scattergun.

Jacob swung his horse around. "You boys know what you're getting yourselves in for? Those Mexicans are playing for keeps."

"I reckon," Vasily Petrov, the huge Russian blacksmith, said. "That is Patrick up there, Mr. O'Brien."

The colonel called the two other men with Petrov and Amos *footmen*. But they did odd jobs around Dromore—waiting at table, opening doors, and assisting the gentlemen to dress. Chosen for their height, rather than ability, they looked so alike that Shawn had named them the Dromore Bookends.

"We're going up the mesa shooting," Jacob said. "And the Mexicans will shoot back."

"We'll stick, is that not so, Mr. Brownlee?" one footman said to the other.

"Most assuredly, Mr. Godfrey," the second replied. "I'd say we are prepared for any desperate encounter."

Jacob slid his Winchester from the boot under his knee. "All right, then, "let's get 'er done."

Lorena watched the men leave, led by Jacob who understood the ways of the gun and the manner of gunfighters better than her husband ever would. Red-eyed, lean as a wolf but infinitely more dangerous, Jacob had been shot, knifed, and hammered, but never beaten. A black depression on his soul, he rode in a hellish gloom and Lorena felt a shiver of fear . . . for him . . . for her husband . . . and for the Mexicans.

* * *

Jacob led the way to the base of the mesa, swung out of the saddle, and ordered the others to dismount. "I'm going up. Sam, anybody you see on the rim, shoot them off me."

"Jake, you can't go up there by yourself," Samuel said.

But Jacob was already climbing, taking the narrow switchback trail the brothers O'Brien had cut when they were boys. He climbed steadily. Samuel's gaze moved constantly from him to Patrick, who was bloodstained enough to attract the attention of crows that cawed and fluttered around his head.

Every minute of delay as Jacob climbed was a minute closer to Patrick's death. The sun blazed, there was no breeze, and Samuel knew it would be brutally hot on the mesa. Heat waves shimmered off the stunted junipers at the crest. Patrick must be suffering the agonies of the damned.

Then his brother lifted his face to the sky and, shocked, Samuel saw that Castillo had fooled them. The man on the cross was not Patrick.

With that realization came the first shot from the rim as a rifleman cut loose at Jacob.

Samuel threw his Winchester to his shoulder and fired. Beside him, his men were also firing. Shooting uphill was uncertain, but somebody scored a hit because the Mexican rose up on his toes, toppled forward, and screamed all the way down until he hit the flat.

Jacob was maybe fifty feet from the rim, still climbing. He battled brush and cactus that had invaded the eyebrow of trail since it was last used years before and that slowed him.

Several Mexicans ran to the mesa rim, rifles in hand. Steady firing from the Dromore men drove them back.

Samuel heard the distant *pop-pop-pop* of Jacob's Colt as he fired at someone on the mesa's edge. Never great shakes with a long gun, Jacob preferred to use his revolver whenever he could.

"Fire at the crest," Samuel yelled to his men. "Keep their heads down."

"But Patrick—" Petrov began.

"It's not him. Damned Mexican fooled us."

All four Dromore men kept up a steady fire on the mesa and no more bandits appeared.

Samuel watched Jacob scramble onto the crest, then clamber to his feet. Bent low, gun in hand, he stepped to within a few feet of the crucified man, then stopped. He lifted the crucified man's head and Samuel was sure he heard Jacob cuss all the way from the mesa rim.

After a few moments, Jacob headed across the mesa and vanished from sight.

* * *

"They headed across the Pecos and then I lost sight of them in the aspen," Jacob said. "Patrick was with them."

"Are you sure it was him?" Samuel asked.

"It was him. He was wearing long johns and boots and nothing else and they'd made him carry his butterfly net."

Samuel frowned. "Hell, what do we do now?"

The sun had dropped lower, but the west side of Glorieta Mesa was still bathed in bright light. Jacob removed his hat and wiped his sweating brow with the back of his hand. "I'm going after them. It may take me a couple of days, but I'll find them."

"Then I'm going with you," Samuel said.

"No, Sam. You stay at Dromore and keep guard on the house. Castillo already fooled us once, and there's always the chance he'll double back and I'll miss him."

"Jake, we killed one man. Castillo still has sixteen, maybe even eighteen riders. You can't buck those kinds of odds."

"I'm sure going to try, Sam."

"Then Petrov goes with you," the Russian blacksmith said.

The man was well over six foot tall and thick muscle roped his shoulders and arms under his plaid shirt. His left cheek bore a terrible scar from his eye to the corner of his mouth, a reminder of the Cossack saber that laid his face open when he tried to save a Jewish servant girl during a pogrom in his village. Petrov had killed the Cossack and then fled his village and later his country.

"We need you at Dromore, Vasily," Jacob said. "You're the best blacksmith in the territory."

"I go. Save Mr. Patrick." Petrov stood as immovable as a pillar of roughhewn rock.

Samuel said, "You going to argue with him, Jake?"

Jacob smiled slightly. "No, I guess not."

"Me Rooshian man," Petrov said. "I learned from a boy how to shoot rifle worth a goddamn."

"Then mount up, let's go," Jacob said. "And keep that rifle handy."

"Wait, Mr. O'Brien." One of the Bookends untied a sack from his saddle horn. "Mr. Godfrey and I packed some food. We thought the gentlemen might feel hungry from their exertions, but now it will sustain you on your quest. Is that not so, Mr. Godfrey?"

"Indeed it is, Mr. Brownlee. We do not wish to see our gentlemen go hungry under any circumstances."

Jacob took the sack and nodded his thanks. Then he and Petrov mounted.

"Take care, Jake," Samuel said. "You're bucking some mighty long odds."

"Keep a lookout for the colonel and Luther," Jacob said. "Right now they're bucking odds of their own."

Aware of his brother's Irish gift, Samuel felt a sharp pang of anxiety. "Do you feel something, Jake? See something?"

Jacob smiled. "So long, Sam."

Samuel watched the two men ride away, the huge blacksmith and his ragged, moody brother who sat his horse like a sack of grain. A stab of fear dried his mouth and hollowed his belly and he wondered if he too shared the Irish gift.

Or was it the Irish curse?

Chapter Twenty-one

Weary as only men past the years of their youth can be weary, Shamus O'Brien and Luther Ironside rode into Recoil, their horses plodding along a dark street splashed with rectangles of orange and yellow light from the saloons and stores lining the boardwalks. They tied their horses to the rail outside the sheriff's office and slapped off clouds of trail dust before stepping inside.

Jim Clitherow sat at his desk. Dallas Steele sprawled elegantly in a chair opposite him. A bottle of Old Crow and a couple of glasses stood between them.

"Ah, the wanderers return," Steele said. "And if I ever seen men who needed a drink, it's you two."

"Glad you said that," Ironside said. "I thought maybe the whiskey was reserved for lawmen."

Steele rose to his feet. "Sit here, Colonel. You look all used up."

"I won't argue with you, son." Shamus collapsed into the chair. "Pour me a stiff shot of redeye, Dallas."

Clitherow waited until Shamus and Luther had their drinks in hand before he questioned them about their trip to Scout's cabin.

"He said he'll think about it," Shamus said. "If he decides to work for us he said he'd come here to Recoil."

"You can't push an Injun into making a quick decision," Clitherow said.

"Is there anything else?"

"His wife makes good coffee then turns into a cougar," Ironside said.

"Luther, that was just a coincidence," Shamus said. "People don't turn into animals. If they did, it would be in the Bible." He read the question on Clitherow's face and explained. "We saw a cougar in the aspens after we left the cabin. Luther is convinced it was Scout's wife, Abequa."

"I met her just once," Clitherow said. "She's a strange one to be sure. Piute, isn't she?"

"Chippewa," Shamus said. "And a really beautiful woman."

"Yes, she's all of that," Clitherow agreed.

"Why do you need the Indian?" Steele asked.

Shamus looked at Clitherow, who said, "I haven't told him about your idea."

"It's simple really," Shamus said. "Nate Condor and his men are trying to force people out of this part of the valley. He must have a reason, and gold is as good a reason as any. We take the gold away from him and he has no excuse to stick around."

"Maybe there's a lost gold mine around here somewhere," Ironside said.

Dallas Steele looked uncomfortable, and that puzzled Shamus. "You reckon I'm barking up the wrong tree, Dallas?"

"I don't think it's a lost gold mine," Steele said. "It's difficult to hide a gold mine, especially since the territory is teeming with tinpans."

It was an unsatisfactory answer and Shamus waited for more, but the Pinkerton had closed down and lapsed into a tight silence.

Clitherow had also stared at Steele expectantly. When the man offered nothing further, he looked up from the cigarette he was inexpertly building and said, "Maybe the best option is to move against the night riders, like I suggested earlier. Wipe out the whole damned nest of them in one fell swoop."

Steele opened up again. "Too many dead men on the ground and most of them would be the respectable citizens of your fair town, Sheriff.

Recoil would never recover after paying a butcher's bill like that."

The door of the office burst open and a bearded, agitated man in the flannel shirt and lace-up boots of a miner rushed inside. "Torches in the hills, Sheriff. And a heap o' hootin' and hollerin'."

Clitherow sprang to his feet. "Are they planning an attack, Rudy?"

The miner shook his head. "They're plannin' something, Sheriff, but I'm damned if I know what it is."

Clitherow grabbed his gun belt from the rack as Shamus and Ironside stood, but Steele said, "You boys stay right here. You've done enough for one day."

"If it's an attack, we want to be there," Shamus said. "We're not going to sit here and listen to the shooting and wonder what's going on."

"It's not an attack, Colonel. If Nate Condor attacks this town he'll hit without warning." Steele smiled. "You and Luther have another drink. If we need you, we'll send for you." He followed Clitherow out the door.

Shamus checked the loads in his Colt. "Let's go, Luther."

"Damn right. You know what they were saying to us, don't you?"

"I know what they were saying. You don't have to tell me."

"They were saying we're too old, Colonel. That's what they were saying."

Shamus smiled. "Well we're not, Luther, are we?"

"Damn right we're not."

"So why are we standing here jawing instead of doing?"

"What do you make of it, Dallas?" Clitherow said.

"I reckon they're trying to scare us," Steele said.

"Well, it looks like they're succeeding."

People had gathered in the street, women with shawls around their shoulders against the evening chill, one man with a stained napkin tucked under his chin as though he'd just risen hurriedly from supper. The sporting crowd had piled out of the saloons, the girls wearing yellow, red, and blue dresses that added flares of color to the drabness of the respectable matrons and the dark street.

Gamblers were placing bets on the ruckus being the prelude to an attack by the night riders and Long Tom Totthill, once a high-roller on the Mississippi riverboats, was concerned enough to shove his derringer in the pocket of his brocade vest where it was handier.

"You men get your rifles," Clitherow called out to the men in the street. "And get the ladies home." He pointed to a blond woman in a bright scarlet dress. "And that includes you, Roxie, and the rest of the girls."

The woman named Roxie lifted her skirt, revealing a shapely leg and a .22 pepperbox revolver tucked into her garter. "Hell, Sheriff, I'm ready for anything, lovin' or shootin', whatever them gents in the hills want."

"Save the stinger for the customers who play and don't pay, Roxie. We'll do the shooting and let you concentrate on the lovin'."

That drew a laugh from the crowd as Clitherow knew it would.

A man called out, "Hey, Sheriff, you reckon they'll attack?"

"I don't know. But we'd better be ready."

Dallas Steele looked north to the foothills of the Big Hatchets where torches bobbed like fireflies in the distance. He heard howls and roars from the riders, but they seemed to be making no attempt to come closer.

But their tactics were working.

Some of the more hardened Recoil denizens like Roxie and Long Tom Totthill didn't scare worth a damn, but others did. The respectable women had left the street and their husbands with them. So far none of the men had returned with their hunting rifles.

"What do you think, Dallas?" Clitherow said. "Will Condor open the ball tonight?"

Steele's blue Colt was in his hand. "We stay right here in the street for now and see how things develop."

Clitherow looked around him. "The horses are gone."

"Damn it," Steele said. "What are those two old coots up to?"

"Up to no good, I imagine," Clitherow said.

Steele turned when he heard the *tap-tap-tap* of a woman's boots on the boardwalk. Chastity Ludsthorpe put her hand on his arm and said, "What's happening, Dallas? There are men in the hills and mother is beside herself with worry."

"It's the night riders." Then, to ease her fears, Steele said, "But don't worry. I think this is a show and they won't attack."

"You think, but you don't know."

"Not for sure," Steele said.

"I wish I'd never come here to this godforsaken place," Chastity said.

Now was not the time to discuss why the girl was in Recoil, so Steele said, "Go home, Chastity. Tell your mother she is quite safe, but to keep her door locked."

"I'll tell her, but it won't help much." She smiled. "I'm sorry to burden you like this, Dallas."

"It's no burden. Now go home and do like I told you."

Chastity smiled again and turned away, but stopped in her tracks as gunfire hammered through the dark, moon-bladed foothills.

Chapter Twenty-two

The night was cool and Shamus O'Brien sat still on his horse, his tired eyes reaching into the darkness.

"How many do you figure, Colonel?" Luther Ironside said in a hoarse whisper.

"Four, five, no more than that."

The two riders were hidden in a shallow valley, the sweep of a hillside facing them. On the top of the rise torches flared, as the masked night riders rode back and forth, yelling at the top of their lungs.

"Ain't so scary up close, are they?" Ironside pointed out.

"They're damned trash, Luther," Shamus said. "No braver than us and probably a lot more cowardly."

"We ain't cowards, Colonel."

"No, Luther, by God, we aren't. Follow me."

Shamus swung his horse to the east and rode through the valley, no more than a grassy dry wash, heavy stands of juniper and piñon growing on both banks.

As he had hoped, the flat-topped hillside they'd faced petered out onto a low, grassy meadow. Looping to the west he took to the rise at its lowest part and followed the gradual incline upward, Ironside close behind him. Attacking the night riders on the level ground atop the hill was a much better alternative than a headlong charge up a steep slope on tired horses.

Riding at a slow walk, Shamus figured the distance between him and the night riders. Three hundred yards? Maybe less, and most of it open ground as the juniper thinned.

They rode a little closer.

Ironside booted his rifle and drew his revolver. When the ball opened, it would be close gun work in crowding darkness. The Colt wasn't as accurate as a rifle but at spitting distance it would give a good account of itself . . . . if the shooter did his part. And Luther Ironside was better than most with Sammy's iron.

He and Shamus covered another hundred yards and ahead of them the torches still flared, moving back and forth, the riders hurling curses at the town below.

Suddenly, Shamus drew rein and Ironside rode into him. "What the hell, Colonel?"

Shamus turned in the saddle and put his finger to his lips. He reached into his saddle-bags and came up with two Remingtons he'd taken from Clitherow's cabinet and passed one to Ironside.

Echoing what Ironside had decided earlier, Shamus whispered, "Two guns are better than one in these intimate social occasions."

Ironside grinned and showed his teeth like a hungry wolf.

"We'll get a little closer," Shamus said. "Then we charge."

"Lead on, Colonel. I'm loaded for bear."

Both men had dropped the reins and guided their mounts at a walk with their knees.

"Hey, what the hell is that?" a man's voice called from the darkness.

"They've spotted us!" Shamus yelled. He kneed his horse. "Forward at the trot, Luther!" After a few moments, he called, "Charge at the gallop!"

Both mounts broke into a run and, as Ironside had done before, he and Shamus shot into darkness, using the night riders' torches as targets. His hammering guns bucking in his hands, Shamus felt a wild, savage joy, like a young horse soldier again. Beside him, Ironside yodeled his Rebel yell, his lips peeled back from his teeth in a snarl.

"Damn it. They're up there shooting," Clitherow said. "They're attacking like they're back in the war."

"Seems like," Steele said, smiling.

"They're way too old to be doing that. They'll get themselves killed."

"Old, maybe, but by God, they're fighting men. I'm proud to know them."

Clitherow shook his head. "That's the trouble with old Johnny Rebs. Fear doesn't enter into their thinking."

"You should know, Jim. You're one yourself."

"Yeah, I am, and that's why I wish to hell I was up there with them."

"They didn't stand," Luther Ironside said, outrage and disbelief in his voice. "Damn it, Colonel. They ducked out and them on ground of their own choosing."

"You hit any of them, Luther?" Shamus asked.

"I don't reckon so, they were running so fast. You?"

Shamus shook his head. "Refusing to fight on their own ground against a numerically inferior enemy. It's hard to believe. Hell, Luther, I don't want to believe it."

"Cowardice in the face of the enemy, that's what it was. They should all be lined up and shot like dogs."

Shamus was so stunned he worried the thing like a dog with a bone. "They outnumbered us two to one, Luther, and should've stood their ground. We didn't even come under fire. Damn them, may the devil roast their hides for yellow-bellies."

Ironside nodded. "I never in all my born days seen the like, Colonel. Right now there should be men dead on the dirt or gasping their last, but there's not."

"Disgraceful," Shamus said. "Just . . . dis-graceful."

Ironside sighed deeply, then stared at the star-studded sky for a few moments. "Well," he said finally, "the danger is past and a superior enemy has fled the field of honor without fight."

"Disgraceful," Shamus said again. "Just . . . disgraceful."

"Disgraceful," Shamus O'Brien repeated. "The damned cowards fled the field."

Dallas Steele smiled. "I guess they thought discretion was the better part of valor, Colonel."

"Valor?" Ironside said. "There was no valor on that hilltop. Damn them, they didn't fire a shot at us. How low can men be to refuse to stand on their own ground?"

"Maybe they had orders not to fight," Clitherow said. "Just make a show and scare the daylights out of folks."

"No, they were craven," Ironside said. "I always told the O'Brien boys, 'If'n yore knees start knockin', kneel on them.' An' that's what them night riders should've done."

The glow of the oil lamp tinted the sheriff's office the color of unpolished brass and deep shadows gathered in the corners where the spiders lived.

Shamus sighed deeply and rose to his feet. "Well, it's me for my cot. This was a night of shame I'll forever try to forget."

"I guess I should turn in as well." Ironside yawned. "It's been a long day."

"You boys did well tonight," Steele said.

Ironside shook his head. "Yeah. 'Chargin' at hosses' asses.'"

Chapter Twenty-three

Jacob O'Brien and Vasily Petrov crossed the Pecos a few miles east of Hurrado Mesa, riding through a day that was slowly shading into evening. To the north, shadows gouged the El Barro Peaks and dark blue light pooled among the pines.

The tracks left by the Mexicans were plain to follow. Jacob led the way through a vast, empty, wooded land that smelled of timber and the first of the summer wildflowers. After three miles, the tracks made an abrupt turn to the east then looped back toward the river.

"They've headed west again," Jacob said. "It seems like Álvaro Castillo has no intention of running."

"Then we follow them," Petrov said.

"Yeah, we follow them."

But night was coming down fast and already a

few stars hung like lanterns in the pink sky. Wakened by the growing dark, hunting coyotes yipped among the hills and a solitary quail called out in alarm.

Jacob pushed them as long as he could, but by the time he regained the Pecos the darkness crowded close. "We'll make camp here, Vasily," he said, drawing rein. "And take to the trail tomorrow at first light."

"Maybe dark good time to free Patrick."

"Yeah, maybe. But Castillo could've crossed the river anywhere. I lost his tracks about a mile back, so he figured he's being followed and decided to cover his trail."

"We find him in the morning, goddamn," Petrov said.

"Yes, Vasily, in the morning." Jacob felt oddly weary, as though all the life had been drained out of him.

Later, as he and Petrov sat around a hatful of fire and ate the roast beef sandwiches the Bookends had packed, the Russian said, "I have heard you play the piano, Mr. O'Brien."

"Call me Jake. Everybody else does."

"You play with soul, like a Russian."

Jacob managed a small smile. "I play Chopin a lot, and he was Polish."

"He was a Slav. He shares some of the Russian spirit." Petrov had a thick mane of blond hair and his eyes were the color of the sky on a morning in the dead of winter. "I've heard you play the music of Pyotr Ilyich Tchaikovsky."

Jacob nodded. "His First Piano Concerto is a work of genius."

"He is a complex man."

"Yeah, I guess he is."

"But there is darkness in him. Sometimes the Russian soul is dark as night." Petrov sighed. "One day Pyotr will kill himself."

Jacob stared at the Russian, the hollows of his eyes masked with shadow. "I won't kill myself, Vasily."

"No, Jake, you won't. But the darkness will. If you let it."

"It's a black dog that waits its chance to attack me."

"Or a wolf. And on a night like this the wolf always seems larger than he is and the darkness in a man's soul grows even darker."

"Don't you get melancholy, Vasily? You're a Russian after all."

Petrov smiled. "No, never. And do you know why?"

"No, tell me."

"Because the iron lifts my spirit. Iron is not male, Jake. It is female. She can go from a red-hot heat to icy cold in the space of a moment. She sings with the voice of an angel, a high ringing peal that's a delight to the ear, but she can hiss like the devil when a man quenches her fire. Yes, my friend, iron is a woman."

Jacob smiled. "Maybe I should look for a wife."

Petrov shook his head. "I have the iron, you have your music. Neither of us needs a wife. Better to sleep with a paid woman who comes and goes and makes no demands. A woman's love is a heavy responsibility for any man."

Jacob passed the bottle of wine he'd found in the supplies and Petrov drank then wiped his mouth with a hand the size of a bear paw. "Let the melancholy go, Jake. Do not nurture it and make it your best friend."

"You're a wise man, Vasily."

"For a blacksmith," Petrov said, smiling.

"For anybody."

"I will go down to the river and wash," Petrov said.

"You mean all over?" Jacob asked.

"Yes, all over."

"Why? You're a blacksmith. You'll just get dirty again."

"If tomorrow is the last day of my life, I will spare the women the task of washing my body," the Russian said. "I do not wish to impose upon them."

Jacob smiled. "Now who is melancholy?"

"No melancholy in Vasily this night. He merely wishes to meet his God clean."

"Vasily, for heaven's sake, you're making me a-feared. You're not going to die tomorrow. Neither of us is going to die tomorrow, or the next day come to that."

The big Russian said nothing, but rose to his feet and walked toward the Pecos. He stopped, and then said over his shoulder, "We will see, my friend. We will see."

Jacob and Petrov scoured both banks of the Pecos where Castillo could have crossed, but found no tracks.

"He's rode up or downstream a ways," Jacob said. "We could spend days scouting this area and find nothing."

"Then now what do we do?" Petrov asked.

"Head back to Dromore and let the Mexican come to us. My pa would call that fighting on our own ground."

"Maybe Castillo will return to Mexico."

"No. As long as he has Patrick as a bargaining chip he'll stick around."

They sat their horses in the river as the shallow water fussed and flurried around them. Jays quarreled in the juniper and the cool morning air was coming in laundered. On the opposite bank, a flock of quail exploded from the brush and immediately the flat statement of a rifle crashed through the quiet.

Vasily Petrov reeled in the saddle as his chest fountained a scarlet gout of blood. The big Russian fell from the saddle and splashed mightily into the river.

Jacob drew, saw a target, and fired.

The Mexican in the brush was hit hard and he jerked erect, his rifle spinning away from him. Jacob fired again and the man went down, rolled, and lay still.

One glance at Petrov floating facedown in the water told Jacob the man was dead. He had time only for a quick pang of regret before he kicked his horse into a gallop, splashing across the river then climbing the bank.

The Mexican lay on his back, dead as he was ever going to be, but there was no other living thing in sight except for the man's horse tethered a distance away.

Jacob swore bitterly. Castillo had spread men out along the riverbank in the hope of a picking off his pursuers. So the man had known all along that he and Petrov were on his trail.

Cursing his own carelessness, Jacob again rode into the Pecos, dismounted, and dragged the Russian's huge body to the bank. Vasily Petrov was dead and a long way from home.

Jacob had admired the man's strength, his

wisdom, and his quiet dignity. All that had been destroyed in an instant on the orders of an ignorant savage who killed only for profit.

Jacob gritted his teeth, his rage flaring as he made a vow to kill Álvaro Castillo, to shoot him in the belly where it hurt most and prolonged the dying.

Samuel and Shawn O'Brien were in the study when they saw Jacob slowly draw near Dromore leading two horses, one with a dead man on its back. They stepped out of the house and waited in silence until he drew rein.

"Vasily is dead. He was killed on the Pecos, shot from ambush."

"Damn. He was a fine blacksmith." For a moment, Shawn looked stricken, then he said, "That was a callous thing to say."

"As good an epitaph for a man as any. Vasily Petrov bathed in the river last night and he's met his God clean. The women don't need to wash his body." Jacob swung stiffly out of the saddle, his dismount more ungraceful than usual. "Castillo posted a bushwhacker back at the Pecos. He got Vasily with his first shot."

"And Patrick?" Samuel asked.

Jacob's shoulders slumped. "I don't know where Patrick is."

Chapter Twenty-four

Edith Ludsthorpe held up her coffee cup and made a face, causing Dallas Steele to reckon she was in an even sourer mood than usual. "The coffee is not to your taste, Mrs. Ludsthorpe?"

"Indeed it is not," the woman said. She sat at an adjoining table in the restaurant not yet busy with the early morning crowd. "It is unspeakable swill that doesn't merit the name coffee."

Edith crooked a finger at the young waitress. "You there, missy. Did you prepare this vile brew?"

The girl shook her head. "The owner makes the coffee, ma'am."

"He does, does he? Well, I have a notion to go back there to the kitchen and box his ears." Edith sniffed. "Does he have tea? Though God knows it will be just as bad."

"I'll ask," the waitress said, taking a step back

as though she feared Edith would attack with her parasol.

"Well, don't stand there lollygagging, girl. Go at once and determine the availability of tea."

A few more customers entered the restaurant and Steele rose and stood beside Edith's table. "Do you mind if I join you, Mrs. Ludsthorpe?"

"Why not? I suppose your company is as good as anyone else's in this benighted town."

Steele sat at her table. "When can we expect the company of the fair Miss Chastity this morning?"

"In a word, Mr. Steele, you can't. At least not for today." Edith frowned. "That was two words, wasn't it?"

"I hope she isn't ill," Steele said. "Or otherwise indisposed."

"Not in the least. She's gone out with nice Mr. Bird. He's teaching her the rudiments of landscape painting, I understand. His own work has been compared, quite favorably I must say, to the great Thomas Cole and to Albert Bierstadt."

Steele smiled. "They're sticking close to town, I presume."

"Then, sir, you presume too much. Mr. Bird told me he plans to drive in his surrey to a place called Apache Hills where the vistas are quite—"

"Are you sure that's what he said?"

"Of course I'm sure. He said it to me, didn't he?"

Steele swore under his breath. "That damned idiot!" He rose quickly to his feet.

"Why, Mr. Steele! What in the world has come over you? Have you gone quite mad?"

"The night riders, skull riders, whatever you want to call them, are pressing close to town. In the flat country to the west they'll see Bird coming for miles."

Edith looked stricken. "Do you mean to say my daughter's life is in imminent danger?"

"What do you think?" Steele said before he flung out the door and slammed it behind him. He raced to the livery.

"Come on, Jonesy, we've got ground to cover," Steele said.

The donkey, a placid creature, allowed himself to be bridled without fuss.

The old man who ran the livery stepped beside Steele. "I see you ain't got a hoss yet, young feller."

Steele ignored that. "When did Maurice Bird pull out of here?"

"Oh, 'bout an hour ago. Had that real purty Miss Chastity with him an' a picnic basket."

"Picnic basket," Steele said as though he couldn't believe what his ears were telling him. "Don't tell Sheriff Clitherow I'm gone, huh?"

The oldster smiled. "Clitherow ain't about

to go on a picnic, not with them night riders around."

Steele nodded. "Don't tell him anyway."

"I won't. Less'n he asks."

"Don't tell him then either."

"You can take the sheriff's hoss," the old man said. "He won't be needin' it today."

"Jonesy is a fine steed," Steele said. "He can cover ground at a fast clip."

"Whatever you say, mister."

Steele led the burro out of the stable and headed east toward Hatchet Gap. He'd mount Jonesy later when the little animal just might give him an edge.

Having gone east as far as he wanted, Steele turned the donkey northwest toward the Apache Hills. In the distance the sun had cleared the Cedar Mountains and was already hot. Gold, silver, and turquoise had been found around the hills and there was always the possibility Bird and Chastity would meet up with some miners.

But, as a gambling man, Steele knew the odds were against it. The grasslands and brush flats of the Hachita Valley were vast and miners few and far between. His eyes constantly swept the wild land, wishful for his field glasses. They were in his room at the hotel and beyond his reach.

After an hour, he caught a lucky break, picking up the tracks of Bird's surrey heading straight as an arrow toward the Apache Hills before disappearing into the distance in an inverted V.

Steele felt hot and dusty and his boots, sewn for looks on a narrow last by the Lucchese Boot Co., his boot maker in San Antonio, punished his feet.

A buzzard circled in the brassy sky, waiting and watching, as though aware of the tensions going on under him. The breeze was light but restless as it moved across the sand and drove fine grains into the brush with a soft ticking sound. The air smelled dusty from the passage of the surrey that Steele thought must surely be close.

After another fifteen minutes walking under the climbing sun, he led Jonesy around an arrow-shaped outcropping of eroded rock, then swung northeast again and stopped right where he was. Ahead of him, upended between some scattered piñon, the surrey lay on its side. He saw loose horses and three figures moving around—two were men, the other was Chastity.

"Jonesy, now we got it to do." Steele stepped onto the donkey's back, eased his Colt in the shoulder holster, and said, "Gee-up."

Depending on the circumstances, a dude wearing a gray suit and plug hat of the same color could be taken for a danger. But when he's riding a donkey, he goes from possible threat to an object of derision.

And that was exactly what Dallas Steele was counting on.

As he drew closer, he summed up the situation fast.

Maurice Bird lay on his back, dead or alive Steele couldn't tell. Chastity, her dress torn from her shoulders and blood running from the corner of her mouth, had backed up against a piñon, her eyes terrified as two grinning men stalked her. So intent were they on the woman, the men didn't see Steele until he was less then thirty feet from them.

"Howdy, boys," he said when he was within conversation distance. "It's a hot one, isn't it?"

"Well, what the hell are you?" One of the men was a small, mean-faced man with the eyes of a carrion eater.

Steele ignored that. He turned his head and said, "Chastity, are you all right. Did they harm you?"

"Not yet," the small man said, his face ugly, "but we will real soon." His hand was close to his gun. "I'll ask you this just one more time, mister. What the hell are you?"

Steele stepped off Jonesy. "I'm your death, I reckon."

The second gunman was taller, younger, and

wary. "He's slick, Luke. Mighty slick. He'll make fancy moves."

The man called Luke grinned. "Try this fancy move for size, dude." He drew. And died right where he stood. His gun hadn't cleared leather when Steele's bullet hit dead center in the man's chest.

The youngster, thinking he had an edge while the dude was engaged with Luke, went for his Colt. He never made it. Hit hard twice, he stared at Steele, his eyes full of wonder, and fell face-down into the sand.

Panicked by the gunfire the outlaw horses reared and galloped away in the direction of Hatchet Gap, dust spurting from their hooves.

"Damn," Steele said, "I could've sold those."

Chastity, her mouth trembling, said, "Those men . . . they were going to . . . to . . . they wanted to . . ."

"I know what they were going to do," Steele said. "They'll never do it again to another woman." He kneeled beside the younger man and rolled him onto his back.

The kid's green eyes looked up at him. "I should never have left Texas. My ma cried when I left. Maybe she knew how I would end."

"Around these parts a man who isn't fast on

the draw and shoot has no right to wear a gun," Steele said. "You one of those night riders?"

The youngster nodded, then suddenly defiant, he said, "You ain't as fast as English Nate Condor."

"Your time is short, boy. Take your medicine and make your peace with God."

"Who the hell are you, mister?" Blood welled on the kid's lips.

"They call me the Fighting Pink. Or so I'm told."

"I never stood a chance with you, did I?"

"Not a hope in hell, boy."

The youngster closed his eyes and all the life that was in him drained away.

Chastity kneeled beside Maurice Bird and then looked over at Steele. "He's dead, Dallas."

Steele rose and took a knee beside the artist. He studied the bullet hole in Bird's chest and then turned him over. "Two balls went right through his chest."

"He didn't have a chance," Chastity said. "They just rode up and started shooting. And it was for no reason."

"You were the reason, Chastity," Steele said. "I'll get the surrey on its wheels and we'll take you back to Recoil."

"You saved my life, Dallas," Chastity said with promise in her eyes. "I owe you."

"You owe me nothing," Steele said. "Maybe

you owe each of the dead men a life, but I can't say that for sure. It's something I'd have to study on for a spell."

"What do we do with them?"

"Leave them for Nate Condor to find, I guess. They were his men."

Chapter Twenty-five

Steele righted the surrey and hitched up the Morgan again. He was about to lift Bird and put him in the back seat of the surrey when a flicker of movement and a flash of metal in the direction of the Apache Hills caught his eye. Was it more of Condor's gunmen on the prowl?

He punched out the empty shells from his Colt and reloaded all six chambers. It paid a man to be careful and the extra shot might make the difference.

Chastity followed his gaze and Steele heard her sharp intake of breath. "Is it more night riders?"

"I don't know," Steele said, his eyes on the hills. "If it is, I'll make my fight right here. Can you handle a gun?"

"No . . . I can't."

"Pity. But I must say, most ladylike."

The sun was higher and he shaded his eyes,

scanning the distance. Whoever had moved back there was showing no inclination to come closer.

"Chastity, Maurice will have to wait a little longer. I'm going to take a look-see over there. I wonder—"

"Dallas, I'm not staying here with three dead men," the girl interrupted, giving him no time to finish his thought. "I'll come with you."

"Dead man can't hurt you," Steele said. "And Maurice couldn't have hurt you dead or alive."

"I don't care. I don't want to be here alone. Their eyes will look at me."

"All right. Let me help you into the carriage."

As they drove toward the hills, Chastity said, "Who do you think is there?"

"If I'm guessing right, miners. And if my second guess is right, I bet they're hiding something."

"What makes you think that?"

"Just a hunch."

"Do you get these hunches often?"

"Sure do. That's why I've stayed alive so long."

A sudden, spinning wind picked up. For a few moments, it rattled angrily in the brush and lifted veils of sand that tossed grit and dust into the surrey. Chastity and Steele bowed their heads against driving grains that stung their unprotected faces like hornets.

Then, as fast is it had begun, the wind died

and the brush flats lay still again under the blazing sun.

"Where the heck did that come from?" Chastity asked.

"It just happens," Steele said. "The Sioux call it *Mato Wamniyomi*, the desert wind that comes out of nowhere."

Chastity did her best to wipe off her face with a scrap of lace handkerchief, but Steele contented himself by taking off his hat and pouring water from the canteen over his dusty head.

The purple silhouettes of the Apache Hills loomed close, near enough for Steele to see a man and woman standing on the bank of a dry wash, close to the white skeleton of a dead piñon. Fifteen feet from the couple, he reined up the Morgan and said, "Howdy." He turned his head to the woman and touched the brim of his hat. "Ma'am."

The woman was no more than a slip of a girl about the same age as Chastity, but much prettier with a tumbling mass of auburn hair, hazel eyes, and the kind of body that keeps a thinking man awake of nights. She had something in common with the man, the hostile expression on her beautiful face and the equally hostile Henry rifle she held in her hands.

"What do you want, mister?" The man was past

middle age, grizzled and sun browned, his gray beard falling to the waistband of his canvas pants. He had gray eyes that showed memories of distant laughter, but at the moment, they were cold as hoar frost.

"I guess you heard the shooting, huh?" Steele said.

"Heard it," the man said. "Didn't think much of it, though."

"It was night riders. I drove over to make sure you were all right."

"Heard o' them night riders. They don't bother me none."

"They might, if you've got a claim back there somewhere."

"I've got me a claim," the man said. The muzzle of his Winchester lifted an inch. "Nobody is taking it from me."

"Glad to hear that." Steele smiled, trying to take the ice out of the air. "My name is Dallas Steele and this is Miss Chastity Ludsthorpe."

"Dallas Steele?" the old man said. "I've heard o' you. You're the man they call the Fighting Pink. I read about you in one o' them dime novels."

"Don't believe everything you read. I never in my life held off a bloodthirsty band of Apaches with my trusty revolver while the captive prairie maiden escaped." Steele smiled. "Unless, of course, it happened and I forgot about it."

"Well, this will test your memory as well," the old man said. "You ever hear tell of a ranny by the name o' Skate Sutton?"

Steele shook his head. "Can't say as I do."

"Well, you should. You shot him up Colorado way, in a town they called Graham's Flat. He was kin o' mine."

"Sorry about that. You have my deepest condolences."

"No need for that. He was treacherous and needed killin'." The old man seemed to make up his mind about something, then said, "Name's Lum Park and this here is my daughter Rhody."

"Pleased to make both your acquaintances," Steele said.

"What you doin' in this neck o' the woods?" Park asked. "There ain't no wild towns around here to tame as far as I know."

"I'm just here on boring Pinkerton and government business," Steele said. "Mostly about water and grazing rights."

"Strange that. There not being many ranches around these parts."

"Ah, well it only takes one troublemaker, you know," Steele said, blinking.

"It wouldn't be that you've been listening to wild stories, now would it, Steele?" Park said. "Maybe one wild story in particular got you headed in this direction?"

"What kind of story in particular? A man in my line of work hears a lot of stories."

"Oh, let's say about the army an' Apaches an' a lost pay wagon filled with gold? That kind of wild story."

Steele hesitated, and Park read the signs. "You have heard about it."

"I believe I was told something about a stolen pay wagon that was stashed around these parts by the Apaches," Steele said. "I don't quite remember where or when."

"You got a real bad memory for stuff, ain't you?" Park said. "It's a kind of affliction with you, huh?"

"I think you could safely say that."

"Well, the story about the pay wagon is just that, a big story. There's not a word of truth in it. Probably got started by a drunk tinpan and some folks took him serious."

Steele nodded. "That's always the case, isn't it? Tall tales about lost gold mines and such that don't have a word of truth to them."

Rhody spoke for the first time. "Pa, I've got a stew on the stove. Best I get back before it burns."

"These folks were just leavin' anyhow." Park pretended an affability he obviously didn't feel. "Well, Mr. Steele, I guess you'll be on your way an' thankee fer the visit. Me an' Rhody don't get many visitors."

Steele didn't push it. "I'm glad you're safe here. Maybe I'll drop by sometime just to check on you."

"No need fer that. Me an' Rhody can take care of ourselves just fine."

Steele smiled and touched his hat. "Well, so long. Nice meeting you, Miss Rhody."

"It's Mrs.," the girl said, her voice cold. "Skate Sutton was my husband."

Chapter Twenty-six

English Nate Condor's face was black with rage. "Two more? You're telling me we lost two more?"

"That's how it shapes up, Cap'n," Barney Merden said. "Luke McLennan and Tom Barden left dead on the ground."

"Who did it? Damn you, Barney, give me a name."

"Lum Park says it was Dallas Steele."

"Steele? He gunned two of my boys?"

"Seems like. It's not a story Park would make up."

"McLennan was good with a gun, fast on the draw. He killed his share."

Merden, who was wasn't hearing anything he didn't already know, nodded. "I guess Steele was faster."

"Why did he kill McLennan and the kid?" Condor asked.

"Lum says Steele had a girl with him when he came snooping around his place," Merden said. "You know how them two boys were about women, Cap'n. I guess they wanted to screw the girl and Steele shot them."

"Steele is dangerous," Condor said. "I have a bad feeling about this. The Pinkertons didn't send him into the territory to a dung heap like Recoil without a real good reason."

"You think he knows about the wagon?"

"He might suspect something, or the government does. The damned army and the Pinkertons are close as two fleas on a frozen dog."

"Want me to take a couple boys and do for him?"

A contemptuous smile touched Condor's lips. "No, you damned fool. You can't take Steele even if you have ten more just like you backing your play." English Nate was silent for a while, then said, "No, I'll take him myself, and I'll kill him in a fair fight. The man who guns Dallas Steele will earn a rep that fighting men will be talking about a hundred years from now."

Condor rose to his feet and stepped to the cabin window. "There's a couple hours of daylight left. We'll go talk to Lum."

"He found the wagon, Cap'n," Merden said. "You know he wants a half share."

"Rhody found the wagon, not Lum," Condor

said. "But I'll take care of him when the time comes." His smile was unpleasant. "And Rhody."

"Did Steele mention the pay wagon?" Condor asked.

"No, I did," Lum Park said.

"You did!" Condor almost jumped out of his chair.

"I told him it was just a big story. What was wrong with that?"

"You damned—" Condor stopped himself in time and waited a moment until he calmed down. "I'm convinced Steele knows the wagon could be here, or at least he suspects it. I reckon that's why he was sent to the Playas, to ferret out the wagon and its one hundred and thirty thousand in gold and silver."

Park shook his head. "Hell, I should've gunned him and the woman, and we'd be done with him."

"Well, it's too late to cry over spilled milk," Condor said. "The damage has been done."

"What now, Cap'n?" Barney Merden asked. "I say we hit the town and get it over with, once and for all."

"No. One thing we're not doing is moving against Recoil," Condor said. "Steele is there and those two troublemakers O'Brien and Ironside.

All three of them are good with guns and the two old men routed your riders last night."

"We had orders not to stand," Merden said, his face aggrieved. "You told me plain to do plenty of hollering and no shooting, Nate."

"Nonetheless, you ran from two men," Condor said. "I can't risk an attack on the town, not with Dallas Steele there."

"Then what?" Park said. "What the hell do we do with the wagon and the gold?"

"We move the gold earlier than I planned and head for Mexico," Condor said. "We can spend it there without anybody asking questions."

"Hell, I don't want to spend my money in Mexico," Merden said. "What the hell is there in Mexico to interest a man?"

"Whiskey and women, Barney," Condor said. "They both taste the same, no matter what side of the border you're on."

"Half of the gold is mine, remember." Park's wrinkled face shone with greed.

"Rhody found it," Condor said. "I'd say the half share is hers."

"She's my daughter and she'll do as I tell her or she'll get the back of my hand."

"Nate," Rhody said, "Dallas Steele is the man who killed my husband."

"Did he now? What a pity, Skate being such a fine, upstanding gentleman and all."

"No matter what he was, and he was evil, he was still my husband."

"Don't worry about it, Rhody," Condor said. "I'll take care of Steele in my own good time."

"So when do we move the gold?" Park asked. "I'm itching to get all them double eagles under my bed."

"Soon, I reckon. I'll talk to the boss tonight."

"Hell, Cap'n, is that wise?" Merden asked. "You going to Recoil would be like sailing a loaded slave ship into Boston harbor."

"I need the go-ahead from the boss to move the gold and I need it now," Condor said. "I have no other choice. There's always the possibility that Steele knows he's on to something and he could come back here with a cavalry regiment."

The Park cabin was a small lean-to and when Condor rose he filled it. "I want to take a look at the wagon."

"No need," Park said. "It's there and it's not going anywhere."

"Nevertheless I want to see it," Condor insisted. "It will put my mind at rest, Lum. You understand that, don't you?"

"I'll show it to you, Nate," Rhody said, getting to her feet.

"You sit down, daughter," Park said. "I'll take him to the gold since he's so all-fired determined to see it."

Condor's eyes hardened. "She's showing me the wagon, Lum. You and Barney sit tight and keep an eye open for Steele and those other two old gun-slinging reprobates."

The sun was setting in the west, the sky above the Little Hatchet Mountains banded with ribbons of rust, red, and jade when Condor and Rhody stepped out of the cabin. The evening was cool and a low breeze carried with it the scent of sage and pine.

Rhody led the way into a waterless, rocky draw that rose gradually between stands of juniper and piñon. After fifty yards, the ground leveled and Rhody stopped and pointed to her left. "It's there, Nate. In the break in the rock."

"All I see is the rock face," Condor said. "I don't see any damned break."

"Come closer, you'll see it." Rhody walked ahead and Condor followed.

Then he saw the break. It was as though the rock had split open during some ancient earth shake. The gap was shaped like an arrowhead; no more than eight feet high by same wide. The interior was dark.

"How the hell did you find this place? What brought you up here?"

"Sometimes I come up here to be alone and get away from Pa," the girl said. "I think it was on my second or third visit I noticed the break and stepped inside. The wagon is in the cave, where the Apaches left it ten years ago."

Condor pushed the girl aside and stepped into the darkness of the break. He thumbed a match into flame and held it high, revealing an army escort wagon designed to be drawn by four horses or mules. It seemed to be in good shape. Even its paint, a blue exterior and dark red interior, was still bright.

He let the burning match drop, rubbed it out under his boot, and lit another. Burlap sacks, each bearing the letters, *US*, were stacked in the bed, When he pushed on one, the coins inside chinked.

He lit a third match and slit a sack with his Barlow knife. Gleaming double eagles tumbled into the box and Condor smiled. The shine of gold was the stuff of dreams.

Rhody stepped to his side. "We could live like royalty with that much money, you and me. Ever think about that, Nate?"

"You and me?" Condor said, grinning. "No, I never thought about that."

"Yes, Nate, it would be just the two of us."

"Living in a little rose-covered cottage with a tree in the yard, you mean?"

"Yes, Nate, if that's what you want."

"What about your greedy pa and my equally greedy boss?"

"They can be gotten rid of, both of them. It would be easy to kill Pa."

Condor smiled. His hands moved to her neck, then lower over her breasts, belly, and hips, like a man assessing the riding potential of a saddle mare. "I'll think about it, and let you know."

"I'll give you anything you want, Nate, anything. Just take me away from this hellhole. I can't stand it here any longer."

Condor's hand cupped a breast and he squeezed hard until Rhody cried out in pain. "I told you, I'll think about it." He walked out of the cave and the girl followed him.

He turned to her. "How would you get rid of your Pa?"

"Shoot him, of course."

Condor smiled. "A real loving daughter, aren't you?"

"I'll kill anybody for a hundred and thirty thousand dollars,"

Chapter Twenty-seven

Before he rode into Recoil, Nate Condor packed his guns in his saddlebags. He sat his horse with his head lowered, hat brim pulled low over his eyes.

The saloons were bustling. The male patrons, mostly miners in from the hills for a one-night soiree, were already halfway drunk and the sporting gals were noisy. No one gave him a second glance.

It was a Friday evening and the street was unusually busy with buckboards and freight wagons. A stage stood outside the hotel, its sidelights glowing scarlet in the gloom.

Condor was pleased that no one even glanced in his direction as he sought out the boss's house. It was exactly the way he'd planned it.

But he was very wrong. He was noticed by a tall, grim-faced old man with shoulders an ax handle wide. The man stood in the shadows and recognized the rider for who he was.

Luther Ironside watched and waited until Condor swung into an alley. Then he shouldered off the saloon wall and followed. He pushed aside a drunk who stumbled into him and offered a swig from his bottle, and walked quickly to keep Condor in sight.

The outlaw rode out of the far end of the alley and Ironside followed. He watched the outlaw angle toward the sprawling gingerbread houses that marked the outer limits of the town. Condor rode at his ease, seemingly in no hurry to arrive at his destination.

Ironside made up his mind. It was time—while the man was still out in the open, a moonlit target. He stepped out of the alley and yelled, "Condor!"

The outlaw looked as though he'd ridden into a wall of icy air that had instantly frozen him solid. He sat his horse immobile and didn't even turn his head.

Ironside stepped into the patch of open sand and brush between himself and the houses, his hand hovering over his holstered Colt. "Condor, you murdering sorry excuse for a man. This time stand your ground and get to your work," he yelled.

Ironside badly underestimated Condor and overestimated his own age-slowed reaction time.

The outlaw exploded into movement. He sawed his mount's head around then raked the vicious rowels of his Mexican spurs across its flanks, drawing blood. The horse galloped directly at Ironside who drew then dived to one side. He slammed the sun-baked ground hard, too hard, and his breath burst out of his chest.

Condor was past him, galloping for the alley.

Ironside sat up and fired, missed, and had no time for a second shot. He got to his feet, gasping in air, and ran into the alley. He emerged into the street in time to see Condor hammering out of town, invisible behind a cloud of rising dust.

Ironside aired out his tortured lungs, letting rip with every cuss he'd ever heard and some he just made up.

A single gunshot was not all that unusual in Recoil and the sporting crowd stayed in the saloons, no doubt figuring that some drunken rooster had taken a pot at the moon.

A man's voice behind Ironside was unsteady with anxiety. "What in God's name is going on here?" he demanded.

Ironside turned and saw a short man dressed in a shirt, pants, and carpet slippers step out of the alley into the street, his face riddled with concern.

Ironside recognized him as Silas Shaw, the

man who'd killed one of the stagecoach robbers and feared he would be thereafter branded as a gunslinger. "I think he was headed for your house."

"Who was headed for my house?"

"Nate Condor, the lowdown skunk who leads the night riders."

"Oh, dear God," Shaw said, adding some considerable dramatic effect as though he was about to swoon away on the spot. "What could that desperado possibly want with me? We could've been murdered in our beds. Oh, my poor lady wife. My poor Martha. I must go to her."

"It could be he wanted to rob you, Shaw," Ironside said. "You being a wealthy merchant and one of the town's leading citizens."

"I'm not wealthy. He would've found only slim pickings in my home. Unless . . ."

"Unless what?" Ironside said.

"Unless he lusted after my dear Martha. Other men have done so in the past." Shaw turned and took a step toward the alley. "I must go comfort her. She heard the shot and it alarmed her terribly. When I left she was all a-tremble, poor thing."

"Just hold on a minute, Silas," Sheriff Jim Clitherow said as he and Shamus O'Brien emerged from the darkness along with Deputy Steve Sparrow, who'd been feeling poorly since he discovered the burned bodies.

Clitherow stared at Ironside as being the likeliest culprit and said, "Who's doing all the shooting?"

"Yeah, that was me, Jim," Ironside said. "I took a pot at Nate Condor and missed."

Clitherow was shocked. "He came into town as bold as brass?"

"Sure did, bold as brass," Ironside said. "I figured he was headed for Shaw's house. He either planned to kill him or rob him, or both."

"Oh dear God in Heaven," Shaw wailed. "Night riders in my front yard. What's to become of us all?"

"Any idea why he would pick on your house, Silas?" Clitherow asked.

"None, Sheriff, unless he knows that I usually keep money in my safe at home. It's just a small amount, hardly enough to attract a dangerous outlaw."

Clitherow turned to Shamus. "They're getting more bold, Colonel, working closer to town. First Maurice Bird murdered close to Recoil, and now this."

"Then we have to find what's keeping Condor in the Playas before he does," Shamus said.

"There's only one thing that can explain the actions of the night riders," Shaw said. "It has to be a gold or silver mine. There is a history of claims in this part of the territory that were prematurely abandoned and later hit pay dirt."

"You seem pretty sure about that, Silas," Clitherow said.

"It's the most logical explanation, Sheriff."

"Sheriff . . . do you m-m-mind them g-g-grangers that was massacred out by B-Black Mountain Draw?" Sparrow said.

"How could I forget? What about them?"

"I r-r-reckon they were l-l-looking fer the same thing the night riders want."

"Hell, boy," Ironside said. "You just said yourself they were sodbusters."

"M-m-maybe at one time. But they wasn't carrying f-f-farmer's tools. I reckon they were searchin' fer s-s-something they knew could be c-c-carried away in a wagon and maybe that's why they was all k-k-killed."

"Like a treasure, you mean?" Clitherow said.

"S-s-something like that," Sparrow said.

"There's no buried treasure around these parts," Shaw said. "If there was, it would've been discovered long ago. And who would've buried it, the Apaches or the Spanish? It doesn't seem likely."

"You're right, Silas, it doesn't," Clitherow said. "You can go home now."

"Thank you, Sheriff. Poor Martha is probably hysterical by this time. I'll sleep with a large revolver on my nightstand, I assure you."

After Shaw left, Shamus said, "How come you missed, Luther?"

"It was dark and ol' Condor was at a full gallop. I only had time for one shot, and I was on the ground at the time."

"I suggest when we get home to Dromore you busy yourself with target practice," Shamus said. "From your performance here tonight, it would be time well spent."

Under his breath, Ironside muttered something about certain folks bein' in no position to criticize other folk's shootin' . . .

"What did you say?" Shamus demanded.

"Nothing, Colonel. I didn't say nothing."

"And I should hope you didn't. A man should not deflect blame by criticizing others, Luther. Remember that."

"An odd occurrence, though," Dallas Steele said, sitting back in a chair in Clitherow's office. "I mean that Condor headed directly for Shaw's house as though he knew right where he was going."

"Maybe he planned to kill him," Clitherow said. "Silas Shaw is a prominent citizen of this town and his death could've started a stampede of folks out of here."

"It's possible, I suppose," Steele said. He turned to Ironside. "Luther, it might've been better if you'd just kept an eye on Condor, watched where he went, and then reported back to Sheriff Clitherow or myself."

"Shaw and his old lady could've been dead by the time I did all that reportin'" Ironside said, irritated.

Steele nodded. "Yes, there's always that possibility, I suppose, but somehow I think it unlikely."

"Dallas, you've got influence in Washington," Clitherow said. Could you get the army down here and clean out that nest of robbers and killers once and for all?"

"I don't have that much influence," Steele said. "Sure I could send a request, in triplicate, for an army presence in Recoil, but it would sit on some second lieutenant's desk for a month before any action was taken."

"And by then it would be too late," Shamus said.

"Well, let's just say that the troubles of a hick town—sorry, Sheriff—in the Playas Valley would not be at the top of the list of current military priorities," Steele said. "Especially now that there's unrest on the Plains and talk of some new dance getting the Sioux and Cheyenne all riled up."

A breeze whispered around the eaves of the

sheriff's office and guttered the flames of the oil lamps. In one of the saloons a pianist played "She Was Only a Sodbuster's Daughter, but I Loved Her Just the Same," and a female voice joined in the chorus.

> *"She had dirt in her fingers and dirt in her toes,*
> *Dirt in her hair and dirt on her nose,*
> *But her heart was as pure as the driven snooow . . ."*

Much affected by the song, a lovesick ranny stood in the middle of the street and howled at the moon . . . then someone scratched on the door.

"Come in. It's open," Clitherow said as his hand dropped to his gun.

"It's Scout."

"Then come in, damn it."

The door creaked open and the Navajo slid inside, his Sharps in his left hand. Behind him stood a huge black man wearing a fashionable frockcoat and checked pants, but his head and shoulders were covered with the pelt of a wolf, its upper jaws jutting over the man's forehead. Like Scout, he carried a rifle.

"You've decided to help us," Shamus said, rising to his feet. "I'm really glad to see you again."

"I will look for what you seek, and you will pay

me when I find it," Scout said. "That is our agreement, is it not?"

"Indeed it is," Shamus said. "And I'll stick by it, never fear."

"And this gentleman is . . ." Clitherow said. The black man was at least seven foot tall and the sheriff looked uneasy.

"His name is Lucian T. Hyde," Scout said. "He's my hired man."

Hyde's voice rumbled from deep in his chest, like the warning grumble of an erupting volcano. "I'm so pleased to meet all of you. I'm afraid we meet under the most singular and distressing circumstances."

Steele was the first to recover from his surprise. "Have you been in the territory long, Mr. Hyde?"

"Only a six-month. Before that I was a consulting detective in New York City, but was forced to flee after I killed a man." Hyde smiled. "He was a white man, so I knew my chances of escaping the gallows were slim to none, so I left the city forever. Then, wandering like Odysseus of old, I met Scout while I was in the desert, close to death from hunger and thirst."

"And he gave you that hat?" Ironside eyed Hyde's barbaric headpiece with obvious disapproval.

"No, this is not a gift. You see, I was attacked by

a wolf, a fierce beast and we fought long and hard for three days and two nights. In the end I prevailed and when I saw the creature lying dead at my feet, I decided to keep his pelt." He smiled again, revealing bone-white teeth. "I think it becomes me, don't you?"

"Yes, yes, very nice," Shamus said. Then to Scout he said, "Mr. Steele here thinks he has a fair idea where the . . . whatever it is . . . is located."

"It is a great treasure," Scout said. "This I know. In a dream, I saw much gold and many dead men." He stared hard at Steele as though he peered into the man's soul. "Where should I start my search?"

"The Apache Hills. There is a man named Lum Park who says he has a claim there, but I think he's hiding something." Steele made a decision. "I believe it could be an army payroll wagon that was stolen by Apaches ten years ago."

"You never told us that afore, Steele," Ironside said.

"Well, Luther, I'm telling you now. There's a hundred and thirty thousand dollars in that wagon and the army wants it back."

"And that's the reason you're here in Recoil," Shamus said.

"Yes, Colonel. The army hired the Pinkertons to investigate."

Ironside whistled between his teeth. "Hell, that's a lot of money. Men like Nate Condor will kill for less."

"And I believe so will Lum Park," Steele said. "He has a daughter. Her name is Rhody and she's just as mean as he is. Besides that, she says I killed her husband."

"You don't remember whether you did or not?" the Navajo asked.

Steele shook his head. "No, I'm afraid I can't bring him to mind."

"You should take scalps or trigger fingers," Scout said. "It would help you remember the men you have killed."

"I'll take your advice into consideration," Steele said.

"We will go now," Scout said. "When we find the gold, we will return."

"You takin' the big feller with you?" Ironside said to the Navajo.

"Yes, Lucian will go with me. The wolf whose pelt he took bit him many, many times and now he knows the way of the pack."

Steele and Shamus exchanged glances, but there was no way to follow up on that comment, so they remained silent.

"One thing more," Scout said. "Colonel O'Brien, your sons are in great danger."

Shamus jerked upright in his chair, his face

alarmed. "Jesus, Mary, and Joseph, what kind of danger?"

"That I cannot see. But heed me. They are in peril." Scout turned and said, "Come, Lucian." Without another word, he and Hyde walked into the street.

Ironside, interested to see what breed of horse the big man rode, stepped outside. Both men were jogging toward the darkness at the edge of town, and soon vanished from sight.

Ironside walked back into the office. "Them two don't have horses, they're . . ."

His voice trailed away as Clitherow finished what he'd been saying. ". . . hold it against you, Colonel."

"Thank you, Jim," Shamus said, "but I'll stick. It wouldn't set right with me to run out on you when you need us most."

Steele's voice was remarkably gentle. "No one can blame a man for putting his family first, Colonel."

"We're talking about the Injun saying there's danger at Dromore, huh?" Ironside said.

"What's your opinion on that, Luther?" Shamus said.

Ironside smiled. "If he's right, then I say God help the rannies stupid enough to try and corral the O'Brien brothers on their own ground."

"Then do we stick?" Shamus asked.

"Your sons are all grown up now, Colonel," Ironside said. "They can handle themselves. If you was an outlaw, would you want to go up against Jake and Shawn in a shooting scrape?"

"Then we stick?" Shamus asked again.

Ironside nodded. "Yup, until this here is over."

Shamus smiled. "Then so be it. And no, Luther, I wouldn't care to go up against Jacob and Shawn in a shooting scrape."

"Damn right," Ironside said.

The smile quickly fled Shamus's face and was again replaced by a look of concern. "I'll say a rosary for my sons tonight. And for Dromore."

Chapter Twenty-eight

"If the Colonel was here, he'd say a rosary and then have at it," Samuel O'Brien said.

"He'd have to find them first," Jacob said. "Just like we have to do."

"Then I say we pull the vaqueros off the range and go on the scout right away," Shawn said. "It's better that than hanging around Dromore, sitting on our gun hands, while we worry about Pat and await Castillo's pleasure."

"What do you say, Sam?" Jacob said. "Do we go after them?"

"So far, Castillo has been calling the shots," Samuel said. "He took Pat hostage and he murdered one of our own. I'm getting pretty tired of being pushed around and I want the Mexican dead."

Little Shamus toddled to Jacob's knee and

showed him his new toy, a wooden horse carved by one of the hands. Jacob lifted the two-year-old onto his lap. "Pretty horse, isn't it?"

The boy nodded his blond head. "Pretty horsey."

Shawn rose, stepped to the parlor window, and gazed into the waning day. "A full moon tonight. I reckon I'll head out now and bring in the vaqueros."

Jacob talked over the little boy's head. "Be back here by first light, Shawn, with or without the hands."

"Depend on it." Shawn looked at Lorena. "You've been quiet, sister-in-law. Is all this talk of fighting troubling you?"

"Vasily Petrov, as fine a man who ever lived, lies stiff and cold in the chapel with candles smoking around him and the wind singing his requiem. Patrick is a captive, perhaps wounded and ill-treated, and we are his only hope." Lorena laid the sock she was darning on her lap. "Dromore takes care of its own and avenges their deaths. I will not stand aside and let you do any less. Yes, I am troubled, but it is time for Dromore to fight those who would do us harm, as we've always done."

Jacob smiled. "You sounded like my mother then, Lorena."

"And I pray I can remain as strong as Saraid was."

"Then I guess it's all settled," Shawn said. "I'm riding."

After his brother left, Jacob rose and passed little Shamus to Samuel. "I'm going out for a scout around. I'm restless being caged up like this."

"Be careful, Jake," Samuel said. "We can't predict what Castillo will do next. The man is obviously crazy."

"I'll be on guard."

Jacob stepped into the foyer to buckle on his gun then stepped outside into the growing darkness. The moon had not yet risen, but the night was clear, already bright with stars. He walked to the rise that stood opposite the house, sat, and fetched his back against a pine. He built a cigarette and smoked, listening to the distant bark of the coyotes and the wind that whispered secrets to the trees.

Alone with his thoughts, a man of black moods and echoing loneliness, he was still there when the newly minted moon came up, round and shiny as a silver coin.

Patrick O'Brien stared across the moonlit clearing to the Mexicans gathered around the fire. He counted them again, just to be sure, and came up with the same figure—eighteen including Álvaro Castillo.

That was too many for Dromore to handle if they all went against it at once.

The new moon rose high, surrounded by a hazy ring that predicted inclement weather. "Count the stars inside the ring, and they will tell you how many days from now the rain will start." Patrick smiled. Luther had told him that, so it must be true.

The Mexicans around the fire seemed to be arguing, but then the discussion stopped and Castillo staggered toward him, a bottle in his hand. "My very good friend, Señor Patrick," the Mexican said, spreading his arms wide. "How are you tonight? Well, I hope."

"Same as I was last night, Castillo, wishing I had a gun so I could put a bullet in your fat belly."

"Ahh, that is not good, because you are Álvaro's friend again. See, I have even brought you whiskey." He looked sly. "A woman? Is that what you want? Would you like a woman?"

"I'd like you to get the hell away from me," Patrick said.

"That is not a nice thing you say to a friend." Castillo was stinking drunk. The cruelty that was never far from his eyes made them gleam. He kneeled beside Patrick and pushed the bottle to his lips. "Drink, my friend. Your friend Álvaro wishes you to be as happy as he is this night."

Patrick turned his head away, his mouth clamped shut.

"I said drink, you pig!" Castillo yelled.

The shout attracted a crowd and drunk, grinning Mexicans surrounded the two men. They pointed at Patrick and laughed as though the sight of him was the funniest thing they'd ever seen.

"Drink!" Castillo said again. He grabbed Patrick by the hair and forced his head around. The Mexican slammed the bottle against Patrick's mouth so hard his lip split and he tasted blood with the raw whiskey.

"Drink!" Castillo said, grinning. He shoved harder on the bottle and slammed the neck against Patrick's clenched teeth. Then the Mexican grabbed his jaw and forced his mouth open. "Drink, damn you!" he yelled, pushing hard on the bottle. "Drink like a man."

Despite his efforts, whiskey flooded into Patrick's mouth and he was forced to swallow, his throat bobbing.

"See, *compadres*," Castillo said, looking up at his men. "The butterfly-catching gringo can drink like a man."

The Mexican rose to his feet then kicked Patrick in the ribs, his thudding boot going in once . . . twice . . . three times. . . .

Patrick stifled the urge to cry out in pain, refusing to give Castillo the satisfaction.

"Next time Castillo asks you to take a drink, you take a drink, understand?"

"Go to hell," Patrick said.

"It is just as well you're not my friend again." Castillo smiled. "But tomorrow perhaps you will be, when you lead my charge against your father's fine house." The Mexican's smile grew into a grin. "A house that will soon be the hacienda of Don Álvaro Castillo."

That drew a cheer from the bandit's men and Castillo yelled, "This time tomorrow, *mis compadres*, we will roast a pig at Dromore!"

More cheers, then staggering, slapping each other on the back, the Mexicans returned to the fire, leaving Patrick alone.

He was slightly drunk, puzzled that he would lead the charge against Dromore. He gave serious thought to that as blood from his split lips trickled down his chin.

Through his alcohol haze, it suddenly dawned on him. He'd be riding in front of Castillo's men, lashed to the saddle probably, and that would reduce Dromore's firepower because his brothers would be fearful of hitting him.

He stared at the haloed moon and wished the night would go on forever. He feared what tomorrow might bring . . . .

Could it be the end of Dromore and the brothers O'Brien?

Chapter Twenty-nine

Shawn O'Brien led eight vaqueros into Dromore just before dawn. He'd left three others and a couple of seasonal hands out on the range, choosing only men of proven courage who were good with the iron.

Jacob approved of his selection. "They'll do."

Shawn considered that high praise indeed from his brother. "With you, Sam, and me, we'll be eleven strong. You reckon that's enough?"

"It will have to be enough." Jacob managed a smile. "Hell, Shawn, it's more than enough."

One of the riders kneed his horse forward and Shawn said, "You got something to say to me, Regino?"

"*Sí, señor,*" Regino Vargas said. "Once I scouted or the army of Presidente Porfirio Diaz and he gave me a fine gold medal from his own hand. I an find Álvaro Castillo for you."

"Ride on out of here, Regino," Jacob said. "Get me that no-good Mexican bandit."

"*Sí señor.* I will find him, I promise." Vargas kicked his mount into motion, waved his sombrero at his cheering companions, and galloped east into the violet light of the new day.

Fifteen minutes later the O'Brien brothers led their vaqueros in Vargas's tracks.

Samuel turned in the saddle and said to Jacob and Shawn, "Times are changing and this could be the last battle we ever fight for Dromore, so make the most of it."

"I just wish the Colonel and Luther were here," Shawn said.

"To join in the fun?" Jacob asked.

"No, to boost the courage I suddenly find I lack. In short, I'm damned scared." Shawn grimaced.

"Once the shooting starts, you'll do fine. The smell of burned powder always settles a man."

"Damn it, Jake, if I cut and run, please kill me," Shawn said.

Jacob nodded. "With the greatest of pleasure, brother. Two in the back, I promise."

Samuel grinned. "So now you know, Shawn."

"Yeah. I guess I do."

Jacob winked at Samuel, but caught up in his own gloomy thoughts, Shawn didn't notice.

* * *

The Dromore men stopped to water their horses at the Pecos. There was no sign of Regino Vargas.

The sun was climbing higher, bringing with it a fierce heat that stained the riders' shirts black with sweat. Jacob scanned the far bank of the river, but saw only pines sweeping away in the distance before rising with the rocky crags and merging into stands of aspen and juniper. The normally talkative vaqueros were silent, their eyes searching. No sound disturbed the quiet of the fading morning

"Well, where do we go from here?" Samuel said, more to himself than anyone else. "Pick a direction, boys."

"I'm studying on it." Jacob lifted his head as though his great beak of a nose was testing the wind, and then bowed his head in thought.

After a minute passed, Samuel said, "Well?"

"We'll hold here for an hour," Jacob said, building a cigarette.

"For what, Jake?"

"For one of two things—either Castillo passes this way or Regino shows up with some news."

"Should we at least send out some scouts?" Samuel asked.

"We have a scout out," Shawn said. "And he won a fine gold medal for tracking folks, remember?"

"Feeling better, Shawn?" Jacob said, smiling.

"Yeah, I feel better, Jake. Given your homicidal intentions, if I turned tail, did I have any choice?"

Jacob shook his head. "None that I could see."

Shawn glared at his brother. "Don't you ever get scared?"

"All the time," Jacob said. "I'm scared right now."

"Count me in on that as well," Samuel said.

"I'm glad Luther isn't here listening," Shawn said. "He'd take a stick to us."

"Yeah," Jacob said, "and the colonel would take up another, bigger one."

Samuel posted a couple of vaqueros up- and downstream of their position and led the rest of the men into the trees on the west bank of the river. They made a cold camp, saw to their guns, then dozed in the sunlight and waited for whatever was to come.

Half an hour later, as drowsy insects murmured in the grass around them, a flurry of shots from downstream brought everyone to their feet.

An instant later, Vargas and the guard galloped through the shallows, fountains of river water erupting around the legs of their horses.

"Where are they?" Jacob yelled, gun in hand.

"They're right on top of us!" Vargas hollered, blood staining the left sleeve of his shirt.

He and the vaquero leaped from their horses, turned and fired at a target obscured from Jacob's view by pine and cottonwoods.

Patrick galloped into sight, roped to his horse, bouncing and swaying in the saddle. The Mexicans were right behind him, Álvaro Castillo in the lead.

The Dromore riders recovered quickly from their surprise and guns roared from among the trees.

Castillo, who'd believed he was chasing stragglers, realized he'd charged into a hornet's nest. He stood in the saddle and waved his men back, his broad face frantic. The Dromore riders had scored hits and the bodies of two Mexican bandits bobbed in the water.

Jacob caught a glimpse of Castillo and readied to fire. At that moment, Patrick managed to turn his mount and rode in front of the bandit, heading for the Dromore position.

Jacob cursed and fired at Castillo, but his bullet harmlessly chipped pine bark. The big Mexican had swung away from the line of fire and was galloping back the way he'd come.

A few more shots rang out, then the firing

stopped and the vaqueros cheered a victory that was no victory at all.

Castillo regrouped his men quickly and they charged along the riverbank where there was room to ride four abreast.

With Patrick safely in the cover of the trees, the Dromore men, all of them on foot, spread out and met Castillo's charge with steady gunfire. Suddenly the bank of the Pecos was a kicking, screaming tangle of downed horses and men.

Jacob and Shawn, standing shoulder to shoulder, pumped bullets into the swerving, confused Mexicans. It was close work that gave the advantage to men skilled with the Colt.

Castillo, not being a strategist, had ignored the age-old rule that light cavalry should never charge skilled infantry in an entrenched position, and he was paying the price.

A young Mexican, bloodied from head to toe, staggered out of the confused knot of dying horses and riders and walked toward Jacob, his hands in the air as he screamed for mercy.

In a fight, like Luther Ironside who had tutored him, Jacob was not a merciful man. He shot down the Mexican and stepped over the body as he sought to close the range between him and the yelling Castillo.

The vaquero who'd been sent upstream reappeared. He galloped though the river shallows, levering and firing his Winchester from the shoulder. He was good with a long gun. His bullets tore into the Mexicans.

Watching, Jacob figured the man killed two or three before he was hit and tumbled from the saddle. It was enough.

The Mexicans lost half their number before all they wanted was to get the hell out of there, away from the hammering Dromore guns. Álvaro Castillo was nowhere in sight.

Jacob caught up a riderless horse and swung into the saddle.

"Jake, where you headed?" Shawn yelled.

"Going after Castillo."

Shawn yelled something else that Jacob didn't hear. He was already cantering along the riverbank, his mount sidestepping dead men.

A couple of minutes later, Jacob saw where the opposite bank was broken down, probably by cattle. He drew rein and looked again. It was as good a spot as any for a man to leave the Pecos and head north into the desolate canyon country.

He decided to play the odds and splashed across the shallows, stopping at a wide sandbar. A single set of fresh tracks had been made only moments before, and the odds were about ten to one they were left by the Mexican.

The stirred-up mud silted the river as Jacob rode across the sandbar and into free-flowing water again. He drew rein and glanced downstream. Nothing moved but the wind. The wide sky was pale blue, tufted with only a few white clouds. There was no sound but the gentle eddy of the current along the riverbank.

Not by nature a gambling man, Jacob tossed the dice and rode out of the Pecos, immediately picking up the tracks of the fleeing Mexican, whoever he was. The tracks pointed north.

Ahead of Jacob rose a wall of red sandstone rock, higher than the topmost point of the Dromore roof.

Was Castillo, or one of his men, holed up at its base? Was there just one Mexican, or had he met up with more of his *compadres*?

Jacob checked the loads in his Colt and thumbed a round into the empty chamber under the hammer. He holstered his gun and moved forward warily, his eyes moving constantly.

As he rode closer, he saw that the side of the cliff formed one wall of a narrow arroyo, the other only sixty feet away. There, the rock was more weathered and much lower, a few stunted juniper growing close to its base. After casting around for a while, he picked up the tracks again and saw that the rider, Castillo or someone else, had entered the canyon.

Aware that mounted he was a big target, Jacob swung out of the saddle and led the horse into the break. The arroyo narrowed as he walked through its cool shade, and at one point the walls closed in on him so tight the stirrups scraped against the sandstone on both sides.

The ground under his feet was slowly rising. During the spring melt, water rushed through the arroyo at a tremendous rate. But it was dry, the bottom a mix of sand and pebble and here and there cat claw cacti were rooted into cracks in the rock.

After the best part of a mile, the arroyo rose at a higher angle and Jacob emerged onto the flat top of a mesa. After the coolness of the arroyo, the sun was again hot on his shoulders, but a constant wind blew. It bent the branches of a few dark junipers and stirred the pale orange blossoms of scattered clumps of globe mallow.

He scanned the mesa with extreme care. It was possible a dangerous man did not wish to be seen.

He walked his horse forward. On all sides of him, the mesa stretched away, flat as a billiard table. Borne on rising winds from the flat, the air smelled of sage and pine and Jacob was almost sure he caught the acrid scent of gunpowder from the battle at the Pecos.

He stopped, movement flickering at the corner of his left eye.

A shadow cast on the mesa as a rider rode past a stand of juniper then emerged from behind them. He was a big Mexican, wearing a wide sombrero. Belts of rifle ammunition made a gleaming X on his chest. It could only be one man.

Álvaro Castillo!

Jacob drew his gun and waited.

Castillo was oblivious. His head was bent as his eyes searched the mesa rim. Fearful of going back the way he'd come, the bandit was hunting a way down.

Jacob judged the distance between himself and Castillo at fifty yards, too far for revolver work. He'd never been much of a hand with a long gun and had no confidence in his ability with a Winchester. He had to draw the Mexican closer.

"Hey, Castillo!" Jacob yelled.

Startled, the Mexican's hand dropped for his gun, but he thought better of it and called, "Ah, my good, good friend. You have come to look for Álvaro, no?"

"I've come to kill you, Castillo."

"No, it cannot be. We are very good friends and a friend does not kill a friend." Castillo pushed his horse in Jacob's direction.

Twenty yards away he drew rein and swung out of the saddle. The Mexican grinned, his teeth very white against his dark skin. He waved a hand. "Hell of a country, is it not, my friend?"

"For some," Jacob said.

"I am a poor man, and I only tried to take a little of what you own," Castillo said. "Surely you don't blame me for that?"

"I'm going to kill you for that, Castillo, and for what you did to my brother."

"But Patrick is fine. He is my good friend. Ask him yourself and he will tell you that this is so. I brought him food, I gave him whiskey, and he himself said to me, 'Álvaro, you are my ver' good friend.'"

Jacob holstered his gun. "It's even, Castillo. Make your play."

"No. No guns, my friend," the Mexican said. "I have tequila in my saddlebags and we will drink and then part ways. Soon, I will be gone from this part of the country for good and you can forget you were ever Álvaro's friend."

Castillo made to reach into his saddlebags and Jacob said, "I see your hand vanish from my sight, I'll gun you right where you stand."

The Mexican swung on Jacob, his face black with fury. "Damn you, gringo, now you are not my friend. I don't like you anymore."

"Skin it, Castillo. Or die like a yellow-bellied coward right where you stand."

"Aye. I have no cartridges in my gun. I fired them all away at the river."

"Then that's the breaks." Jacob drew and Castillo, so fast his hand blurred, almost matched him.

Gunfights were measured in seconds. The Mexican was just a half-second slower than Jacob O'Brien, and it cost him his life.

Jacob's bullet slammed into Castillo's chest and the man was already in shock when he fired back. The Mexican's bullet ripped a shallow furrow along Jacob's ribs on the left side, a stinging, burning wound, but one a strong man could shake off. Jacob fired again and again, his bullets slamming into and through Castillo.

His rage building, Jacob roared, "Now you know the cost of Dromore comes too high for a piece of garbage like you."

Castillo, bloody, finished, shot to pieces, swayed on his feet, his eyes wide and unbelieving. He who had once destroyed a whole town and dreamed of being the lord of Dromore crashed onto his back and lay still. Nothing and nobody.

Jacob let Castillo lie where he fell, figuring the

buzzards would find him soon enough. On the off chance that somebody might visit the mesa and wonder at the bones, he got out his tally book, scribbled a few words, and shoved the scrap of paper into the Mexican's shirt pocket. It read *He played out his string*.

Chapter Thirty

What would go down in Dromore family history as the Battle of the Pecos River was over and the victory won. The butcher's bill was eleven Mexicans dead and none wounded. Two vaqueros were shot, but would live. Jacob had burned ribs and Patrick's head had been grazed by a flying bullet that rendered him unconscious for a while.

"Did Castillo put up much of a fight, Jake?" Shawn O'Brien asked in the Dromore parlor as he handed his brother a snifter of brandy.

"He was game. He died fighting with a gun in his hand."

"Please, no more talk of fighting and killing," Lorena said. "It's over. Let's put it behind us." She smiled at Patrick. "How are you feeling?"

"Just fine, Lorena. If the bullet had been an inch to the left I wouldn't be here."

"You poor thing," Lorena said. "Can I get you an ice bag for your head?"

"No, I think I'll be just fine, Lorena, thank you." Patrick gritted his teeth as though he was bravely fighting his pain.

Jacob, whose ribs were hurting like hell, said, "Next time you go butterfly hunting—"

"Collecting, Jake, collecting," Patrick said.

"Make sure you're wearing a gun. I thought Luther taught you better than that."

"Jacob, Patrick isn't feeling well. Please don't chide him." Lorena's brows gathered. "And since we're on the subject of chiding, please tell your cat to stay out of the kitchen. She stole poor Patrick's bacon sandwich this morning, you know."

"I'll tell her, Lorena, but she doesn't heed me much."

"Obviously," Lorena said, icing the word.

Shawn grinned. "Calico cats are like Baptists. They raise hell, but no one can ever catch them at it."

"Come to think about it, you could say the same thing about Luther," Patrick said.

"Talking about Luther, what are we going to do

about him and the colonel?" Samuel said. It was a question open for anybody to answer.

Jacob answered it. "I'm heading down to the Playas."

"When?" Shawn asked.

"I plan to leave at first light tomorrow."

"You figure they're in trouble down there, Jake?" Samuel questioned.

"I know they're in trouble."

"Do you sense it?" Patrick wondered.

"I sense something," Jacob said.

His brothers exchanged glances, and then Patrick said, "I'm going with you."

"Good to have you, Pat, if your poor head can handle it."

"There's nothing wrong with my—"

"We're all going." Samuel ignored the look Lorena threw at him.

Jacob considered that briefly. "Sam, with the gather not even half done, your place is here at Dromore."

"If Pa is in danger, my place is at his side."

"Sam, you acquitted yourself honorably on the Pecos this afternoon," Shawn said. "You have nothing to prove."

"I can prove my loyalty and my love for my father and for the man who reared me."

"If the colonel was here, he'd order you to stay," Jacob said.

"Of course he will stay," Lorena said. "We've got two wounded vaqueros who will be abed for weeks under a doctor's care. Samuel, your presence is needed at the roundup and I will brook no argument on that point."

"Lorena, will you have me turn my back on Pa when he's in danger? What kind of son would I be?"

"I will not have you turn your back on your duty," Lorena said. "And the colonel would tell you that your duty is here, out on the range for the gather."

"You're staying, Sam," Jacob said. "Let there be no argument."

"Jacob, that was a most singularly sensible thing to say," Lorena said. "You and Patrick are quite able to assist the colonel in his endeavors."

"What am I, invisible?" Shawn put in.

Jacob smiled. "Shawn, you're not the best puncher in the world and we could sure use your gun."

"As to your first point, Jake, I don't concur," Shawn said stiffly. "But as to your second, I do agree. Sam talked about duty, and it's my duty to make sure you and Pat don't get your fool heads blown off."

"I still think I—"

"No, Samuel, it's settled." Lorena rose to her feet. "Jacob, if we retire to the parlor would you play some Chopin for us?"

Jacob nodded. "My pleasure, Lorena."

The woman smiled. "Good, I enjoy the company of O'Brien men with my Chopin."

Chapter Thirty-one

"The boys tell me we'll need a mule team to haul the gold to Mexico, Cap'n," Barney Merden said. "Horses are no good for the hard country between here and Sonora."

"Team? How many is that?" Nate Condor asked. It was a sailor's question. He was not a land-lubber.

"I reckon four, maybe six," Merden said. "The wagon itself is heavy and it's got a load to haul."

"Where can we get that many damned mules in a hurry?"

"Beggin' your pardon, boss," one of his gunmen said. "There's a stage station just to the north of the Playas Dry Lake. Always mule teams there." He was a former lawman by the name of Steve Placket. Over the years he'd killed four men.

Condor considered that. "Good. We'll go

round 'em up and then head directly for the Apache Hills and the wagon."

"We got a problem, though, boss," Placket said.

Condor was irritated. He didn't want to hear about problems. "What the hell is it?"

"The station is run by old Hick Gunter and he'll be a handful. By times, he's been a buffalo hunter, army scout, and lawman, and he's tough as a knot in a pine board." Placket grinned. "Got himself a pretty young wife he calls Sally an' a yeller cur dog by the same name."

"He scare you, Steve?" Merden said, his mouth twisted in a sneer.

"Hick don't scare me none, but he's a man to walk around."

"Yeah, well we don't have time to walk around anybody. We kill him and take his mules and maybe his woman if she's pretty enough." Condor's eyes became dangerous. "If that sets all right with you, Steve."

Placket shrugged. "I'm fine with that, boss. Do we wear the masks?"

"No, we're done with that, by God," Condor said. "It was the boss's idea, what he called 'a dramatic flourish,' and it didn't work worth a damn."

He waved a hand at Merden. "Get the people mounted, Barney. We'll go get our bloody mules."

When Condor stepped outside, he'd only eight men sitting their horses. His numbers were dwindling. A couple had recently lit a shuck when they heard Dallas Steele was in Recoil. Apparently they'd run into the Fighting Pink before and wanted no part of him.

Condor shrugged it off. The fewer who were with him in Mexico, the less he'd need to kill.

The stage station was a few miles farther north and east of the dry lake than Placket remembered, closer to the Coyote Hills in harsh desert brush country. It consisted of a single low cabin with two glazed windows to the front, a few outbuildings, a small barn, and a pole corral. Eight years before, it had withstood an Apache attack and the army had counted five Indians dead on the ground after Hick Gunter got through with them.

Condor studied the place through his field glasses and made out a dozen animals in the corral, half of them mules. He turned to Merden. "There are our draft animals, Barney. We make this fast, in and out, you understand? The stage line uses the wagon road and I reckon so will the army if it's around."

"I got you, Cap'n," Merden said. "We'll get it done real quick."

"Keep the shooting to a minimum so we don't draw too much attention. In other words, shoot to kill, man, woman, child, or animal, understand?"

"Aye, aye, Cap'n. It will be as you say."

"We go visit, real peaceable, like we're honest travelers passing through. We'll all look so innocent that old Hick will invite us inside for tea and cake."

This brought a laugh from the men as Condor waved them forward.

But as they drew closer to the cabin, it seemed that Hick Gunter was not entirely a sociable man. He stood outside his cabin, short and stocky, like a figure hewn from granite. He held a Henry .44-40 in his hands and his gray eyes were guarded, wary but not unfriendly. He looked like a man willing to take things as they came, good or bad. "What can I do fer you boys?"

It was a mild surprise to Condor that the man was a fighter, or had been at one time in his life. He had the look of a man who was hard to kill.

"I need mules," Condor said. "I'll take all you have."

"I got mules, but they ain't for sale. They belong to the stage company."

A pretty girl wearing a blue gingham dress and a white apron opened the door. "Hick, is everything all right?"

"Everything is fine, Sally," Gunter said. "Git back in the house while I talk with these gentlemen."

After the door closed, Condor said, "Now, about those mules—"

"They ain't for sale. Clean out your ears, boy, because I already done tol' you that."

"Ah, you're under the misconception that I'm buying," Condor said, his deep-set eyes like stone. "I'm not. I'm taking."

"Is that the way of it?" the old man said. "I took ye fer a thief of some kind."

Condor didn't answer. He was there for mules, and he didn't have time for conversation. He drew and shot Hick Gunter in the chest.

Then the ball opened.

Hit hard, the old man staggered back. But he was getting his work in.

Condor's horse went down kicking as a bullet slammed into its chest. Condor was thrown clear, but he landed with a thud. All the breath gushed out of his lungs and left him open-mouthed and gasping on the ground.

Guns hammered into the hot stillness of the day. Two of Condor's men went down and a third sat slumped over in the saddle, coughing up black blood.

Gunter, on one knee, his face ashen, levered his rifle. The entire front of his shirt was splashed scarlet, but the old man had sand and was game to the last. His body jerking from the impact of round after round, he finally fell on his face and went down.

Screaming, Sally Gunter ran to her husband and threw herself on his body, her slender frame racked by great, heaving sobs.

Able to finally suck in some air, Condor rose unsteadily to his feet. "Get the damned mules!" he yelled. "We've wasted enough time."

But Steve Placket swung out of the saddle, lust and the desire for revenge tangled in his blue eyes. "Ain't she pretty?" he yelled.

He threw himself at Sally and tried to kiss her, but she attempted to ward off his unwanted advances.

Condor stepped around the struggling pair and walked to the corral. "Round up the mules, Barney, on the double. And cut out a horse for me."

"Right, Cap'n," Merden yelled, pointing northward. "Dust to the north!"

"Damn you, get it done," Condor yelled. "We're running out of time."

Within a few minutes the mules were loaded up with harnesses and hurriedly led out of the corral.

"Let's go!" Condor yelled. "Get the hell out of here."

The dust cloud was getting closer.

Placket was still tearing at the girl and Condor roared from the stolen horse, "Steve, leave that alone. Let's go."

The man ignored him, overcome with lust.

Condor glanced to the north. The dust was close and there was no time to lose. "Placket!"

The man ignored him, intent on the girl.

Condor drew and shot Placket in the temple. When the gunman dropped, Condor's gun roared again and the girl collapsed, a red rose blossoming between her eyes.

"Damn shame, Cap'n," Merden said. "I mean, a pretty woman going to waste like that."

They rode south, driving the mules toward the Apache Hills.

Chapter Thirty-two

After the last shovelful of dirt fell on Maurice Bird's grave, Dallas Steele took off the black mourning garment supplied by the undertaker as did the other men who'd come for the funeral.

"Well, they done ol' Maurice just fine," Luther Ironside said. "Laid him out all nice and planted him in a silk-lined coffin. A man can't ask more 'n that."

"This was a most singularly depressing event." Edith Ludsthorpe was dressed from head to toe in black and a weeping veil covered her face under which she continually dabbed her eyes with a handkerchief. "Poor Mr. Bird. Such a great talent to be taken from us so violently by ruffians." She swayed a little. "I feel faint, I really do."

"Please don't distress yourself too much, dear lady," Shamus O'Brien said. "Mr. Steele has thoughtfully provided a picnic basket that will help sustain you in your time of grief."

Ironside listened to the colonel's speech with growing disbelief. He grinned and opened his mouth to speak, but Shamus silenced him with a warning glare.

"Dear Mr. Steele, thank you for the thought, but I declare, I can't eat a single bite," Edith said, taking Steele's arm. "I am so distraught I can barely walk."

"Well, I can," Chastity said, dressed like her mother all in sable, but without the weeping veil. "Funerals always make me hungry."

"Well, perhaps my daughter is right," Edith said. "Pray, what refreshments did you provide, Mr. Steele?"

Smiling slightly, he told her.

Edith said, "Perhaps I can force down a couple pieces of fried chicken and a glass of brandy. I always say that a slice of apple pie settles nicely on top of all that's gone before."

"My sentiments entirely, Mrs. Ludsthorpe." Steele led the woman and Chastity to a tree-shaded area on the top of a low hogback that overlooked the small Recoil graveyard and spread a blanket on the ground.

After the ladies were seated and the picnic basket opened, he said, "Will you join us, Colonel?"

"I don't think so, Dallas," Shamus said. "I reckon Luther and I will head back to town"—he waved a hand—"with Deputy Sparrow here."

"I'm h-h-here in an o-o-official c-capacity," Sparrow said. "It w-w-would not do to s-s-socialize."

"I understand," Steele said. "Well, I'll see you gentlemen back in Recoil."

"Mind if I grab a chicken leg, Steele?" Ironside said. "I'm a little sharp set."

"By all means. There's plenty."

"Luther," Shamus said, "does your mind ever rise higher than your belt buckle?"

"Sometimes," Ironside said. "But never at weddings and funerals."

After the others rode away and the gravediggers packed up and left, Dallas Steele said, "How do you like the chicken, Mrs. Ludsthorpe?"

Edith sighed. "Truth to tell, Mr. Steele, I'm so upset I can hardly taste it." That she was on her third piece gave the lie to that statement and Steele smiled.

"I've been meaning to tell you something, Dallas," Chastity said, laying aside her wineglass. "It may be of the greatest moment, or nothing at all."

"Then let me be the judge," Steele said.

"Do you remember just after we first met I told you I wanted to be an actress?"

"Chastity, really, how could you say such a terrible thing?" Edith exclaimed. "Acting is a profession for whores." A scrap of chicken skin clung to the corner of her mouth.

"We'll talk about this later, mother." Chastity turned to Steele. "Now where was I? Oh, yes, I said I wanted to be an actress and I told you that there were people all over the West who'd trod the boards at one time or another."

"I remember," Steele said, wondering where this was leading.

"Well, before he was killed, Maurice—"

"Poor Mr. Bird," Edith sobbed, lowering her weeping veil. She was on her second brandy and feeling the effects.

Chastity glared at her mother, then continued. "Maurice had traveled around quite a bit and he said he saw Mr. Shaw—you know that nice man who owns the hardware store in town?"

Steele nodded. "Yes, I know him."

"Well, Maurice said he once saw Mr. Shaw and his wife in burlesque at the Royal Strand Theater in London, oh, maybe ten years ago. Apparently they did an American-millionaire-meets-the-English-lady act that was quite popular at the time."

"So Shaw was an actor? I don't see where that's

taking us." Steele removed his coat as the sun rose higher in the sky.

Chastity leaned forward to within whispering distance. "Is Mr. Shaw all that he seems?"

Steele smiled. "Have you been reading detective dime novels?"

"Dear Mr. Shaw"—Edith hiccupped—"what a nice man."

"Tell me what you know about him, Dallas. Mr. Shaw, I mean," Chastity said.

"Well, I size him up as a timid, henpecked little man—"

"Who was bold enough to shoot dead one of the bandits who held up our stagecoach the day we arrived in the Playas," Chastity said.

"I heard about that," Steele said. "I guess it took sand on his part."

"You guess! It took a deal of bravery."

"And some skill with a gun." Steele thought for a moment, then said, "When we get back to Recoil I'll ask Sheriff Clitherow what he knows about Shaw."

Steele had his own suspicions about Shaw, and Nate Condor's recent attempt to visit the man's home had sharpened them, but he didn't want to tip his hand, at least not yet. If Shaw was connected to Condor in some fashion, he could lead the way to the army gold.

Her pretty face eager, Chastity said, "Do you think he could be in league with the night riders?"

Steele laughed. "Catch your breath, Chastity. I think that's highly unlikely. Shaw is a respectable businessman."

"And a church elder," Chastity said. "But that doesn't mean anything. Listen, his wife's name is Martha and from what I've seen of her she has an actress's expensive tastes in clothes and jewelry. Maybe the money is running out and Martha is complaining."

"Actresses . . . whores . . ." Edith said. Her head dropped to her chest and she started to snore.

"We have to get your mother home," Steele said. "She's had a . . . trying morning."

"She's had too much to drink, you mean." Chastity frowned at Steele. "Do you always wear your gun like that?"

"In a shoulder holster? Yes, I do. I have my tailor cut my coats to accommodate a revolver."

"Who's your tailor?"

"I bet you ask ladies, 'Who's your dress-maker?'"

"Oh yes, I do. All the time."

"Brooks Brothers of Manhattan, New York though I often patronize a tailor in Denver, a man called Simon Levy who's a genius with cloth." Steel smiled. "Satisfied?"

"Quite," Chastity said. "Your taste is exquisite.

Now I really must take mother home." She laid her hand on Steele's forearm. "After you speak to the sheriff, you will tell me what he says?"

"Of course. But don't get your hopes up. I believe Clitherow is going to tell me that Shaw is a pillar of society and a shining light that illuminates the church."

"Perhaps," Chastity said, "but my woman's intuition tells me otherwise."

Chapter Thirty-three

The Lordsburg stage had often been late, but when it pulled into Recoil just before noon on the morning of Maurice Bird's funeral, it was a day late, a fact that alarmed Sheriff Clitherow.

If the driver, the dashing, buckskinned Tom Gill, was also concerned at his tardiness, he made no show of it. He stopped the stagecoach and helped his three passengers alight outside the Rest and Be Thankful Hotel, still scarred from the bomb that missed killing Colonel O'Brien and Luther Ironside.

Clitherow crossed the street to the stage. "Tom, what the hell?"

Then he saw the faces of the passengers.

All three were men, a couple of drummers, the third a young counter clerk by the name of Dan Clark who worked for the Recoil Bank and

Trust and had been visiting his ailing father in Lordsburg.

The men looked like the damned who'd just taken their first glimpse into hell. Their eyes were wide, stunned with the remembrance of a horror that, until then, they couldn't even imagine. Clitherow had seen that look before in the eyes of soldiers who'd had a limb amputated, unbelieving, staring around them but seeing nothing.

"Tom," Clitherow said, "what the hell happened?"

"Gunter Station happened, Sheriff," Gill said. "Hick and his wife dead, three more men dead on the ground. It seems that old Hick made his fight."

Clitherow opened his mouth to speak, but Gill talked over him, eager to finish his story. "We buried the dead best we could, me an' Buff Ferguson, who was riding guard, an' the passengers. Never seen them as done it, except for the rannies that ol' Hick shot. They took all the mules from the corral. I spied that my ownself from the tracks. Hick was a mean old codger, but he ran a good station, and his wife was a fine cook an' just as pretty as she could be. She didn't deserve the end she got. Neither of them did."

Clitherow went at it gently. "Tom, where were the tracks headed? Can you recollect?"

"Sure I recollect. They were headed east. Southeast, you would call it."

In his mind's eye, Clitherow pictured the lay of the land from Gunter Station southeast. "They were maybe headed for the Apache Hills. In that general direction anyway, huh?"

"Could be. I wouldn't know. It's off my route." Gill stepped away and said to the passengers, "Are you men feelin' all right? You've been through a lot and look used up."

The drummers exchanged glances, then one of the said, "We will be all right after we have a drink or three." He looked at the bank clerk. "You care to join us, young feller?"

"That woman was . . . was . . ."

"I know," the drummer said. "You want to join us, get them tintypes out of your head?"

"Damn right I do," Alan Clark said.

"How about you, driver?" the drummer asked.

Gill shook his head. "I got mail for Sonora and I'm already running behind. Thanks fer the offer, though."

"Well, good luck."

"Yeah, and good luck to you too."

"So you can see that this thing has come to a head," Sheriff Jim Clitherow said. "Nate Condor is headed for the Apache Hills and I bet he's after the army wagon if it's still there. That's where we'll find him."

"When did Condor raid the stage station?" Dallas Steele asked.

"About this time yesterday, maybe a little earlier."

"He could be long gone by now."

"We'll find him," Clitherow said.

"Who have we got?"

"You, me, and—"

"Us," Shamus said. "Luther and me."

"Five with Deputy Sparrow," Steele said. "Is that enough?"

"It'll have to be," Clitherow said. "We can't depend on anybody else. Not to go up against Nate Condor and his boys we can't."

"What about Shaw?" Steele asked.

"Silas Shaw?" Clitherow said, surprised. "What about him?"

"Chastity Ludsthorpe told me that Shaw handled a gun pretty well at the stagecoach holdup."

"He was lucky," Ironside said. "Any one of them bandits could've taken him without even tryin'."

"Maybe," Steele said, "but I think we should bring him along as an extra gun."

Clitherow sighed. "Whatever you say." He

motioned to Sparrow. "Steve, go get Silas. Bring him here and tell him to wear iron."

The deputy nodded and left.

"After I talk to Silas, we saddle up and head directly for the Apache Hills," Clitherow said. "Damn it, boys, we'll run him to earth this time."

"You'll have to ride a hoss, Steele," Ironside said. "This isn't work for a burro."

"I don't have a hoss."

"I'll find you one," Clitherow said.

"I don't like horses," Steele said. "I never did cotton to them much."

"You'll learn to love them, Steele," Ironside said, his lips twitching under his mustache. "We'll make a horseman of you yet."

The office door swung open and Sparrow stepped inside. Silas Shaw, wearing a brown apron over broadcloth pants and a collarless white shirt, was right behind him.

"What can I do for you, Sheriff?" Shaw asked. "I am very busy, you know, with the hotel being repaired and all."

"Steve didn't tell you?"

"I thought Silas should h-hear it from you, Jim," Sparrow said.

"The night riders are headed for the Apache Hills, and it could be they're after an army pay wagon carrying more than a hundred thousand in gold and silver coin. We're going after them and time's a-wasting."

"How do you know this?" Shaw said, his face drained of color, something Steele noticed.

"They raided a stage station yesterday, killed the owner and his wife and stole a mule team," Clitherow said. "Tom Gill come up on the place and he said the bandits left tracks that headed in the direction of the Apache Hills. Just for your information, Silas, the leader of the killers is a man by the name of English Nate Condor."

"Condor is a former pirate and slave trader," Steele said, watching Shaw's reaction closely. "He's a man that needs killing."

"Why are you telling me all this?" Shaw rubbed his left arm and his eyes were wary, guarded, and pained.

"I'm forming a posse and I intend to trap Condor in the hills. I'd like you to join us, Silas."

"But I'm not a gunfighter. And I have my poor wife . . . and my store to consider."

Steel smiled inwardly. Perhaps the man doth protest too much.

"I can't force you to do this, Silas," Clitherow said. "I'm asking you as a friend."

"Then I'll do it." Shaw's eyes hardened to chips of gray flint. "When do we leave?"

"Now." Clitherow rose to his feet and extended his hand. "You're a brave and honorable man, Silas." He and Shaw shook.

Steele, silently observing, did not share Clitherow's opinion of Silas Shaw.

Chapter Thirty-four

"Landslide down the Burro Mountains way took the track out, but it should be repaired by nightfall," the ticket agent said. "Sorry boys. But on the bright side, you can spend a few hours enjoying the pleasures of Deacon Brody Flat."

Shawn jerked a thumb over his shoulder. "That's it?"

"Hell, mister, it's all you need," the agent said. "We got a saloon, a general store, and a blacksmith's shop. Saggy Maggie Monroe entertains at the saloon and Tom Grant over to the general store makes a right tasty sowbelly sandwich."

"If the train leaves at dusk, when will we reach Lordsburg?" Patrick asked.

"Oh, not later than midnight, depending on the state of the track." The agent picked up a pen and bent to his ledger. "Now, if you boys will excuse me . . ."

Jacob stepped outside, walked to the edge of the warped wooden platform, and looked across the rails to the town, such as it was. The saloon and store were small, false-fronted buildings showing the effects of weather. They had been painted at one time, but most of the paint had flaked off, leaving just a few forlorn patches of white. Two saddled mustangs stood hipshot at the hitching rail.

"Not much of a place," Shawn said, stepping beside his brother.

"I've seen worse," Jacob said.

"I haven't," Shawn said.

Jacob smiled. "Shawn, you've led a sheltered life."

Shawn turned his head and looked at the Mexican families camped out in the shade of some nearby cottonwoods. They had a fire going and the women were preparing meals as children clung to their skirts.

"That's what we should do," he said. "Make camp and eat tortillas in the shade until the train leaves."

The locomotive and its two cars were a ways down the track, the firebox cold. The afternoon sun gleamed on the rails and in the distance heat shimmered.

Patrick joined his brothers and Jacob said, "Anybody interested in a cold beer?"

"Warm beer, you mean," Shawn said. "In this godforsaken place,"

"No matter, warm or cold, it will still cut the dust."

The agent stuck his head through the ticket window. "Boys, just a word of warning. It looks like Logan Epp and Hank Pickett are in town. They own a one-loop ranch west of town."

"What about them?" Shawn asked.

"Well, they're nasty customers when they're sober, but when they get to drinking they're pure pizen. Logan shot a miner over there to the saloon not a three-month past. He said he could never abide a bald man with a beard so he drawed down and plugged him square. I seen that with my own two eyes."

"Sounds like a real nice fellow," Shawn said. "The kind of man you would invite home for tea and crumpets."

"Well, Logan was drunk at the time, so nobody got down on him too much."

"We'll be careful to step around both gentlemen," Shawn said. "We're just travelers stranded in a wasteland and none of us wears a beard."

"I told the white passengers to wait in Grant's store," the agent said. "He sells sody pop and bottled beer and he usually has cigars."

"Thank you," Patrick said. "For the warning about the ranching gentlemen, I mean."

"I do what I can to ensure the safety of my passengers and their goods," the agent said, as though he recited words he'd read on a printed page. His head disappeared through the window.

Shawn said, "Well, where do we have our beer?"

"At the saloon of course," Jacob said.

"I knew you'd say that." Shawn stepped off the platform, followed by Jacob and Patrick.

They crossed the dusty street, pushed open the batwing doors and entered the saloon.

"Hello, boys, just in from the range, are ye?" Saggy Maggie, enormously fat in a loose-fitting, blue silk dress, fluttered toward the O'Brien brothers like a schooner under full sail.

"I guess that about sums it up," Jacob said. "Our train is stuck here because of trouble farther down the track."

"Then get yourselves a drink and if any of you gents feel the need to throw a leg over the bucking pony, just let me know."

Patrick, polite to a fault, said, "We'll be sure to do that, dear lady."

Maggie laughed and turned to the other patrons in the saloon. "Hear that, boys? The schoolteacher here called me a lady. More than any of you ever done."

A tall man with the golden eyes of a cougar looked in the saloon mirror at the woman.

Without turning his head he said, "Maggie, you were never a lady. You gave up all claim to that title when you shacked up with a Mississippi lowlife for five years in a cabin just back of this saloon."

"He was good to me. So why not? A man's a man and they all want the same thing. You'd no call to gun him the way you did, Logan."

"I was tired of looking at his ugly black face. That was reason enough."

"That's tellin' her, Logan," said a small man who sat at a table nursing a beer. His daddy might have been a weasel.

"Shut your trap," Epp said. "Let a man drink in peace."

"What can I do you for, boys?" the bartender said, his voice timid.

"Three beers," Jacob said. "Is it cold?"

"No, it's warm as hoss piss." Epp was drunk and getting drunker.

"Then it'll have to do, I guess," Jacob said.

The bartender poured the beers and Jacob laid a coin on the counter. "And a drink for my two friends at the end of the bar."

Logan Epp turned to face Jacob. Hank Pickett, with the impassive, sun-browned face of a cigar store Indian, took a step to the rancher's left.

"I pay for my own drinks, mister," Epp said, his

eyes ugly. "And I don't care to be beholden to saddle tramps."

Jacob smiled. "A man who's always on the prod should stay away from whiskey. It makes him irritable and downright unfriendly."

"Is that a fact?" Epp said.

"Yup, that's a natural fact," Jacob said. "But I'm buying you one, anyhow."

"The hell you are," Epp argued. "Now you run next door and stay with the women and the rubes until I decide to leave town."

"I don't hardly have time." The old, reckless light was in Jacob's eyes, the one his brothers had seen many times in the past. "Because after you finish the drink I'm buying, you're leaving town real quick."

"What the hell are you?" Epp demanded, his hand close to his gun.

"Me, I'm a man who didn't make a reputation as a gun hand by shooting old miners and black sharecroppers."

"Let it go, Jake," Shawn warned. "We've done enough killing to last us for a spell."

Epp's eyes opened a little wider. A niggling doubt was added to his certainty that he could kill the tall, shabby puncher with the sweeping dragoon mustache who faced him with such easy, relaxed confidence.

In a small voice, Hank Pickett said, "Who the hell are you, mister?"

"I don't give a damn what he is," Epp said. "He can crawl out of here on his hands and knees or be carried out by his pardners. The choice is his."

Jacob ignored that, "Name's Jacob O'Brien, out of Texas and then the Glorieta Mesa country."

That last was a conversation stopper and a man could've heard a pin drop in the saloon.

Epp swallowed hard. "I didn't know it was you."

"I don't enjoy a man calling my beer hoss piss and I don't like a man threatening me," Jacob said. "Do you understand that?"

Epp was silent.

Patrick said, "For heaven's sake, say you understand that."

"I understand that," Epp said, shrinking in size like a deflated balloon.

"If you'd drawn on me, I would've killed you," Jacob said. "You're a wanna-be bad man, mister, a piece of back-shooting trash. As soon as I walked in here, I figured you for a scoundrel. You're not in my class. A thing to remember."

"Logan," Pickett said, "let's head back to the ranch. You'll have another day."

"No," Jacob said. "There will be no more days for Logan. Pretty soon he'll kill some other poor, scared to death, fumble-fingered rube, just to prove to himself that this was all a bad dream and he's still a real mean hard case. I won't stand aside and let that happen."

Jacob drew and fired.

Epp's right hand froze in place, clawing over his gun, Jacob's bullet cut the man's thumb clean off, as though it had been severed by a butcher's cleaver.

Epp held up his mangled hand, blood running down his arm. "Damn you," he screamed. "You shot off my damned thumb."

"I sure did, didn't I?" Jacob said. "From now on if you draw down on a man he'll get an even break."

"I won't forget this, O'Brien," Epp said. "Damn your eyes, I won't forget this."

"I hope you don't. Now get the hell out of here or I'll shoot off your other thumb."

"Let it go, Logan," Pickett said. "When we get back to the ranch I'll bandage that hand."

"He gave me no warning," Epp said. "He just grinned and gunned me."

"You don't mess with men like him, Logan," Pickett said. "He's all kinds of hell."

Jacob turned to the door. Several curious on-lookers had gathered there when no more shots were fired. "You folks come inside. You can drink in the saloon again. My brother is buying."

A muscular man in a leather apron stepped through and grinned. "That's good enough for me." The blacksmith was bald and sported a thick beard.

A dozen thirsty train passengers followed him inside.

"Logan, are you still here?" Jacob said, looking at Epp. "I'm really surprised."

"We're leaving, Mr. O'Brien," Pickett said. "No need for more fancy moves." He helped the whimpering Epp through the door, and moments later the two men were riding out of town.

"That's strange," Patrick said.

"What's strange?" Jacob asked.

"When Logan Epp walked into this saloon he was over six foot tall. When he left, he was just a nubbin'. You cut him down to size, Jake."

"I can't abide bullies." Jacob turned Shawn. "I believe the bartender wants you to pay him."

The train pulled out at four in the afternoon. The ticket agent had assured the O'Brien brothers that the track was clear all the way to Lordsburg. "You'll fly to your destination on wings of steel," he'd said, reinforcing Patrick's belief that there's a bit of the poet in everybody.

Patrick was looking out the window at the passing terrain, then turned to his brother. "How do you figure Pa and Luther are making out, Jake?"

"We'll know soon enough, I reckon."

"Still got a bad feeling?"

"Bad enough."

"Maybe you're just upset about gunning that Epp ranny," Shawn said.

"You know, I've been studying on that," Jacob said. "Instead of blowing off his thumb, should I have put a bullet in his belly and put him out of the gun-slinging business forever? It's a thing for a man to consider, you know, ponder the right or the wrong of the thing."

Shawn shook his head. "Jake, you're an unforgiving feller and that makes you a mighty dangerous enemy."

Jacob nodded. "Don't it, though."

Chapter Thirty-five

Sheriff Jim Clitherow and his small posse rode out of Recoil.

A couple of things about Silas Shaw troubled Dallas Steele. The first was the belted Colt he wore and the Winchester in the boot under his right knee, hardly the armament of a timid storekeeper. The second was that Shaw sat his horse with jut-jawed determination, as though he planned to see things through to the bitter end, no matter the cost to him or anyone else. It was not the demeanor of a man who'd been pressed into posse service.

It seemed to Steele the store owner had an axe to grind and it involved Nate Condor. Steele was convinced the two were in cahoots. As to their exact relationship, he had no idea.

"Hey, Steele," Ironside said, "I thought you said you couldn't ride a hoss?"

"I said I didn't particularly like horses. I didn't say I couldn't ride one."

"Well, you look good, all dressed in fancy duds and sitting straight up and down in the saddle like a Yankee general on parade."

"Maybe I should try to look like a Confederate general," Steele said.

"Nah," Ironside said, shaking his head. "You don't have the breeding for that."

"Luther," Shamus O'Brien said, turning in the saddle, "Southern gentlemen do not cast aspersions on another gentleman's breeding. Now watch your tongue."

"No harm intended, Colonel. What does cast aspersions mean?"

"It means—"

"It means, Luther, that you're a plain-talking man," Steele said, smiling at Shamus.

"Damn right," Ironside said. "That's me all right. As plain talking a man as ever was.

"Dallas, thank you for your patience," Shamus said. "Luther can be a trial and a tribulation sometimes."

"Apache Hills s-s-straight ahead." Steve Sparrow glanced at the sky. "And it l-l-looks like we're in f-f-for it, boys."

Building ramparts of black clouds loomed over the Cedar Mountains to the northeast and lightning flickered. The wind rose quickly, tossing the brush and skittering leaves and small branches across the ground.

Clitherow turned in the saddle. "We go in easy and with our eyes skinned. Condor and his damned night riders could still be there."

Steele kneed his mount forward. "I'll scout ahead, Sheriff. Make sure there are no unpleasant surprises waiting for us."

The lawman nodded. "Take care, Dallas. We're not dealing with pilgrims here."

Steele touched his hat and then galloped for the hills gouged with shadow as the storm threatened. Thunder rumbled in the distance and the wind pummeled him mercilessly.

Slowing his horse to a canter, he reached under his English tweed hacking jacket and drew his Colt. His eyes scanned the hills, but only the wind moved.

He reached the dry wash with the skeleton of the dead piñon on the bank and rode into it as thunder muttered closer. He followed the wash for a hundred yards before a cabin came into view on his left.

Not a horse fighter, Steele dismounted and approached the cabin on foot. The door hung partially open on its rawhide hinges. He called out, "Anyone home?"

No answer, just the endless sigh of the wind.

Gun in hand, Steele stepped inside into silence.

There is nothing quieter than the quiet of the dead. Lum Park, looking old and shrunken in death, lay sprawled on his back. He'd been shot in the chest several times.

A porcelain clock decorated with tubby cherubs ticked on the mantel, a small sound joined by the patter of rain on the cabin roof. Steele heard a noise behind him and spun around, his Colt coming up fast.

"Hold up. It's only me, Dallas." Shamus looked at the old man on the floor. "Condor did for him?"

"Seems like," Steele said.

Shamus crossed himself. "Where is the gold?"

"Well, I believe the gold is gone for sure, but maybe we can find where it was. If it was the army wagon, it would leave tracks."

"This rain and wind will wash away any tracks, I imagine."

Steele nodded. "That would also be my guess, Colonel."

Shamus stepped to the table. Three coffee cups, half full, still sat in their saucers with a platter of uneaten salt pork sandwiches nearby. A chair was tipped over where someone had risen in a hurry.

Shamus picked up a sandwich. The bread was curled and dry, the pork already odorous. "I'd say they left yesterday after something scared them."

"Condor doesn't strike me as a man who's easily scared," Steele said. The horseshoe-shaped diamond pin in his cravat caught the gray light angling in from the cabin window.

"He left in haste," Shamus said. "That's all I can gather."

"Shot the old man, then scampered?" Steele asked.

"I'm not a detective, but that's how it looks to me." Shamus stepped to the mantel and stared at the clock for a moment. "Austrian," he said to himself. "Made in Karlstein, I would say."

"Where's the girl? Did she go with Condor, do you think?"

"No, Dallas, I fear we'll find her body very soon."

Sheriff Clitherow stepped into the cabin and glanced at the body on the floor. "Lum Park."

"As ever was," Steele said. "Shot through and through. Did you find his daughter, or her body?"

"No, but we found someone else," Clitherow said. "You'd better come outside and take a look."

They walked through dashes of rain and gusts of wind to a patch of heavy brush and a few junipers near the bank of the wash, where a dead man lay on his back. His spurs had gouged the damp ground when he was dragged from the undergrowth.

Steele stared at the corpse. "He's a gun hand. No puncher could afford those boots."

"Then he must be one of Condor's boys," Shamus said.

"Look at his throat," Clitherow said. "Look real close."

Steele squatted beside the corpse. "My God. His throat's been torn out."

Shamus, not trusting his legs, bent over and saw what Steele had seen. "May God and all his holy saints in Heaven grant this poor man eternal peace," Shamus crossed himself and straightened up. "An animal did this? A wolf or a bear?"

"Whatever it was, it scared Condor and them out of here, Colonel, just as you had it figured," Steele said.

Ironside stepped beside them, wearing a slicker. He passed the one in his hand to Shamus. "What happened to him?" He pointed to the dead man.

"Look closer, Luther," Shamus said. "His throat's gone."

"Hell, I thought that was gunshot blood," Ironside said. "Damn it, Colonel, you're right. Something bit him, and it was big."

"A wolf, you think?" Shamus said, shrugging into the slicker.

"Could be," Ironside said. "Or a mighty mean grizz."

"Sheriff!" Silas Shaw stood farther up the wash,

wind-blown rain slamming at him. "Come see this," he yelled.

Beside him, Steve Sparrow stood hunch shouldered and miserable.

"What is it, Silas?" Clitherow hollered.

"A cave! And the army pay wagon!"

They met up with Shaw and he led them into the rocky draw and to the break in the rock. The wagon had been pulled out of the cave, but it teetered to one side like a bird with a broken wing. The right rear wheel lay flat on the ground and even from a distance it was obvious the axle had shattered.

"Dry rot," Shaw said. "When they pulled the wagon out of the cave the axle broke in about three places. And look"—he dug into a pocket and produced a couple of double eagles—"they were in so much of a hurry to get the hell out of here they dropped these."

"I guess they loaded the sacks of coin onto the mules," Clitherow said.

"Yes, that's exactly what they did. Damn their eyes." Shaw's face was bitter, shadowed with anger, and at that moment Steele knew for a certainty that Nate Condor had crossed him.

Clitherow thought for a few moments. "It's only six, seven miles from here to Chihuahua, and it's all flat country. They're in Mexico by now, damn them."

"Aren't we going after them?" Shaw rubbed his left arm and kept working his jaw muscles by opening and closing his mouth.

"They could be anywhere," Clitherow said. "It would take a regiment of cavalry to search that desert country, and that might not be enough. Besides that, it's out of my jurisdiction."

"Why, you damned fool, you're letting Condor get away with a hundred and thirty thousand dollars," Shaw yelled.

"Don't call me a fool, Silas," the sheriff said, his voice low and flat.

"Then if you're not a fool, you're a damned coward," Shaw said.

"Don't call me a coward either, Silas, unless you're prepared to back your words with a gun."

"Enough," Shamus said, stepping between the two angry men. "We're all a little tense here, today."

"Why do you care so much, Shaw?" Steele asked. "It's not your money."

The man was taken aback, but only for a moment. "I wish to see justice done. Condor is a murderer and I plan to stand at the gallows and watch him hang."

"Well, he isn't going to hang, at least anytime

soon," Clitherow said. "Like it or not, the pirate turned outlaw has won."

"Jim, at least the danger to Recoil is over," Shamus said.

"Yes, I guess it is. Condor has what he wanted and he's flown the coop. Colonel, I guess your task here is done. I'm grateful for your help, yours and Luther's."

"We didn't do much, Jim, and in the end . . . well, as you say, we lost."

Clitherow looked at Steele. "What about you, Dallas? Is your job done here?"

"Let's step into the cave and I'll tell you what I think, Jim. The rain is doing nothing for my tailoring."

"Damn you, you can all go to hell," Shaw said. "I'm riding after Condor."

"We don't even know he's headed for Old Mexico," Shamus said. "He could've gone in any direction."

"Mexico is the closest place of safety for him. It's somewhere he can spend his money in peace. Well, I won't let him get away with it."

"He's a man to be reckoned with, Shaw," Steele said. "He's real fast with the iron, maybe the fastest there is."

"Unlike you damned cowards, I'll take my chances." Shaw stomped away through the rain toward his horse.

Ironside said, "Now there goes an angry man."

"Yes. But maybe too angry." Steele waved toward the break in the rock. "Shall we?"

Once out of the rain and wind, Clitherow said, "You were planning to tell us something, Dallas?"

Steele took time to light a cigar, a damp one he observed. "Through the Pinkertons, I was ordered by President Cleveland to investigate the murders in and around the town of Recoil, and something else—the whereabouts of Lowery's gold."

"Lowery's gold? I'm not catching your drift," Clitherow said.

"The major in charge of the guard detail for the pay wagon was named Lowery," Steele said. "Apparently, that's what Washington now calls the missing money that they'd dearly love to get back, especially since the president is pushing for a gold standard to back up our currency."

"Hell, Steele, it's gone," Ironside said. "They can't blame you for that."

"They can and they will," Steele said. "Washington always needs a scapegoat."

"Dallas, you can always come work for me at Dromore," Shamus said.

Steele smiled. "That's very kind of you, Colonel, but I wouldn't make a very good cowboy. I'm going after the gold."

"When? Now?" Clitherow questioned.

"Of course now, Sheriff. That is if I can keep the horse for a little longer."

"Keep it as long as you want."

"I can understand your haste," Shamus said. "It's your duty. Luther, give Dallas your slicker. He can't ride in this weather without one."

"Hell, Colonel, I'll get wet."

"Yes, but you're heading back to town and can dry yourself. Dallas is riding into the wilderness."

"Thank you, Luther," Steele said. "I appreciate it."

With a deal of ill grace, Ironside took off his slicker, muttering about the young whippersnapper . . . and the damned rain. "Buy his own slicker . . . too much favoritism around here . . ."

"What did you say, Luther?" Shamus said.

"Nothing. I didn't say nothing."

"I should hope not. Flatter not thyself if thou hath no charity for thy neighbor, Luther."

A smile touching his lips, Steele took the dripping slicker from Ironside's hands. "I really do appreciate it, Luther."

Ironside caught Shamus's glare and growled, "You're quite welcome, I'm sure."

Clitherow turned his attention back to Steele. "Dallas, if you can bring Nate Condor in alive, I want the pleasure of hanging him."

"What about Shaw?"

"Silas Shaw?"

"Yes, Sheriff. I believe he's every bit as guilty as Condor and probably more," Steele said. "I'm beginning to think he was the brains behind the night riders and the killings."

"Hell, we just let him go," Clitherow said.

Steele nodded. "Recovering the government's money comes first. Silas Shaw can wait. I'll round him up later."

Chapter Thirty-six

When the brothers O'Brien rode into Recoil the town was in a festive mood. Sheriff Clitherow had spread the good news that the threat from the night riders was over. The bomb-damaged Rest and Be Thankful went as far as hanging red, white, and blue bunting from the second story balcony and the proprietor hinted that cake and ice cream might be available for all guests.

"Looks like we arrived just in time to join the party," Patrick said as they rode past a brightly lit, roaring saloon.

As though the man in the moon wanted to be a part of the celebration, his face was flushed as he beamed down on the town.

But Jacob didn't figure it that way. "Blood on the moon. That's never a good sign."

"Good enough sign for me." Shawn grinned

"After we find Pa and Luther, I'm going to do some celebrating myself."

"So where do we start?" Patrick asked. "The hotel?"

"No, right there." Jacob pointed down the street. "The sheriff's office is as good a place to start as any."

The O'Briens stepped inside. Shamus and Ironside were talking to Clitherow. He looked up at their entrance and was immediately alarmed by the sudden appearance of three rugged young men who bore the stamp of gun hands.

Shamus saw the look on the lawman's face and said, "Relax, Jim. They may look like desperadoes, but they're my sons."

After the smiles and hugs and the how-the-hell-are-you greetings of rough-hewn men, Jim Clitherow declared that a celebration was in order and produced a bottle of Old Crow. When everyone had a whiskey in hand, Shamus and Ironside took turns recounting all that had happened after they rode away from Dromore.

"Pa," Patrick said, "you two could've easily gotten yourselves killed. You can't go around inviting gun trouble like that."

"The two-bit gunman hasn't been born yet who can kill the colonel and me," Ironside said. When nobody volunteered a comment, he added, "Damn right they can't."

"English Nate Condor is a man to step around, Luther," Jacob said. "He's fast and he's a killer."

"You've met him, Jacob?" Shamus asked.

"No, heard of him is all. I understand he was a slave trader at one point in his life and the sick and old ones he couldn't sell he used for target practice."

"Sounds like the kind of thing he'd do." Clitherow sipped his whiskey and made a face. "Now he's enjoying wine, women, and song in Old Mexico, unless Dallas Steele succeeds in tracking him down."

"Dallas was here?" Jacob said, surprised. In telling his story Shamus hadn't mentioned the Pinkerton by name.

"He was here, investigating the lost army payroll for the government," Clitherow said.

Shamus looked at his youngest. He said he knew you, Jacob."

"He does. And I owe him a favor from way back."

"What kind of favor, Jake?" Ironside asked. Then, with enthusiasm, "I'm thinking that gunplay was involved, huh?"

"It was four years ago. I got hit over the head with a bottle—"

"A bottle!" Ironside said. "Damn, was it empt or full?"

"Luther, allow Jacob to tell his story." Shamus nodded to his son. "Go ahead, Jacob."

"Well, to make a long story short, I got hit over the head—with an empty bottle, Luther—and rolled when I walked out of a grog shop on the Barbary Coast. I guess the robbers didn't want to leave a live witness, so they came back to make sure I was dead. But Dallas showed up and scared them off. I had a headache for a few days and since they took all my money, I was flat broke. Dallas insisted on paying my way."

"Did you get them robbers, Jake, like I teached you?" Ironside asked eagerly.

"As Shawn said to me recently, I'm not a forgiving man," Jacob said. "As soon as I was well enough I went looking for those two. Found them in a dance hall and stated my intentions. They drew and I killed them both. After that I had to skip town. I've met a Dallas a few times since then, and every time we talk, I tell him I owe him and that I'll pay him back one day."

Shamus's face was slack-jawed with amazement. "Jesus, Mary, and Joseph, boy, you lead a life none of us know anything about."

Jacob smiled, but said nothing.

"Well, you done fine, boy," Ironside said. "And it's real good that them two scoundrels were informed. That's a Southern gentleman's way of doing things, just like I taught you."

"It's also the way a Southern gentleman repays his debts," Shamus said. "I can understand why you feel beholden to Dallas Steele."

"What about Dromore?" Ironside asked. "Anything interesting happened since we've been gone?"

"And how are Samuel and Lorena and little Shamus?" the colonel asked.

"They're just fine, Pa," Patrick said. "But—"

Jacob interrupted quickly. "We had a run-in with Mexican bandits, but nothing much came of it."

"Nothing much!" Shawn said. "Jake, you've still got a scar across your ribs where Álvaro Castillo's bullet burned you and Pat almost got shot in the head." He smiled at the colonel. "And we won a battle, Pa."

"A battle!" Shamus said. "Tell me about it now, and tell me no more."

"We call it the Battle of the Pecos River, Pa," Patrick said. "As the Duke of Wellington said after Waterloo, 'it was a close run thing.'"

"Tell me the story," Shamus said, his face flaring. "Now!"

"Yes, Colonel," Patrick said.

He, Shawn, and Jacob took turns describing what had happened and Jacob described his killing of Álvaro Castillo on the mesa. "Maybe i Pat hadn't decided to go butterfly hunting—"

"Collecting, collecting, collecting. How many times do I have to tell you that, Jake?"

"—it might have turned out differently," Jacob said.

Ironside was stunned. "You went hunting butterflies without a gun, Pat?"

Patrick gave him a long-suffering look. "They're not dangerous game, Luther."

"Damn it, boy, you're damned lucky I wasn't there," Ironside said. "You're not so growed up that I wouldn't have dropped your britches and tanned your hide. Didn't I tell you, not once, not twicet, but a hundred times, never to walk out of the house without your iron?"

"Luther, it's eighteen eighty-seven," Shamus said. "The time for carrying guns everywhere is past. Patrick didn't need a Colt to go butterfly hunting."

"Collecting, Pa," Patrick said wearily.

"Well, all that aside, when we get back, I'm going to erect a monument with a brass plaque commemorating the Battle of the Pecos River," Shamus said. "You boys did very well and I'm proud of you."

"And your sons should be proud of you, Colonel O'Brien," Clitherow said. "You and Luther stood up like men and played your part."

"Thank you, Jim," Shamus said. "Anytime—"

"I'll send for you," the sheriff said, smiling.

Shamus nodded. "Well, we'll ride for Lordsburg tomorrow morning, catch a train for Santa Fe, and then on to Dromore."

"Not me, Colonel," Jacob said. "I reckon I'll pay back Dallas Steele the favor I owe him."

"I don't understand, son."

"I'm headed for Chihuahua down Old Mexico way."

"Jake, that's long-riding country," Shawn said. "Finding Steele will be like looking for a needle in a haystack."

"I pay my debts, Shawn. Dallas headed southeast from the Apache Hills into Mexico and that's where I'll start looking."

"How many men does Condor have, Sheriff?" Shawn asked.

"I don't know. Enough, I reckon. And I think he may be traveling with a woman. We didn't find her body, at least."

"Then you're not going it alone, Jake," Shawn said. "I'll ride with you."

"We'll all ride with you," Shamus said. "I will not stay behind and watch my sons ride into mortal danger. What do you say, Luther?"

"I'm goin', Colonel. Ain't nobody gonna stop me, an' that includes you, Jake."

"Luther, I wouldn't even try."

"Damn right you wouldn't."

Shamus looked at his second born. "Patrick?"

"Count me in, Pa."

"Don't bring your butterfly net, Pat," Shawn said.

"Shawn, that's quite enough," Shamus said. "Don't tease your brother. If he wants to hunt butterflies, then let him."

"Collect, damn it!" Patrick yelled. "It's collect!"

Everyone looked at him in surprise.

Chapter Thirty-seven

Silas Shaw was out of the rain and out of water.

To the east, the green peaks of the Sierra Alta sky island stood in stark contrast to the surrounding desert brush country, thick with creosote, yucca, and mesquite. A single buzzard glided in lazy circles above his head as Shaw rode steadily south on a tired horse.

Darkness would fall soon and he needed a place to hole up, get water and grub.

He'd not come across the tracks of Condor's mules, nor could he see any living thing in the shimmering distance ahead of him. It was lost, lonely country, once a refuge for the Apache and Comanche, but they were long gone and had made no mark on the land.

Shaw's head ached, his eyes burned, and his mouth was dry as mummy dust. His left arm ached—had since he left the Apache Hills. He wondered if he'd injured it.

Only his searing hatred for Nate Condor drove him on. . . .

A hundred and thirty thousand dollars was enough for a two-way split, sixty-five thousand each, plenty to last a man the rest of his life if he was careful. He'd wanted the money for Martha. He'd watched her wither like a rose in the sun, so far from the Eastern cities she loved and the boisterous, artsy theater crowd that sustained her body and soul.

When they'd arrived in Recoil they knew it was the last stage stop on the road to hell. There was no escape, no return to what once had been. Their life had suddenly become one of scraping, scratching, penny-pinching, and making do.

He blamed the world for their misery—the audiences that no longer applauded, the agents who ignored him, and the miserable clerical job he was forced to accept in a bank that later accused him of embezzlement and hounded him all the way to the western frontier and oblivion.

On a business trip to Lordsburg, Shaw's life took a sudden and dramatic turn. He'd talked with another storekeeper in a saloon who told him they were hanging a man named Dixon Trent in the morning and asked if he planned to stay on and watch the show.

Only mildly interested, Shaw asked why the fellow was being hung.

"Knifed a man. But from what I hear, the killing was over a fortune in gold that the dead man wanted to keep for himself." The storekeeper shrugged. "That's the way I heard it, anyway."

Still not biting on the hook the other man dangled, Shaw brushed it off. "Probably a squabble about a mine that's never produced an ounce of gold in a twenty year," Shaw had said. "It happens all the time."

The storekeeper shook his head. "It's no mine, friend. Trent says he knows the whereabouts of an army pay wagon that was captured by Apaches about ten years ago. He says it's in a place where nobody can find it but him."

At that, Shaw was interested. "How much gold?"

"At least a hundred thousand dollars' worth. Maybe more. Hey, it's down in your neck of the woods, in the Hachita Valley someplace." The man laughed. "Maybe you'll find it."

"Maybe I will," Shaw said, smiling.

Silas Shaw was an uneasy man. As he rode, he constantly checked his back trail. After his third or fourth turn of the head he saw what he feared most . . . a rising plume of dust behind him.

He didn't hesitate or take time to think anything through. He stepped from the saddle, slid his Winchester from the boot, and lay belly down under the meager shade of a mesquite. With a fortune at stake, anybody riding the desert country was his enemy.

The day was well gone and the Sierra Alta gathered shadow around itself like a great dusky cloak. Heat waves still danced in the distance and the lowering sun was warm on his back. Sweat running from under his hair to his cheeks, he waited, his red-rimmed, burning eyes on the approaching dust.

Five minutes passed . . . then ten. . . .

The dust was much closer. Shaw saw a dark speck that grew in size until it became as large as a fly on a windowpane.

It was a mounted man and he was coming on at a walk.

Shaw grinned. "Come on. Just a little closer." He racked a .44-40 round into the chamber and waited with a predator's patience. A man born with a natural skill at arms, he was confident of his shooting ability. This would be real easy.

A minute passed . . . another. . . . The rider came on as though he was out for a canter in the park.

Shaw settled his sights on the man's chest where it showed wide above his mount's lowered head. He took up the slack in the Winchester's curved trigger. Took a deep breath and let part of it out. . . .

Now!

Shaw fired. But the rider still sat upright in the saddle.

Then, like an axed pine the man swayed slowly to his left side, gathered momentum, and thudded into the sand where he lay still.

Grinning to himself, Shaw got to his feet. He'd always been a dab hand with a long gun and he'd proved it again. He gathered up his horse, swung into the saddle, and headed south again.

He didn't look back at the man on the ground.

The solo rider was dead. Nobody lived for long after a hit to the center of the chest.

Damn, his arm hurt and so did his jaw. And the gnawing pain was getting worse.

As the day slowly shaded into night, Shaw knew what ailed him. It was thirst. He needed water and soon.

By nightfall, with the Boca Grande Mountains in sight, Silas Shaw had not come across tracks, not even those of an animal. He camped by a dry creek and made his bed in the sand. He was hungry, thirsty, and his throbbing, pulsating headache gave him no peace. He felt sick enough to throw up and everywhere he looked he saw flashes of light.

He needed Martha to comfort him. But Martha was not there. There was only him. Somewhere out in the darkness, a campfire lit the sneering face of Nate Condor as he drank hot coffee, never sparing a thought for the man who'd been his boss.

The anger and envy spiking at him only made Shaw's headache worse. The ache in his arm was a living thing, giving him no peace. He groaned and buried his face in his trembling hands and wished for morning.

Chapter Thirty-eight

Jacob O'Brien rode through the pale light of the aborning day, his eyes searching the distance. He was following two sets of tracks, both still fresh in the windless desert. Ahead of him, he saw what he took for a pair of ancient volcanic boulders.

As he rode closer he made out a droop-tailed horse, head hanging low, standing still on a patch of open sand. Beside the animal stretched the body of a man. Before he reached the still figure, Jacob knew who it was.

Dallas Steele lay on his back, unmoving. The dun horse took a couple of steps away from Jacob, then stopped and lifted its head to look at him with curiosity.

Covered in dust, his faded blue shirt already showing arcs of sweat in the armpits, Jacob stepped out of the leather saddle, grabbed his canteen, and took a knee beside Steele. To his relief, he saw that the man was still breathing, but Steele's hair was thick with blood and the front of his shirt was stained scarlet.

Jacob lifted the wounded man's head and put the canteen to his lips. After a few moments, the Pinkerton drank and his eyes fluttered open. At first, all he could manage was a dry croak. Jacob gave him more water.

Steele found his voice, weak and strained though it was. "Why, Jake O'Brien, what a pleasant surprise. What brings you to these parts?" After a moment's hesitation, he coughed away the dust in his throat. "Are you just visiting?"

"I've been following you since yesterday, Dallas."

"Why?"

"Let's just say I'm trying to repay an old favor."

"As I recall, the favor I did you in San Francisco was a small one. Of no account."

"I've added interest." Jacob looked for bullet wounds and found plenty of dried blood, but no holes. "What happened?"

"I was riding along, singing one of Mr. Gilbert and Mr. Sullivan's latest ditties as I recall, when a person or persons unknown took a pot at me."

"Shaw?"

"Likely him, but it could've been Nate Condor. Whoever the gentleman was, he didn't stay around to introduce himself."

"Where are you hit, Dallas?" Jacob said. "I have to tell you, it looks bad."

"Tell me nonetheless, Jake, though I really don't think I want to know."

It was the blue Colt in Steele's shoulder holster that told the tale. The bushwhacker's bullet had hit the revolver and driven the cylinder into Steele's ribs with considerable force. The mangled ball had then ranged upward and torn across the Pinkerton's scalp, stunning him.

"Hell, it's not near as bad as I thought. You'll live," Jacob said.

"Am I shot through and through, Jake? You don't need to spare my feelings, and I promise I won't scream."

"The bullet hit your Colt and then bounced and slammed against your head. The ball drew blood but did little damage."

"Are you telling me I've got a thick head?"

"Something like that." Jacob held up the Colt and let the shattered cylinder drop into the sand. "You may have some broken ribs and your iron is ruined."

"Damn it all, that was a seventeen dollar Colt," Steele said. "Cash on the barrelhead at Tam McLean's Rod and Gun in Denver."

"I guess it saved your life before and it surely did it again."

"Three cheers for Sammy Colt. I always said he made the world's best revolvers, bless his heart."

"Let's get you to your feet. The bump to your head has made you a little loco." Jacob pulled Steele to a standing position.

Steele swayed and touched his bloody head. "Damn, I feel sick and I've got a headache. And my ribs hurt."

"A couple may be broken or maybe they're just bruised," Jacob said. "Can you ride?"

"I can ride. I sure as hell can't walk."

Jacob stepped to his horse, reached into his saddlebags, and produced a short-barreled Colt. "I always keep a spare," he said, handing the revolver to Steele.

The Pinkerton felt its weight. "It's almost as well-balanced as my old one."

"We do what we can."

"Strangely enough, I'm hungry," Steele said. "How can a shot-up man be hungry?"

Jacob reached into his saddlebags again and gave Steele a strip of jerky. "It was all I could get in Recoil at short notice."

"It'll do," Steele chewed on the jerky for a few moments. "Any ideas, Jake?"

"I'm studying on it. The Colonel and Luther are to the west of us, my brothers to the east, scouting for Condor's trail. If they don't have any luck I told them to meet me on the San Miguel

River to the north of the Boca Grande. If you're still in a mind to go after Condor, we can make our plans then."

"I must try to get the payroll back, Jake. It's what they're paying me for."

"Then so be it. It's about a fifteen-mile ride from here to the San Miguel across some mighty rough country. Can you make it?"

"I can make it."

"Then we'll get going."

"You don't think I've a chance in hell of catching up with Nate Condor, do you, Jake," Steele said as they rode south, the sun high above the Alta peaks.

The waning morning was hot and the dusty air smelled of desert shrubs and far distant pines.

"There's always a chance, Dallas. Maybe my brother Pat will come up with something. He's pretty good at figuring things." Jacob smiled. "If we do find Condor, we'll have a scrap on our hands. The man is a demon with the iron."

"Talking about being good with the iron, you'll never guess who I met in Denver about three months ago," Steele said.

"I've no idea, Dallas. I guess you meet a lot of folks."

"Doc Holliday. He asked after you."

Jacob was speechless for a moment, then said, "I want nothing to do with Doc. Seems like every time we meet he brings trouble with him, usually with the law."

"He was frail, Jake. I don't think he's got long to live."

"Doc's lucky he's lived this long."

"He told me he'd made only two friends in his life. One was a lawman by the name of Wyatt Earp and the other was you."

"I'm not Doc's friend. I never was and I never will be. He's a menace to society is what Doc is. He mentioned this Earp feller from time to time. Who is he?"

"He was a lawman in the Arizona Territory, a place called Tombstone," Steele said. "All I know about him is that Doc helped him out in a shooting scrape. He doesn't talk about it much."

"If Doc calls Earp a friend, I don't want to know about him anyway. Hell, he could be as big a damned pest as Doc."

"He's dying, Jake. Doc's not the man he was."

"Doc was never the man he was."

"I told him about Dromore."

Jacob shook his head. "Now what did you go and do that for?"

"Like I said, he was asking after you. I mentioned Dromore in conversation. At least, I'm sure I did."

"It's no matter. If Doc decided to come visiting, he wouldn't make it as far as Dromore. The high country air is thin as a whisper. It would kill him."

Steele smiled. "And here I thought you'd be glad to hear about an old friend."

"Old friend, my patoot. Doc almost got me hung in El Paso for a killing that was all his work. Three years later, I met up with him again and we escaped another hemp posse up on the Picket-wire after he cut a whore the local punchers set store by. Doc's pure poison. I want nothing to do with him, not now, not ever."

"Sorry to hear that, Jake," Steele said, grinning. "He's such a nice Southern gentleman when you get to know him."

"Dallas," Jacob said, "go to hell."

After an hour, riding through a landscape distorted by heat in every direction as though painted by a drunken artist, Steele said casually, "Dust behind us."

Jacob turned in the saddle, "It's probably Shawn and Patrick."

"Probably."

"Keep your iron handy."

"It's always handy."

A couple of minutes later, Steele said, "Two men running."

"Running?"

"Looks like."

Jacob drew rein and Steele did the same. They swung their mounts around.

"Hell, looks like Apaches," Jacob said.

"No, it's a Navajo and a black giant," Steele said. "The Indian's name is Scout and the giant is called Lucian T. Hyde. They're shape-shifters."

"What does that mean?" Jacob said, his hand on the butt of his Colt.

"They can themselves turn into wolves or any other animal you care to mention."

"You joshing me, Dallas?"

"Honest truth."

"Unless they come up on us real friendly like, I'll shift their shapes into corpses pretty damn quick."

"Dear old Doc Holliday taught you a lot, didn't he, Jake?" Steele said.

Jacob ignored that and watched the two men come closer, both running with the easy, loping grace of lobo wolves.

"The giant is the one on the right," Steele said.

"Figured that. Looks like his top half's already turned into a wolf."

"Changed his mind midway through, maybe."

When the Navajo and Hyde stopped in front of Steele's horse neither man was breathing hard nor had broken a sweat.

Not a man to mince words, Scout said, "The man Nate Condor is not in this place. You seek him in vain."

"Where is he, Scout?" Steele said. Then, as an afterthought, "This here is Jacob O'Brien, a friend of—"

"I know who he is," Scout said. "How do you fare, Jake?"

"Well. I didn't recognize you at first."

"A man changes over the years. You have not changed. Maybe your nose is bigger."

"It's my finest feature, Scout. That's why it tends to grow on people."

The Navajo gave a ghost of a smile and said, "Nate Condor fooled you. He pushed into Chihuahua for a few miles, then swung north again. I say he's headed for Silver City where he can sell the army payroll for folding money and no questions asked. A man can't drag around a heavy weight of gold coin without attracting unwanted attention."

"Where is he now, Scout?" Jacob said.

"Last I saw him, he was driving his mules to the east of the Cedar Mountains. He can follow the north star to Silver City."

"How many men with him?" Steele said.

"Only Condor and one other. We found the bodies of three men and a young woman in the desert. All had been shot. Mr. Hyde was forced to kill another at the cabin in the Apache Hills."

"I saw that man," Steele said.

"A most unfortunate occurrence," Hyde said. "I feared he might discover me as I watched the cabin."

"You tore his throat out. Now that was a mite unfriendly."

"Yes indeed, Mr. Steele. But it is the way of the wolf," Hyde said.

"Good a way as any, I guess." Jacob turned to Steele. "We'll round up the Colonel and the others and head for Silver City."

"No need," Scout said. "I have already told them to meet us in the village of San Mateo a mile north of Johnson Mountain."

"Hell, Scout, for men on foot you two sure get around," Jacob said.

The Navajo nodded. "In the desert, a man can outrun a horse."

"What about Shaw, Dallas?" Jacob asked. "There's no doubt in my mind that he tried to kill you."

"Right now, getting the payroll back is more important than Shaw."

"You heard the man, Scout," Jacob said. "Lead the way. And don't run too fast for the horses."

Chapter Thirty-nine

Silas Shaw led his lame horse south, walking under the slamming heat of the merciless noon sun. His head ached and his lips were swollen and cracked under his skull mask. Nausea curled his belly like a green snake, but one thing he knew . . . one thing that kept him going . . . he'd meet up with the cur Nate Condor soon.

And then he'd kill him. And take what was rightfully his.

Around Shaw stretched a searing wasteland of sand, yucca, mesquite, and vast acres of tarbush. In the distance the mountains stood tall and silent, the abodes of the long winds that once cooled the old Comanche Trail. He figured he was hundreds of miles from the nearest white man, but neither knew that for sure nor cared.

His skin itched under the skull mask, but he was damned if he was going to take it off. He'd wear it when he gunned Condor; give him a foretaste of what he'd meet in hell.

Somewhere along the trail he'd lost his hat. He didn't know when or how. He knew only that it was gone and he wasn't going back for it. No time. He was catching up with good ol' Nate, he was sure of that. The showdown was near.

Shaw stumbled and fell on all fours. He lay there for a while. His head felt like it had been split open by a wood axe and steel nails driven into his brain. Lightning flashed around him in vivid shades of scarlet, yellow, and dazzling white. His arm pained him like a nagging toothache.

He staggered to his feet again.

"Damn you, Condor!" Shaw yelled, spreading his arms wide. "You can't hide from me. I'm coming after you." For some reason he thought that very funny and laughed until his sides ached.

Then he walked on, the suffering horse dragging behind him.

When Shaw saw a wagon in the distance he thought he'd found Condor, He drew his gun and got ready. He dropped the horse's reins and staggered toward the wagon, dragging his feet like a man wading through deep water.

He fell a couple of times and getting to his feet again was becoming a problem, but he managed to stagger on, his Colt up and ready.

When he reached the wagon, he dropped to a

squatting position and smiled. "Well, hello you two." His lips were swollen and cracked and his voice was thick.

Two skeletons, scraps of tattered clothing clinging to their bleached bones, sat side by side on the driving seat. One was a woman, parts of a blue prairie bonnet still covering her skull.

A strap-iron arrowhead was embedded in the man's breastbone. The woman showed no sign of a wound that Shaw could see, but there had been one, he was sure of that. It looked like the couple had been dead for many years. Ten, twenty, a hundred. He didn't know.

His left arm buzzed and his fingers tingled as he stood and stared at the skeletons, his skull mask making him one with them.

Shaw put the tip of his right forefinger to the wooden chin of his grotesque mask and said, "Now, my dears—may I call you . . . what can I call you? Ah, yes. How about Tom and Mary?"

The yellow skulls grinned at him.

"You like that? Well, jolly good. I was an entertainer, you know. I mean, on stage. I acted and sang and danced with my dear lady wife."

Shaw cupped a hand to his ear. "What did you say, Mary? Oh, what kind of songs did I sing? Well, all kinds. My favorite? I don't know. They were all my favorites."

The woman's skull grinned at him.

"I'll sing you one. But my throat is dry and croaky, so you must forgive me. First I'll sing you a little ditty I sang when I trod the boards of the music halls in London town. With the Prince of Wales, God bless him, in attendance, don't you know."

Shaw cavorted a little, kicking up puffs of sand, and then he sang.

"Champagne Charlie is my name,
Drinking champagne is my game.
I love to hear the corks go pop!
I love champagne and I'll never stop.

"Hmm . . . those weren't quite the words, were they? If my lady wife was here she'd set me right, never fear. Ah well, not to mind, Tom and Mary. Come sit down here with me and we'll have a nice little chat."

Shaw reached up and grabbed hold of the woman's skeleton. Bones clattered onto the boards of the wagon as he lifted his bizarre burden and propped it against a wheel. He did the same for the man, but by the time he got the skeleton down, only the ribcage, spine, and skull were still connected.

Shaw sat on the sand. "Are we sitting comfortably? We are? Good. Now, Tom and Mary, let me tell you a story about a lowdown, thieving skunk by the name of English Nate Condor. Oh, by the way, you wouldn't have a little water about your persons, would you? No? Well, it doesn't matter. I'll drink Condor's water soon."

Shaw smiled. "You're both grinning at me. Is it because you like my mask? It makes us all look the same and that's nice, don't you think? It's as though we're all in this thing together."

Pain stabbed through Shaw's left arm and he felt as though an iron crab was crushing his chest. "Now, where was I?" he said, gasping. "Oh yes, I was about to tell you about that lowlife Nate Condor and his evil ways."

The lifeless eye sockets of the skeletons stared at him, their teeth bared in grins that would end only when their bones turned to dust.

"Condor . . . he . . ." The pain in Shaw's chest and arm reached a crescendo and there was a clamor in his head like the clanging clash of symbols.

All at once, the left side of his body died.

Shaw groaned and slumped onto the sand, aware of what had happened to him.

He'd once seen a man who'd had a stroke. One half of him was dead and useless, and he talked out of a corner of his mouth, stringing saliva, cursing God and the mother who'd borne him for his fate.

The man had been an English lord of high

estate, but death is not impressed by wealth and title and had struck him down as it would any other man.

Shaw knew then in those awful moments that Nate Condor had won.

Unable to face that fact, unable to endure the prolonged death that awaited him, he reached for the gun at his hip. He moved the skull mask aside and shoved the muzzle of the revolver under his chin.

He pulled the trigger.

The racketing echoes of the shot hammered across the silent desert and the skeletons of Tom and Mary watched the dead man and grinned.

High overhead, the cold-eyed buzzards dipped lower.

Chapter Forty

The village of San Mateo consisted of a dozen adobe houses, a small church, and a cantina grouped around a small, dusty, central plaza where scrawny chickens pecked. The Mexican peons who lived there were silent and sullen, wary of white men who carried guns.

Shamus O'Brien and Luther Ironside managed to buy coffee, tortillas, and a slab of bacon at exorbitant prices while the others filled their canteens at a nearby creek.

The proprietor of the cantina told Shamus that no other white men had visited his modest establishment recently and no, he had not seen nor heard of gringos in the surrounding area.

When Shamus and the others met again in the plaza, Jacob said that Scout and Hyde had gone on ahead, searching north.

"Then we'll follow their trail." Steele thought.

Shamus looked used up, and to a lesser extent so did Luther. "I can see it through from here," he said, offering the older men an out.

But Shamus would have none of it. "We said we'd help you, Dallas, and that's what we're going to do. I want to be in at the end."

"Damn right," Ironside said.

Shawn grinned. "You can't butt heads with these two ornery old range bulls, Dallas. But it was a nice try."

"Shawn, I'll be asking you to keep a respectful tongue in your head when speaking of your father," Shamus said. "The Fifth Commandment says to honor thy father and thy mother."

"Damn right," Ironside said again. "Didn't I teach you to respect your elders, boy?"

"You know, Luther, I don't recall that you ever mentioned the Fifth Commandment," Shawn said.

"Well, I maybe I should've," Ironside said.

"There are many things you should've taught my sons, but didn't, Luther," Shamus said.

Ironside was quiet for a while, and then he muttered something that sounded like . . . "Taught them plenty . . . no one else did . . ."

"What did you say, Luther?" Shamus snapped, made irritable by heat and pain from long riding.

"Nothing, Colonel, I didn't say nothing."

"I should hope not. A little holy scripture

added to your teaching would not have gone amiss. And don't mumble, man."

Patrick came to Ironside's rescue. "I've been thinking, Pa. Suppose Nate Condor heads for Deming. He can ride the rails from there all the way to Silver City."

"I thought of that my ownself," Jacob said. "But I don't think he'd want to attract any attention to those money sacks."

"He won't take the risk, Jake," Shawn said. "It's sixty hard miles between here and Silver City, but he'll go that route."

"Dallas, what do you say?" Jacob asked. "Do we head north or swing over to Deming?"

"North," Steele said. "I've got a feeling that's where our trusty scouts will find Nate Condor."

"Damn that man to hell," Shamus said. "And when he gets there may the devil swallow him sideways."

"Now there's a good old Irish curse that'll stop Condor in his tracks. So let's get the damn thief." Shawn smiled. "And that's some good old American cussin'."

Chapter Forty-one

Nate Condor and Barney Merden camped in flat brush country a mile east of the Victorio Mountains. They found a narrow, sluggish creek that smelled of sulfur but provided enough water for the mules and horses.

Merden stirred the coals under the coffeepot that smoked on the fire and inclined his head toward Condor. "How much will the Gimp pay, you reckon?"

"As little as he can."

"How much is little?"

"Don't worry. Enough to keep you in whiskey and whores for years."

"There's law in Silver City, Nate," Merden said. "We'll need to step around real careful, like."

"Humphrey the Gimp owns the law, like he owns most everything else in the town. The only thing we need to be careful about is not to let him beat us up on the price."

"What you gonna do with your share of the money, Nate?"

"Buy a house back East with an oak tree out front, violets in the window boxes, and a yellow-haired woman in the kitchen."

"And now you're pulling my leg."

"The hell I am," Condor said. "The West is getting smaller and smaller and pretty soon there will be no room for men like us, Barney. When this is over, I'll hang my guns on a nail and retire."

"Jesse tried that, remember? Look what happened to him."

"Jesse didn't retire, and neither did Frank, at least not until after his brother was killed. I might move to England. There are no Bob Fords in London."

"Yeah, and then somebody recognizes you and you'll get hung fer a pirate rogue and a slave trader."

"Boston then. Or New York, where no one knows me or cares."

Merden grinned. "Nate, you'll spend your money on whiskey and wild women and raise hell, just like me."

Condor nodded. "I guess so. It would be nice though, wouldn't it? I mean a house in the country where everything is peaceful and quiet and the birds sing in the morning."

"It ain't fer us, Cap'n."

There was a touch of regret in Condor's smile. "No, you're right. It isn't for us and it never was."

"Hello, the camp!" A man's voice, harsh and confident, rang out from the darkness.

Condor and Merden jumped on their feet, instinctively stepping out of the firelight.

"What the hell do you want?" Merden yelled.

"We're honest travelers with something to trade," the man yelled.

"You got nothing we want," Condor said. "Ride on, feller."

"Hell, you ain't seen it yet," the man hollered.

Two men emerged from the darkness, sitting astride wiry mustangs, a shadowy figure behind them on foot. Both riders were dressed in buckskins, the fringes on the arms a foot long. They cradled Winchesters and one had the stub of a clay pipe stuck in the corner of his mouth.

"I told you fellers to ride on," Condor said. "There's nothing for you here."

Clay Pipe's gaze fixed on Condor and sized him up as a man to be reckoned with. "Jes' came in fer a warm up and a cup of coffee. And some honest tradin' if'n you have a mind."

"We've nothing to trade and only enough coffee for ourselves," Merden said. "Now move on like the cap'n said."

"Cap'n, is it?" Clay Pipe said. "Cap'n o' what?"

"Of your destiny, feller," Condor said. "Now you git and take your friends with you."

"You best take his advice, boys," Merden said. "You done woke up the wrong passengers on this trip."

If the buckskinned riders were intimidated, they didn't let it show.

"What you got in them pokes back there?" Clay Pipe motioned with his chin.

"None of your business," Condor said. Then, "And don't push it any further, mister."

The man turned his head and barked something. A young girl stepped out of the shadows. She wore a buckskin dress, but she was black, with short-cropped hair and huge frightened eyes. She had a thin string of red and white beads around her neck.

"I'm selling her for forty dollars," Clay Pipe said. "She cost me twice that over to Missouri way a spell back, so I'm takin' a loss. She's young and she don't know much yet, but she'll keep you gents' bellies warm."

Condor was not in the mood for a gunfight but he'd had all he was going to take. "I'm spelling it out. I don't want blood and dead bodies all over my camp, so I'm giving you one more chance—shut the hell up, ride out, and take the black with you."

"Harsh words," Clay Pipe said. "Harsh words to men engaged in an honest trading venture."

"Mister, I'm done talking." Condor drew both guns and thunder rolled.

Hit hard, the men tumbled off their horses, dead as ragdolls when they landed on the ground.

After his ears stopped ringing, Merden grinned. "I guess them two never come up against a real gunfighter before."

Condor nodded. "Right now, that's what they're telling each other in hell."

He holstered one gun, motioned to the terrified girl with the other, and said to Merden, "You want that?"

Merden shook his head. "I'll have no truck with her kind. Damned animals."

Condor pointed the gun at the girl. "You, get up on one of those mustangs and git the hell out of here."

The girl stood frozen in place with fear.

Condor fired and a V of dust flew up an inch in front of her toes. "Git!"

Startled, the girl ran for a horse and jumped into the saddle. After one scared glance at Condor, she rode away into the darkness.

"Hell, Nate, why didn't you gun her?" Merden asked.

"We will have two bodies to drag away from here. Why make extra work for ourselves with three?"

Merden smiled. "Or maybe just then you was thinking good thoughts, like the house with the tree out front."

"Maybe," Condor said. "But I doubt it."

Chapter Forty-two

It was going on noon when Patrick O'Brien, riding scout, came upon a black girl in a draw south of the Victorio Mountains.

Her face frightened, the girl ran for her horse, but stumbled and fell.

Patrick rode into the draw and swung out of the saddle. "What are you doing alone out here, and you just a young 'un?"

The girl shrank from him and dug her feet into the sand as she tried to back away.

Patrick smiled and fetched his canteen from the saddle. "Drink? There's no water in the draw, girl."

The girl's face showed interest and she rose to her feet.

Patrick approached her slowly, holding out the canteen. "If you strain it through your teeth, it's good water," he said, pushing his round eyeglasses higher on his nose.

The girl snatched the canteen from his hand and drank greedily.

Patrick took it from her. "Whoa, you'll give yourself a bellyache. Some now, some later, that's the ticket."

Patrick was a tall man and he towered over the girl. He squatted on his heels to appear less intimidating. "What's your name?"

It took a while, but she finally said, "Abby."

"That's a pretty name. Mine is Patrick."

Abby said nothing.

"How did you get out here by yourself?"

"White men brought me," the girl said.

"Where are they?"

"Dead." The girl pointed north. "That way."

"Do you know their names, Abby?"

The girl shook her head.

"Can you take me to the bodies?"

"I can take you there."

Patrick helped the girl into the saddle. Her mustang seemed tired, but it had been well cared for and took to the trail without protest.

It took a deal of scouting around before Abby pointed out the camp. She was reluctant to go near it, but Patrick rode in front of her and it was he who discovered the bodies.

Both men showed chest wounds and had died almost instantly.

Patrick's face was grim. The men had been killed by someone who knew his business and that could only be English Nate Condor.

The campsite revealed little, but the tracks told Patrick that two men had ridden north, pushing half a dozen pack mules. He led the horses to the creek to drink their fill. Then he and Abby hunkered down in the meager shade of a mesquite and waited for the colonel and the others to catch up.

"Did Nate Condor kill those two?" Patrick asked.

The girl looked at him, but her eyes drew a blank.

"Well, it was probably him. I wonder why he didn't kill you, Abby. From what I hear, Condor is not a merciful man."

"The man who killed the two others told me to leave."

"Well, I'm glad he did. How old are you?"

Abby shook her head. "I don't know. I was an orphan. One of the men—I think he was called Frank but I'm not sure—bought me from a farmer. He tried to sell me to the men in the camp for forty dollars, but they didn't want me."

She drew patterns in the sand with a twig and

without looking up, she said, "I'm an ugly, black Negro, you see."

Patrick figured the girl had been used and abused, but didn't ask about her life. Some questions were better asked by womenfolk, who understood such things.

He rose to his feet. "The others are coming. I see their dust."

To his surprise, Abby clung to him and he could feel the girl tremble.

"Don't worry. These men won't hurt you. One's my pa and my brothers are with him."

Abby still grabbed on to him and her breath came in quick, frightened little gasps.

The O'Briens, Ironside, and Steele rode into the camp.

"Pat, your orders were to scout ahead, not dally in the sun with a dusky maiden," Shawn said.

"Condor was here," Patrick said, ignoring Shawn's remark. "He killed two men and then scared away this girl." He pushed up the glasses that were forever sliding down his nose. "Her name is Abby."

"Pat, how far ahead of us is Condor, do you reckon?" Jacob asked.

"Half a day, maybe less. The mules are heavily loaded and they're slowing him down."

Shamus looked at the girl. "Don't be frightened, Abby. We won't harm you."

"I think she's scared of all white men, Pa," Patrick said.

"Well, apart from you, Pat, obviously," Shawn said.

"All right then, Pat, you can take care of her," Jacob said. "I mean, since she's taken such a shine to you."

"She's only a child."

"All the more reason why you should look after her," Jacob said. "We've got half a day to make up and it's a rough trail."

"Then let's hope Scout and his friend stick to their job," Steele said.

Patrick smiled. "Ah yes, Dr. Jekyll and Mr. Hyde." Surrounded by blank stares, he said, "Robert Louis Stevenson's latest novel, published last year. In the book, which is excellent by the way, Dr. Jekyll is a shape-shifter of sorts."

"Pat, you've got to quit readin' them dime novels," Ironside said. "They're ruining your eyes and makin' you plumb loco, huntin' bugs an' such."

"It is a good book, Luther," Steele said. "I've

read it myself and the title is a very apt description of Scout and his friend."

Ironside shook his head. "Everybody's gone nuts around here except me." He caught Shamus's glare and added quickly, "And the colonel, of course."

Chapter Forty-three

A man can take a lot of punishment, a fact he learned real fast when he was driving mules.

Nate Condor figured enough was enough. He had the sailor's inborn dislike of riding and the gunfighter's disdain for any task that even hinted at manual labor. On top of that, he'd been eating dust for miles and he was hot, sweaty, and itched all over.

Mules were a chore. They were sorry, spiteful creatures born with a streak of meanness and murder. Unloading them every night and burdening them all over again in the morning tried a man's soul.

Condor and Merden rode past three peaks to their west—Bessie Rhoads Mountain, the Soldier's Farewell Hill, and finally JPB Mountain—one following close after the other. Finally, they were among the foothills of the high Big Burro peaks.

"Barney, look for a place out of sight where we can corral the mules for a day or two," Condor said.

"How come, Cap'n?" Merden's face was covered in a layer of gray dust, just like Condor's.

"I'm going on ahead to Silver City. I need to talk to the Gimp before we bring in the gold."

Merden didn't look any too happy. "Hell, Nate, we can stash the mules in a canyon and both go."

"And leave a hundred and thirty thousand dollars unattended?" Condor said. "Are you out of your damned mind? I'm sure that gun-fighting Pinkerton is somewhere behind us."

"We can handle Dallas Steele."

"Maybe so, but I'd rather not put it to the test. And neither would you if you had any sense."

After a mile, Condor noticed a slab of bedrock that slanted upward and lost itself in a mixed stand of pine and aspen. He'd no way of telling if the rock ended at the towering cliff face behind it or if there was a space between wide enough to hold the mules.

He left Merden and rode around the bedrock, a distance of about fifty yards, then looped back, keeping to the bottom of the cliff. To his joy, Condor saw that the rock shelf did indeed stop short of the cliff to form a fairly large arroyo. The rock was at least twenty feet high and the canyon was invisible from the trail.

He explored farther and saw grass and water. Not a great deal, only a steady drip that fell from a break in the cliff and splashed into a stone tank, but it was enough. Black circles of old fires scarred the grass and Condor reckoned the Comanche had once used this place.

He rode onto the flat again and rejoined Merden. "I found a spot where you can hole up, Barney. It's behind the shelf of rock."

"What kind of spot?" Merden was suspicious, not liking this one bit.

"There's enough grass for two, three days . . . and water. You'll have tortillas and whiskey and be cozy enough." Condor slapped his forehead. "What the hell am I thinking? Before I leave we'll unload the gold and stash it at the back of the arroyo. When I come back I'll bring a wagon. We can turn the damned mules loose and you won't have to deal with them."

Merden smiled. "Now you're thinking real good, Cap'n. The mules will scatter to hell and gone and leave false trails all over the place."

"But no fire, Barney. Make a cold camp."

"Hell, I know that, Nate."

"Right, then let's get it done."

* * *

As Nate Condor rode north he smiled to himself. Turning the mules loose was a stroke of genius. The gold in the sacks was enough to tempt any man and by times, Barney was easily tempted. With the mules loose, there was no way he could load up the gold and strike out for himself, heading back south into Old Mexico.

There was always the possibility that he would tie a couple of sacks to his saddle and light a shuck, but Condor dismissed that possibility. He decided Barney was just stupid enough to take his chances, but the man must know Chihuahua was infested with bandits who would pretty soon strip him of his gold and his life.

The Gimp may be a damned cheating crook, but trading with him was a sight safer than heading into Mexico.

Besides, Barney Merden was loyal to a fault and when the time came, as it was coming soon, he'd be easy to kill.

Condor ignored the thronged streets of Silver City with their colorful, noisy mix of miners, cowboys, soldiers, whores, Mexican peons, stately dark-eyed señoritas, and shifty young men on the make. He rode into the city's business district and drew rein outside a gloomy building in a gloomy street in what was the gloomiest part of town.

The place of business of Silas Strangewayes, nicknamed the Gimp, but never said to his face, was a dingy, narrow storefront on the ground floor of a rickety timber building. Three stories of offices and storerooms towered threateningly above.

The large window was painted black. Faded gold lettering announced

SILAS STRANGEWAYES
Egg and Cheese Importer

Condor had done business with Strangewayes before, and to his certain knowledge, the man had never imported a single egg nor a morsel of cheese in his life.

He dismounted and looped the reins around the iron ring on a post that stood at the edge of the sidewalk. Strangewayes' door was never locked and Condor opened it to the sound of a clanging bell and stepped inside.

He walked into a single room of moderate size that contained only a desk, two chairs, and a grandfather clock that ticked with a solemn resonance.

Silas Strangewayes sat at his desk, scratching a steel pen across a ledger that was at least four inches thick. He didn't look up, his eyes puddles of darkness under a black visor. He was a bent, scrawny, scarecrow of a man, dressed in frayed broadcloth, his linen yellowed with age. Strands of thin, white hair fell over his rounded shoulders and tufts of darker hair sprouted from his nose and ears. He was said to be worth a million dollars, but nobody really knew.

"What can I do for you?" Strangewayes' voice sounded like the creak of a rusty gate.

"It's me, Silas. Captain Nate Condor as ever was."

"Bah! The Arab slave trade is gone, destroyed by the damned, infernal British navy and the meddling Dutch."

"I'm not here to talk about the slaves," Condor said. "I've got something much more important in mind."

"Then what do you want to talk about? Damn your eyes, speak up, man. Time is money."

"I want to talk about one hundred and thirty thousand dollars, mostly in gold coin."

Strangewayes laid down his pen and looked up. His face was long, narrow, bony, and gray. "What is all this to me?"

"Silas, I can't walk into a bank and deposit a wagonload of gold. And I can't lug it around with me."

"What do you want me to do with it, huh? And where did you get this gold?"

"It was taken from an army pay wagon," Condor said.

The old man waved his pen. "Get the hell out of here."

"Apaches stole the wagon ten years ago. Its trail has long since gone cold."

"Ten years, ye say?"

"Yes."

"And there's nobody after the gold, trying to get it back?"

Condor thought briefly of Dallas Steele and the Pinkertons, but he said, "I told you. It's a cold trail."

Greed gleamed in Strangewayes eyes. "Where is this gold now?"

"It's hidden in an arroyo south of here."

"How did you transport it and from where?"

"The gold was hidden in the Apache Hills and we brought it this far by mules."

"We?"

"I have a partner." *But not for long,* Condor thought but didn't say.

"So, you can't carry sacks of gold around with you everywhere you go, is that it?"

"Yes, that's my problem. I don't want to raise any suspicions, not with the army all over the territory. There are a lot of men who will kill for that much money."

"What do you want from me, Captain Condor?"

"Deposit the gold coin for me in a sound bank. I want it clean, no questions asked, and no trail leading back to the territory."

"Where?"

The suddenness of his decision surprised Condor when he heard himself say, "Boston would be preferable."

"I can do that, but it will cost you," Strangewayes said. "Your money will be deposited in several Boston banks as insurance and, as you say, no questions will be asked."

"How much is your cut?" Condor said. "Speak plain now."

"Thirty percent. Let's say forty thousand dollars as a round figure. Take it or leave it."

It was a chunk and it hit Condor hard. That left ninety thousand for himself. But it was enough for a man to live well if he was careful. "Done and done. Here's my hand on it, matey."

"I don't clasp hands with the likes of you," Strangewayes said. "Bring the gold here to my office. My associates will take care of it from there."

Stung by the refused handshake, Condor said, "How do I know I can trust you?"

"You don't. That's the chance you take, Captain."

Condor's anger always shimmered near the surface. "Silas, I could reach across this desk and wring your scrawny neck. It would be real easy and quick."

Strangewayes' eyes lifted. They were almost colorless, tainted, like cholera-infected well water. "Yes you could. But since my associates know you are here, you'd never get out of Silver City alive." He jabbed his pen at the ceiling. "I have watchers up there and they miss nothing."

Condor backed off. He should've known Strangewayes would have guards. "I was talking in jest, of course."

"Yes, of course you were."

"I need a wagon and a couple of good horses to pull it." Condor had had enough of mules.

"I thought you said you got it this far by pack animals?"

"I let them go."

"Careless of you." Strangewayes was perched in his chair like a scrawny parrot on a stand. He rose to his feet, a frail hunchback no bigger than a ten-year-old charity orphan. "Go to Church Street, to the Blue Coyote livery stable, and tell Ebenezer Cobham that I sent you. He will supply what you need. The cost of the hire of a wagon and horses will be deducted from your share of the proceeds."

Condor fought back his anger. Strangewayes, the poisonous little dwarf, was trying to bleed him dry. "How do I find Church Street?"

Strangewayes pulled on a cord behind his desk, then turned and said, "One of my associates will guide you and he'll stay with you until you recover the gold."

"I don't need help."

The most unfortunate thing Strangewayes did was attempt a smile. He showed teeth that were long and yellow, an ape grimace totally devoid of humor. "No, but I do. Let's just say I'm protecting my investment."

The door jangled open and a small, slender man wearing black broadcloth, a bowler hat, and a scowl stepped inside.

"This is Mr. John Gaudet. He will be your shadow until the gold is safely delivered into my hands," Strangewayes said.

Gaudet was a gun, Condor decided, taking his measure of the man. Hard-faced, thin-lipped, with the eyes of a Louisiana alligator, he'd be sudden and hard to kill.

"I'll be back in a couple of days, maybe sooner," Condor said. "I don't know who's riding my back trail and I may have to take care of them."

Strangewayes gave a dismissive wave of his pen. "Do whatever you think is best. Now, good evening to you, sir."

"One thing," Condor said. "Don't forget those Boston banks."

"I never forget anything, Captain Condor."

Chapter Forty-four

Night had overtaken Dallas Steele and the Dromore riders and so had a sense of frustration.

"Those mules we found running all over God's creation mean only one thing," Steele said.

"That Condor has stashed the gold somewhere," Shawn O'Brien said.

"Exactly. But where?" Steele said.

Shawn shrugged off Steele's question.

"We could search, I suppose," Shamus said.

"This is a big territory, Colonel," Luther Ironside said. "Where would we start?"

"That answer to that, Luther, is that I don't know," Shamus said.

"There's one thing," Jacob said. "If he stashed the gold, Condor has to come back for it. That's when we might nail him to the barn door."

"Pat, you know these things," Ironside said,

looking around him into darkness. "Just where the hell are we at?"

"If I remember my maps correctly, we're just east of the Continental Divide and about twenty miles due south of Silver City."

"In a mountain wilderness that looks like it goes on forever in every direction," Steele said.

"I can't argue with that," Patrick said.

The mesquite fire burned without smoke, casting a rippling scarlet light as Shawn intently sliced bacon into a skillet. He looked up and said, "My guess, Condor is in Silver City, making arrangements to exchange folding money for his gold or a good chunk of it."

"Jacob, you, and Patrick could ride up there in the morning while the rest of us stay here and watch for Condor if he heads back this way," Shamus said.

"It's as good a plan as any," Jacob allowed. "But it's not easy to find one man in a town that big."

"I'll go with Jacob and Pat," Steele said. "An extra pair of eyes could make the difference."

"If you see Condor, go to the law," Shamus said. "Don't try to take him by yourselves."

"The colonel is speaking to you, Jake," Ironside said.

"If I see Condor a-strolling down the street on a morning promenade, I'll set the law on him, Luther, I promise."

"I found that less than convincing, Luther. Did you?" Shamus said.

"Jake's a heller, Colonel," Ironside said.

"If that's the case, I'd rather have a live son than a dead heller," Shamus said.

"Damn right." Ironside winked at Jacob.

The moon had spiked itself on a pine and the darkness was shot through with tarnished silver. Coyotes yipped close by, drawn by the smell of frying bacon. The air was cool and crisp, fragile as spun glass.

Scout and Hyde suddenly appeared just beyond the rim of the firelight. Ironside holstered his gun and yelled, "Damn it! Don't you boys know better than to walk into a man's camp without a howdy-do? I could've dropped you both."

The Navajo smiled. "What is it white men say, Ironside? Ah yes, that you're a nervous nelly."

Ironside drew himself up to his full height, outraged. "And right about now you're mighty lucky you ain't a dead Injun."

"Luther, sit down and behave yourself," Shamus said. "And remember that Scout's ways are not ours."

Ironside took his place by the fire with ill grace,

muttering under his breath about redskins in general and Injun-lovers in particular.

"What did you say, Luther?" Shamus demanded.

"Nothing, Colonel. I didn't say nothing."

"I should hope not. Many a time a man's mouth broke his nose." Shamus's back pained him. Reluctant to stand, he looked up at the visitors. "There's coffee in the pot and bacon in the pan."

"Coffee is good," Scout said, "but no food. We killed earlier today."

After he and Hyde had taken a seat by the fire, Scout said, "Condor is in Silver City."

"We figured that much," Jacob said.

"He talked with a man named Silas Strange-wayes and then left his place of business. That is all I know."

"Did you find out where he is now?" Steele said. "The name of a hotel?"

"No. Mr. Hyde and I left the city then, because we must return home. We've already been gone too long."

"Scout, do you have any idea where Condor hid the gold?" Shamus asked.

The Navajo shook his head. "None. It is hidden from me."

"And us," Patrick said.

Scout rose to his feet. "We will go now."

"I must pay you for your efforts, Scout," Shamus said. "You've been a great help to us."

"No, Sheriff Clitherow will pay me. That was our agreement." Scout stepped away from the fire and he and Hyde disappeared into the darkness.

"Right strange fellers, them two," Ironside said.

"I can't disagree with you there," Steele said.

Jacob bent over and grabbed the knife from Shawn's hand and speared himself a slice of bacon. "Hot, hot, hot," he said as he chewed open-mouthed.

"Hell, Jake, you could've waited," Shawn said.

"No time for that," Jacob said, swallowing. "Condor is in Silver City and I don't plan to lose him. Dallas, Pat, are you ready to ride?"

"Night riding. Haven't we had enough of that?" Patrick said, but he smiled and looked eager to go.

"How do we find him, Jake?" Steele asked.

"We have the name of a resident, Silas Strange-wayes. Find him and we can find Condor."

"Then let's do it."

"Be careful, all of you," Shamus said. "I'll say a rosary for you before I seek my blankets."

Jacob nodded, seeming to make up his mind about something. "Pat, you stay here. You've got Abby to see after and if Condor gives us the slip, the Colonel could use another gun."

"I'd rather go with you and Dallas, if it's all the same to Pa."

Shamus thought about that. "Your brother is right, Patrick. The girl doesn't trust anyone but you . . . and I'd rather you stay."

"Pat, if this all goes bad and Nate Condor comes this way, the Colonel is going to need you," Jacob said.

Patrick understood the logic of that. Nate Condor was no ordinary man and he'd be a handful. Finally, Patrick said, "Well, I guess I'll stick."

"Jake, you sure you don't want Shawn and me along?" Ironside asked. "Suppose you get in a shooting scrape?"

"No, Luther. I want both your guns here. There's a good chance we'll miss Condor in Silver City."

"We'll be on the scout for him. You can depend on us."

Jacob nodded. "I know I can."

Steele put his hand on Ironside's shoulder. "Luther, I want you to know that I consider you one of the best and bravest fighting men I've ever met."

"Damn right," Ironside said, his words broken. He turned away quickly so no one could see his face.

Chapter Forty-five

Dawn was breaking when Jacob O'Brien and Dallas Steele rode into Silver City. The streets in front of the businesses were deserted except for the cur dogs that sniffed around the false fronts of the stores and slunk into the shadowed places between buildings.

But in the open spaces behind the businesses were stirrings of life—the sound of freight wagons being loaded and unloaded and the coughs and hoarse voices of men who talked in different languages working unseen at dozens of different tasks. At the train station, a locomotive clanged cars together.

If anyone noticed the two tall riders, they paid them no mind.

"I could use a cup of coffee, Jake," Steele said. "Up there beyond the saloon, what's that place?"

"Looks like a restaurant. We'll see if anyone is awake."

The place was already open, its front windows steamed up. Oil lamps glowed inside in a smoky haze.

Jacob and Steele reined and dismounted in front of the restaurant. They entered and took a seat. Ten or so other customers sat at tables, one stout man with the prosperous look of a banker making a start on an enormous steak topped with half a dozen eggs.

A middle-aged, handsome waitress poured coffee without even waiting for their order. It was good and strong.

She appeared talkative and had her own opinion when they asked about Silas Strangewayes. "You boys steer clear of him. He's a mean, grasping old beggar who would cut his mother's throat for a dollar."

"Is he a moneylender?" Steele asked.

"He's an importer, or so he says, but usury is his game and more besides, including murder, if you ask me."

"Is he rich?" Jacob said, trying to assess the man.

"As Midas. He owns half of Silver City, cowboy, and he's got his greedy finger in every other pie, legal and illegal, in the town."

"You ever hear of a ranny by the name of English Nate Condor?" Steele asked.

The woman shook her head. "Name doesn't ring a bell with me."

A man's voice yelled, "Bessie!" from the kitchen. The waitress said, "I got to go. But remember what I told you. Steer clear of that old rogue Silas Strangewayes." She hustled away.

"After all that, I'm quite anxious to meet the gentleman," Steele said.

"Then drink up, Dallas. Condor won't wait for us."

Across town at the Blue Coyote livery stable, Nate Condor was having his own problems.

"The wagon will be back by noon," said the proprietor, a fat man who walked in a fragrant aura of horse dung and sweat. "You can wait until then, surely."

"Where the hell is it now, Cobham?" John Gaudet said, his reptilian eyes angry. "Mr. Strangewayes said it was all arranged."

"Nothing was arranged, and that's why the only wagon I've got is out at the Rafter-T delivering barbwire. It will be back by noon, like I said."

Condor glanced at his watch. "Five hours from now. Is there any other place in town we can hire a wagon?"

"Nope," Cobham said. "At least not a Studebaker that will carry a heavy load over rough country. As soon as it gets back, I'll change the horse team and you'll be on your way." His red, polished face took on a sly look. "Why are you in such an all-fired hurry, mister?"

"That's none of your damned business," Condor said.

"But it is my business." Cobham didn't look in the least intimidated by Condor. "I'm mighty particular about them as I rent a wagon and horse team to."

"You're renting it to Mr. Strangewayes," Gaudet said. "That's all you need to know."

"Silas's marker is as good as cash in the bank. You're right about that." Cobham picked up the bridle he'd been repairing. "You boys look sharp set. There's a restaurant at the other side of town by the name of the Hungry Hunter. It's a fair piece, but the grub is worth it and the walk will kill time until Bertie Yates gets back with the wagon."

Twenty minutes later, Nate Condor and John Gaudet sat in the same seats recently vacated by Jacob O'Brien and Dallas Steele.

The middle-aged waitress took their orders, but didn't engage them in conversation.

* * *

The sun had not yet cleared the peaks of the Mimbres Mountains forty miles to the west and the street where Silas Strangewayes did business was even gloomier than usual. A dim light glowed behind the black-painted window as Jacob and Steele dismounted and hitched their horses.

"Egg and cheese importer," Jacob read. "Sounds innocent enough."

"Maybe he'll sell us some eggs at cost," Steele said, smiling. He bowed and extended his arm. "After you, Mr. O'Brien."

The bell above the door jangled as Jacob stepped into the office, Steele right behind him.

The man Jacob took to be Strangewayes sat behind a desk like an emaciated troll, the steel pen in his hand scratching across a thick ledger. Without looking up, the troll said, "What can I do for you?"

"Silas Strangewayes?" Jacob asked.

"Yes, yes, that's me. Now what do you want? Be quick of tongue, man."

"A dozen eggs and a pound of English cheddar, extra sharp," Steele said.

Now Strangewayes looked up. "You are pleased to be funny."

"Just trying to attract your attention," Steele said.

"You have it. Now what do you want?"

"We're trying to find a man and we believe you know where he is," Jacob said.

"This is a place of business, not a lost and found bureau," Strangewayes said. "If you have no business to transact, then good day to you both."

"His name is Nate Condor." Jacob said. "He visited you here, Strangewayes."

The man didn't flinch. "A lot of people visit me here. As I told you, this is a place of business. Now, if you have none to transact, then be gone. Get out of my office."

"We could beat it out of you, old man," Steele said.

Without a word Strangewayes got to his feet, hopped like a seedy crow to a bell rope and yanked on it. "Now I'll have you thrown out,"

A few moments later two men stepped into the office, the bell over the door clamoring above their heads. They had the look of knuckle and skull fighters who'd learned their trade in saloons and waterfront dives around the country. Both were big, brawny, and mean and seemed eager for a fight.

Strangewayes sat back at his desk, picked up his pen and bent to his ledger. "Throw them out."

The broken-nosed faces of the bruisers broke into sadistic grins and their fists bunched at their sides. Not employed for their intelligence or perception, they saw a fancy-pants dude and a ragged, dusty puncher and figured it was going to be easy and fun.

It was a bad mistake.

They had not reckoned on gunfighters.

As Steele drew, Jacob took a couple of long, swift steps, and was at Strangewayes' desk quickly. The little man opened a drawer and reached for a gun, but Jacob slammed the drawer shut on Strangewayes' wrist. The man squealed in pain.

Jacob grabbed Strangewayes by the front of his coat, jerked him out of his chair, and pressed the muzzle of his Colt against the man's temple. He turned to the bruisers who were momentarily rooted to the spot, their slow minds grappling with the implications of Steele's revolver and their boss's plight.

"Stay right where you are or I'll scatter his brains," Jacob said.

"The man means what he says," Steele said, his Colt up and rock steady in his hand.

"Boss, what do we do?" one of the bruisers asked.

"Stay right there and don't move," Strangewayes said, his crow-croak of a voice quivering. "He'll kill me."

"Count on it, mister," Jacob said. "Now, where is Condor?"

"Damn you to hell," Strangewayes said.

Jacob shoved the Colt muzzle harder into the man's temple. "You live or die by your next words, Strangewayes. Where is Nate Condor?"

"The Blue Coyote livery stable."

"Is he still there?"

"No, he's probably gone by now."

"Where is he headed?"

"South. That's all I know."

"Tell me, damn you." Jacob shook the man.

"He wouldn't tell me where he was headed. South . . . just south."

"Where is the Blue Coyote?"

"The north side of town. Take Hudson Street and you can't miss it."

Jacob turned to Steele. "You reckon he's telling the truth, Dallas?"

"I'm telling the truth," Strangewayes said. "You'll find Condor there and God help you when you do." The man's voice rose to a hysterical shriek. "He'll kill you . . . kill you . . . kill you . . ."

"Yeah, he's telling the truth." Steele smiled. "But maybe he's lying about the kill you part."

"Maybe." Jacob dragged Strangewayes from behind the desk. "Call off your apes."

Strangewayes hesitated and Jacob said, "I will blow your brains out, you know."

The man heard the truth in Jacob's voice and said to the bruisers, "You two, get back upstairs."

"Boss, we—"

"Now!" Strangewayes yelled. "This here is a madman and he'll kill me if you don't leave."

Reluctantly, the men left.

After a minute passed, Jacob said, "Dallas."

Steele nodded and he too stepped outside.

The racketing roar of a Colt followed a moment later, followed by the crash of glass and the heavy thud of bodies hitting the concrete sidewalk.

"Seems like your friends had other ideas about letting us leave, Strangewayes," Jacob said.

"That was none of my doing." The man shivered with fear.

"No, I guess not," Jacob said. "I'm in a good mood today and I'm willing to give you the benefit of the doubt. Have you any more stashed away upstairs?"

"No, only those two. Are they both dead?"

Strangewayes question was answered when Steele stepped inside, clanging the bell again. He frowned. "Damn that bell. It makes me jump every time."

"What happened?" Jacob said.

"They were at the window, laying for us with rifles. Looks like they're now both deceased." Steele opened the jangling door again. "I suggest we leave before the law gets here." He nodded at Strangewayes. "Are you planning to gun him, Jake?"

"No!" the little man cried. "Spare me, please."

"Two dead hardcases outside, Strangewayes. I'd say you've got some explaining to do," Jacob said.

The little man bit his lip and looked worried. "I won't tell them it was you who killed them, I promise. Robbers. It was robbers. Yes, that's what I'll tell them."

"Explain it any way you can," Steele said. "Jake, are we riding? We've got an appointment with Nate Condor to keep, remember?"

Jacob nodded and holstered his Colt. "Yeah, so let's go keep it."

Chapter Forty-six

"Hell, Jake, we don't have time for this," Dallas Steele said. "Condor could light a shuck."

"It will only take a moment. Trust me. We'll catch up with Nate Condor, all right."

"Jake, I always knew you were a kneeler, but this is ridiculous," Steele said.

"Look at it, Dallas. It's calling out to me and I'm damned if I know why."

"There's nobody been inside that place for years, maybe a hundred years," Steele said. "All you'll find in there is pack rat nests and bird droppings. If God ever lived in there, he moved to better quarters a long time ago."

"Stay outside on watch, Dallas. If Condor passes this way, come a-running."

Steele shook his head. "Anything you say, Jake. I know better than to argue with an O'Brien when he's got his mind set on something."

The old mission chapel lay off the tree-lined street in an acre of ground overgrown with brush and cactus. Its adobe walls had long since faded into a dirty cream color and the oak doors were dry and stained as ancient parchment. A bronze bell, green with mildew, still hung in a timber tower. The few headstones and marble crosses in front of the building that marked the graves of forgotten dead leaned over at impossible angles.

Still clinging to cobwebs of morning mist, it had a lost, forlorn, neglected air and Jacob reckoned Steele had it right. God had long since abandoned the place.

He swung out of the saddle and tethered his horse to the limb of a wild oak, then stood outside the church door. He had no idea why he was there, why he'd interrupted a manhunt to visit the old place. The chapel called out to him. That's all he knew.

When Jacob opened the creaking door he smelled the mission's musty breath, but its heartbeat was gone, stilled when the last worshipper after the last mass closed the place for the last time.

To his surprise, though the mission was empty of pews and the pulpit had crashed to the floor some time in the past, a sanctuary lamp glowed red at the right side of the ornate altar. The light meant consecrated hosts were present in the tabernacle. Jacob took in the single statue of a bearded man struggling against massive iron chains standing in a niche in the wall before he removed his hat and kneeled in front of the altar. He crossed himself and bowed his head.

"Welcome to the mission San Pedro en Cadenas, my son." The male voice, heavily accented, came from Jacob's left.

He turned his head and saw a tall, thin man of late middle-age dressed in the rough brown robe of a monk step out of a doorway to the left of the altar.

Jacob rose to his feet. "I thought there was no one here."

The monk smiled. "The sanctuary lamp is lit and that means Our Lord Jesus Christ is here, present in the altar." He stepped closer to Jacob and held out a pale hand. "I am Father Karl Friedrich von Weisen, the pastor of this mission."

Jacob shook the priest's hand. "Judging by your name and accent, I'd say you're a far piece off your home range, Father."

The priest nodded. "Far from my native Prussia, yes. But then, any church is my home range, even this one."

"What did you do to deserve St. Peter in Chains?" Jacob smiled to take any possible sting out of his question.

Von Weisen smiled in turn, his sky blue eyes

amused. "The short answer is nothing. I was sent here two years ago to take over the flock. But there is no flock. Silver City has more fashionable churches than one that threatens to fall down on the heads of the faithful. I expect I will be recalled to Europe again soon." His face became serious. "Why are you here? Only to visit?"

Jacob dropped to one knee. "I want your blessing, Father."

"I suspect you're troubled about something."

Jacob nodded. "I'm on my way to kill a man."

If Father von Weisen was shocked, he didn't let it show. "This man, is he a good man or is he evil and that's why you must kill him?"

"Or he might kill me, Father. And yes, he is a man of evil, past and present."

"Years ago, I blessed the soldiers of the Prussian army before they set off to fight the French," the priest said. "The French were not evil, but they were the enemy."

"English Nate Condor is evil and an enemy, Father," Jacob said. "Your blessing will give me the courage to face him. At least, that's what I tell myself."

Von Weisen smiled. "I can't withhold from you what I conferred on the Prussians. But if you'd asked to confess your sins I would have refused, since it's possible that in God's eyes you were already planning to commit the sin of murder."

"I understand," Jacob said.

The priest laid his left hand on Jacob's head and made the sign of the cross with the other. "Almighty and eternal God, protect this warrior as he discharges his duties. Protect him with the shield of thy strength and keep him safe from all evil and harm. Amen."

"Amen." Jacob rose to his feet.

Von Weisen smiled again. "Perhaps, my son, you were lucky that you met a Prussian priest this morning, one who's seen his share of war."

"Perhaps that's why I was drawn to this mission," Jacob said.

"Yes, God works in mysterious ways. Now, let us both hope we haven't mortally offended Him."

Jacob nodded his thanks and returned to the street where Steele waited patiently.

"Hell, Jake, you were talking to a priest? You probably offended the hell out of him," Dallas Steele said. "Did you tell him you're planning to kill a man?"

"Yeah, Dallas I did. I told him English Nate Condor was evil and needed killing. And I didn't offend him."

Steele shook his head. "Well, they sure don't make preachers like they used to."

"He's Prussian," Jacob said.

"Who?"

"The priest."

"Ah, that explains everything," Steele said, the puzzled expression on his face revealing that it didn't.

Before Steele could say anything else, Jacob said, "Did you catch sight of anyone who might be Nate Condor?"

"Look at the street, Jake. It's beginning to get busy, and it seems that everybody walks in this town. Condor could easily lose himself in the crowd."

"A two-gun man who looks like a pirate isn't difficult to spot," Jacobs said.

"All right, then, I didn't see him."

"Why didn't you say that in the first place?"

Steele shook his head and grinned. "You know something, Jake, with the possible exception of the colonel, the O'Briens can be a pain in the arse."

Jacob smiled in return. "Can't we though?"

Chapter Forty-seven

As livery stables went, the Blue Coyote was better than most.

It was a large, white-painted building with stalls for twenty horses, an attached tack room, and a blacksmith's forge set up on flagstones. For the comfort of customers, there was a waiting room with a couch and chairs and the luxury of a two-holer outhouse in the back.

"Where the hell is the wagon?" Condor said. "It should be here by now."

Ebenezer Cobham said, "Just a little longer now."

"It's four hours longer, damn you," Condor said. "Can't you find me another wagon?"

Cobham shook his head. "Freight wagons are hard to come by in Silver City. The big mining companies have all the independent hauling firms tied up and looking for more."

John Gaudet, mean as a snake, sneered. "What are you afraid of, Condor?"

"I'm afraid of nothing," Condor said. "But I want the hell away from here. The army is too damned close and I may have been followed."

"I can take care of whoever is following you," Gaudet said. "I ain't sceered of no boogeymen."

Condor's mouth twisted in a feral snarl. "You be scared for yourself, Gaudet. I will only be pushed so far and you're mighty close to my limit."

The gunman was not intimidated. "I heard you were a pirate once, before you took to the outlaw life. Is that true?"

"That's a damned lie. I was a trader," Condor said.

Ebenezer Cobham had been listening to the exchange between the two gunmen. "What kind of trader?"

"Black slaves. I bought them cheap on the West African coast and sold them to the Arabs."

"Was there money in that?" Cobham asked.

"Sure there was, once you figured a way to keep the blacks alive, or at least most of them."

"If there was money in slave trading, why did you quit?" Gaudet's sneer was a permanent fixture on his face, as though he'd been born with it. He probably had.

"The British, the Dutch, and the French navies began to sink slave ships on sight, even if there were blacks in the holds. Then the Americans joined in and the game was over."

"Too bad," Gaudet said.

"Yeah, wasn't it?" Condor's dislike for the little gunman was palpable.

"Now I understand why you're so all-fired worried about the freight wagon," Gaudet said. "You got nothing left."

"You should be worried too, Gaudet," Condor said. "If the wagon doesn't show, I'll have no need to keep you around any longer."

"Is that a threat?" Gaudet shouldered off the wall of the livery office and laid his coffee cup on the desk.

"Take it any way you want." Condor's body tensed, ready.

"Keep that until later," Cobham said. "We got a visitor and he don't look happy."

Silas Strangewayes scuttled like a crab toward the livery, a crooked man leaning on a crooked cane, a crooked scowl on his face.

Condor greeted him. "Why are you here? What the hell happened?"

"Two men happened," Strangewayes said. "They invaded my office and forced me to tell them where you were. One of them—his name is Dallas, curse him—killed two of my men."

"Dallas Steele." Condor saw the shock of recognition in Gaudet's pale face and took pleasure in it. "And I'm willing to bet the other is Jacob O'Brien."

"O'Brien? The gunfighter out of the Glorieta Mesa country?" Gaudet said. "They say he always plays the piano before he kills a man."

"That would be the one," Condor said. "But don't worry, Gaudet, there are no pianos around here."

Gaudet was quiet for a few moments, then he said, "Hell, I can shade him."

Condor smiled. "Yeah, sure you can."

"Unless you can get rid of those two, Condor, the deal is off," Strangewayes said. "I've already tried to explain away the corpses of my men in the street as the result of a robbery attempt, but I don't think the law believes me."

"I'll kill Steele and O'Brien for you, Silas," Condor said. "Now quit your bloody whining and calm down."

"Don't kill them here, damn it," Strangewayes said. "Two more dead men is two too many. Louis Kennon is the deputy marshal here and he's already got his suspicions, I swear it."

"I'll take care of him as well, if you want," Condor offered.

"Leave Kennon be. Killing a lawman could bring nothing but trouble. Get O'Brien and the other one and that's all. At least for now."

"Consider it done."

"Ride north out of the city. Lure them into the mountains a ways and then do for them." The little man scowled at Condor. "Those two could be here soon. What the hell are you waiting for?"

"Just make sure the wagon is here when we get back, you old reprobate," Condor said. "Or we'll serve this town another dead man for breakfast."

Strangewayes' words lashed at Condor. "The wagon will be here. Any more threats from you and you'll find yourself with a noose around your neck, you damned pirate."

"You heard the boss, Condor," Gaudet said, tensed. "Now shut your trap."

"You want to shut it for me, Gaudet?"

"Here, enough of that!" Ebenezer Cobham stepped between the two gunmen. "You heard Silas. Be about your business."

Condor nodded, his eyes cold on Gaudet. "Later."

Gaudet smirked. "I'll accommodate you any time you feel up to it"

That brought a sneer to Condor's lips. "You damned idiot."

Chapter Forty-eight

"What can I do for you gentlemen?" Ebenezer Cobham asked.

"We're looking for a feller goes by the name of English Nate Condor," Jacob O'Brien said.

Cobham pretended to be eager to help. He gave a little bow and rubbed anguished hands together. "Oh, dear me, you just missed him. He left . . . well, not fifteen minutes ago."

"Did he have a wagon?" Dallas Steele asked. "And did he say he was heading south?"

"No, he didn't have a wagon. But he did mention that he and his associate were planning to do a little bird hunting up Bear Mountain way. That's northwest—"

"I know where it is," Jacob said.

Cobham's eyes grew wide as the muzzle of Jacob's Colt slammed between them.

"Where is Nate Condor?"

"North, mister. Honest." Piss ran down Cobham's pants leg. "That's all I know. Him and another man rode north fifteen minutes ago, like I said."

"Who's the other man?" Jacob shoved the gun into the livery man's midsection.

"His name is Gaudet," Cobham said. "He works for Mr. Strangewayes."

"I reckon he's telling you the truth, Jake." Steele shook his head. "Oh, dear me, Mr. Cobham, it seems like you just pissed yourself."

"It'll dry." Jacob looked at Steele, puzzled. "Why would Condor head north? The gold is south."

"He plans to kill us out of town where there are no witnesses, I reckon."

Jacob lowered the hammer of his revolver and dropped it into the holster. "Well, he's going to get his chance." He stepped to his horse, Steele walking behind him.

Gunshot roared loud within the walls of the stable.

Jacob heard Steele groan as the bullet hit him. He turned and pulled his gun as he eased the Pinkerton to the floor.

Silas Strangewayes, holding a smoking revolver at eye level, stood outside the open door of the tack room.

They fired at the same time. Strangewayes'

shot burned across Jacob's neck, but the little man staggered under the crushing impact of two .45 rounds dead center to his chest.

"Damn you!" Strangewayes screamed, taking an unsteady step forward. "You've killed me." The little man fell on his face, twitched like a stepped on bug, then lay still.

Cobham, his face ashen, backed away. He looked at Strangewayes' body. "I thought he'd never die."

Jacob ignored that and kneeled beside Steele. He held the Pinkerton's head. "You lay still, Dallas. I'll get a doctor."

Steele, his lips pale, shook his head. "The hell you will, Jake. Get after Condor."

"You're hit hard, Dallas."

"Yes, I know." His face puzzled, he said, "Who shot me?"

"Strangewayes, and I did for him."

"I'll survive, Jake. Now go get Condor."

Cobham stepped closer and Jacob said, "Bring a doctor." The man hesitated and Jacob yelled. "Now, damn you!"

Cobham fled.

"Now leave me be, Jake." Steele winced. "I hurt like hell. What the hell did he shoot me with?"

"Looks like a .38-caliber British Bulldog."

Steele smiled. "British? Good, at least it was a gun with class." He grabbed Jacob by the front of his shirt. "Go now, Jake. I'll be fine until the doc gets here."

Jacob eased Steele's head onto the floor, and then rose to his feet. "I'll bring you Condor's scalp."

"Just put an extra bullet in him for me." Steele's eyes fluttered closed and he drifted into unconsciousness.

Jacob stepped to Strangewayes' body and with his boot rolled the little man onto his back. His water-colored eyes were wide open, but he was dead as he was ever going to be.

Later, the *Silver City Miner* newspaper would speculate on why Silas Strangewayes remained at the Blue Coyote livery stable after Nate Condor and John Gaudet left instead of immediately returning to his place of business. The only explanation reporters could come up with was that the old man, known citywide for his mean and nasty disposition, had homicide in mind.

The unfortunate events that followed were laid at Strangewayes' doorstep. The *Silver City Miner* stated that, "It is our opinion that the crook and moneylender Silas Strangewayes had escaped the gallows for too long. He is no great loss."

Understandably, that was also Jacob O'Brien's opinion.

* * *

Jacob O'Brien rode into the high timber country north of Silver City, the sky above him like the inside of a blue ceramic bowl. It was not yet noon but the day was hot and the mountain air was thin as muslin and hard to breathe.

His horse tight-reined to a walk, Jacob constantly scanned the rugged land ahead of him. But, familiar with the code and conduct of skilled, gun-fighting men, he did not fear an ambush.

English Nate Condor was a named gun. To outdraw and kill Jake O'Brien would greatly enhance his reputation among other belted men, but the deed must be done face-to-face, *mano a mano*, or it would not stand. On this point, the code was strict and unforgiving, a thing Nate Condor understood and would therefore act according to its mores.

Thus, Jacob rode without fear of a bushwhacking, but with fear of a different origin . . . the fear that he wasn't fast enough on the draw and shoot to shade a man like Nate Condor, said to be the best with Colt's gun there ever was or ever would be.

Fear ices a man's belly and Jacob accepted that. But he'd inherited his sand from Irish warrior kings and there was no backup in him. Condor was indeed an enemy to be reckoned with, but as the Colonel once told him in the old

Gaelic, "*Laech cach fer co forrager.*" Every man is a warrior until he's defeated.

Jacob bore that in mind as he rode on through the brightening day . . . along with the certain knowledge that he would meet up with Condor soon and have it to do. The tracks he followed were fresh, two horsemen heading north and they were not more than a few minutes ahead of him.

The trail led across a grassy meadow bright with wildflowers hemmed in on one side by a thick stand of timber, a craggy parapet of weathered rock on the other. Two hundred yards ahead of him it rose gradually to a treed hogback, a boulder-strewn clearing at its crest.

Nate Condor sat on a small rock in the clearing and watched Jacob. A second man stood a few yards apart from him, holding the reins of the horses.

Jacob rode within talking distance and swung out of the saddle, walking his horse forward.

Condor, grinning, rose to his feet. "Jacob O'Brien is your name, matey, is it not?"

"It is, and there's no need to tell me yours, Condor."

"Ah, then let me introduce my associate, Mr. John Gaudet."

Jacob's eyes flicked to the man. He'd stripped to his shirt and pants and wore a gun in a shoulder holster rig. Little else about Gaudet caught his interest.

"So, Mr. O'Brien, what brings you all the way out here?" Condor asked.

"I've come to kill you. That's the short answer to your question."

"I must confess I'm a little disappointed Mr. Steele is not with you. He's not ill, I trust."

"He's otherwise engaged today."

"What a pity, I was rather looking forward to meeting him," Condor said.

Jacob slapped his horse away from him, out of the line of fire. Then he took time to study Condor.

The man stood with his legs apart, his slim hips crossed by two gun belts. There was no fear in his eyes, just a glint of triumph, as though he was glad to finally see the famous Jacob O'Brien in the flesh. "You can't shade me, O'Brien, you know that. But it's a beautiful day and I'm willing to do you a favor."

"I don't want any favors from you."

"At least have enough manners to hear me out and stop acting like a raggedy-assed Irishman fresh out of the bogs."

"Talk then, and be damned to you."

"Turn around, mount your horse, and I won't kill you. When I get back to Silver City all I'll do is spread the word that I put the crawl on the famous Jake O'Brien, gunfighter of the top rank." Condor turned to Gaudet and spread his arms. "Mr. Gaudet, can I say fairer that that?"

Gaudet grinned, but said nothing.

"See, Mr. Gaudet agrees that I've made you a magnanimous offer," Condor said.

"You're finished in Silver City, Condor," Jacob said. "Silas Strangewayes is dead and you've got nowhere else to go with your gold."

Condor was shaken, a sight that pleased Jacob greatly.

"You're a damned liar, O'Brien. You piano-playing blackguard, you're lying."

"Mr. Strangewayes ain't dead," Gaudet said. "He can't die. Everybody knows that."

"Well, when I left him he was laying on the floor of the Blue Coyote livery, his beard in a pile of horse dung," Jacob said.

"That's a lie, O'Brien," Condor said.

"You're making fighting talk, Condor. Do you have the sand to back it up?" Jacob asked quietly.

"I can back it up. Catch this!" Condor made a two-handed draw, his guns slicking fast from the leather.

Jacob's own Colt was suddenly bucking in his fist, his draw as fast and smooth as Luther Ironside and constant practice could make it.

Too slow by a heartbeat, Nate Condor took Jacob's bullet in the chest. Condor's breastbone seemed to cave in as his shoulders jerked forward and his entire upper body bent around the blossoming wound. His own shots went wild, missing Jacob by inches.

Insane with fury, Condor screamed in frustration and desperately tried to bring his Colts to bear.

Jacob shot him again and again, the *smack-smack* of the bullets an ugly sound. And Condor was done.

Jacob didn't wait to see the man fall. He turned on Gaudet, thumbing back the hammer as he spun, but the gunman wanted none of it.

He stood frozen to the spot and shrieked, "No quarrel! No quarrel!"

His heart pumping, his nerves raw, Jacob thought about it, but finally lowered his gun. "You got lucky today, Gaudet."

"Is . . . is he dead?" Gaudet said, staring at Condor's sprawled body.

Jacob nodded. "As dead as three bullets to the chest can make a man."

"I never saw a man draw and shoot as fast as you did, O'Brien. Never thought it was possible."

"I reckon." Jacob punched shells out of his Colt and reloaded.

The expression on Gaudet's face was a mix of shock, wonder, and admiration. "I can't draw near as fast as you did."

"Few men can," Jacob said as he gathered up the reins of his horse.

"Then why the hell am I wearing this?" Gaudet said, gesturing to his holstered revolver.

Jacob turned his head and looked at the man. "Wear it, boy, just don't try to draw down on mean fellers like me."

"The hell with that." Gaudet stripped himself of his Colt and threw the gun into the trees where it struck a branch, then thudded into underbrush.

Jacob stared hard at Gaudet. "That's the second wise thing you've done today."

Chapter Forty-nine

Patrick O'Brien was certain the little butterflies fluttering around the scrub oaks were Sleepy Duskywings, a species that had often eluded him in the past.

He'd been scorned and warned by Luther Ironside never to go on a butterfly hunt without a gun and he had two of them, the Colt on his hip and the Winchester in the boot under his knee. He was a mile north of Saddle Mountain, keeping an eye on the main wagon roads heading south out of Silver City. Shawn was farther west and the colonel and Ironside were somewhere along Walnut Creek to the south.

There had been no sign of a wagon or even a rider for hours and Patrick was bored. "Abby," he said to the black girl at his side, "you see those butterflies over yonder by the scrub oak?"

The girl nodded, and Patrick said, "Those are Sleepy Duskywings, not real rare, but seasonal."

"They're brown," Abby said, seemingly unimpressed.

"Not as pretty as swallowtails, I allow, but I'd surely like another for my collection."

"You collect flutterbyes?" the girl said.

"Butterflies, Abby. They're called butterflies."

The girl shrugged. "They're brown."

Patrick looked around him and into the distance where heat waves danced. The land was still and silent, echoing its emptiness. "I could catch one in my hat."

"Catch what?"

"A Sleepy Duskywing."

"Oh."

"You keep watch, Abby." Patrick stepped out of the saddle. "You see anyone coming, especially the big, mean-looking old man they call Luther, holler out. Understand?"

Abby nodded.

"Not much on conversation, are you, girl?"

"I don't know nothing about flutterbyes."

"Well, keep watch and I'll teach you about butterflies later." Patrick smiled. "The worldwide diversity of the *papillio* species is a fascinating subject for study and discussion."

"Ah," Abby said.

Patrick walked to the scrub oak, hat in hand. A

cloud of butterflies soared up in front of him, but he had eyes for only one, a magnificent Sleepy Duskywing more than two and a half inches from wingtip to wingtip.

The butterfly was not only large, it was spry, and it led its pursuer toward a narrow arroyo hemmed in by a pair of high rock shelves.

The thrill of the hunt drove Patrick and made him oblivious to all else.

Finally the butterfly landed on a small yellow flower and folded its wings.

Patrick pounced. "Got you!" he yelled, the crown of his hat covering the insect. He looked up in triumph . . . into the muzzle of a .45 Colt.

"What the hell are you?" Barney Merden snarled.

"I'm a butterfly collector," Patrick said. "But it seems like every time I try to catch one somebody points a gun at my head."

"Is that a fact? Well, four-eyes, this is your unlucky day. On your feet and shuck the gun belt."

Patrick rose and did as he was told.

"Take a couple of steps back." Merden nodded. "There's a good boy. Now me and you—"

"I think that should be, 'You and I,'" Patrick said.

"I don't give a damn what it should be. Walk to the wild oak over there so I got less distance to drag your carcass."

"Let me get my hat," Patrick said.

Merden's smile was ugly. "Where you're going, you don't need a hat."

The exchange about the hat took only about four seconds—but it saved Patrick O'Brien's life.

The rock missed Merden's head, slamming into his right shoulder with a dull thud. Merden instinctively looked up at the top of the cliff face where Abby stood looking down at him.

"Pat, I came up here to watch after you," she called, smiling.

"You black witch!" the gunman yelled. His arm had been numbed by the rock and he struggled to lift his gun.

Patrick took his chance and dived for his gun belt. His glasses flew off his nose, but he grabbed his Colt as Merden turned on him. At a range of only a couple of feet, he fanned three shots into Merden's belly. The bullets ranged upward into the gunman's chest and staggered him.

Merden made no attempt to return fire. A prejudiced man of deep-seated hatreds, he ignored Patrick and thumbed two quick shots at Abby. "Damn you," he screamed. Dying on his feet, he was still a gunfighter to be reckoned with. Both his bullets slammed into the girl's frail body.

Abby shrieked as she crumpled and fell from the cliff wall, crashing hard onto the rocky arroyo floor.

Patrick saw Merden as a fuzzy image and fired

his two remaining shots at the gunman. Both missed, but it didn't matter. Still standing, his eyes staring and a primitive snarl frozen on his lips, Merden was dead.

Stepping to the man, Patrick pushed him in the chest and Merden's body fell back and lay sprawled on the ground. He grimaced and turned toward where Abby lay. He wanted to thank her for saving his life. He wanted to take her hand in his and thank her again and again. But the girl was beyond hearing. Her short, miserable life had reached its end.

Stepping to his hat, Patrick lifted it carefully and let the butterfly go. To his surprise, it fluttered around his head and landed on his hand where it stayed for several minutes before flying away.

In later years, Patrick would say that somehow Abby's soul had entered the butterfly for a while and had tried to comfort him. At least, that's how he very much wanted to believe it had been.

Attracted by the gunshots, Shawn was the first to arrive at the arroyo.

Patrick told his story and then Shawn, a caring man, held his brother in his arms and comforted him as best he could.

When the colonel and Ironside rode up on the

arroyo they read the story from the bodies and silently agreed to let Patrick tell it again at his own pace and in his own time.

It was nightfall by the time Ironside led Jacob and the wagon to the arroyo where a fire burned and coffee simmered. "Near missed him. I was about to give up when I seen him in the distance."

"Jake, where is Dallas?" Shawn asked.

"He got shot." Jacob told his story, and as one gunfighter acknowledging the skill of another, added, "Condor made his stand and he was fast on the draw."

The silence that followed was broken by Shamus. "And where is Dallas now, Jacob?"

"He has a good doctor attending him and is staying with a priest I met."

"Hell, that will kill the poor sod fast enough," Ironside mumbled.

"What did you say, Luther?" Shamus asked.

"Nothing, Colonel. I didn't say nothing."

"I should hope not," Shamus said, frowning. "Holy Mother Church appoints her priests to be the good shepherds of her flock. I am sure Dallas is in excellent hands."

Shamus waited as moment then said, "What did you say, Luther?"

"Nothing, Colonel. I didn't say nothing."

"I should hope not."

Shawn suppressed a grin. "Well Jake, where do we go from here?"

"Now that Patrick's butterfly hunting has led us to the gold stashed in the arroyo, we should take it back to Silver City and hand it over to the army. Then take our leave of Dallas."

"And return to Dromore," Shamus said. "Thank the good Lord. I'm anxious to see my grandson again."

"That sounds like a fine plan," Ironside said.

"For once, Luther, it seems that we can agree on something," the colonel said.

"We always agree on Dromore, Colonel," Ironside said.

Shamus nodded. "I should hope so."

Chapter Fifty

It was early October and winter's first dusting of snow lay around Dromore. Frost had turned the pines to arrowheads of crystal and a hollow moon horned aside the stars over Glorieta Mesa. The hard, cold air smelled like raw iron and chilled to the bone.

A log burned in the fireplace of the Dromore parlor where the O'Briens had gathered after dinner for coffee and brandy.

"So read us Dallas Steele's letter, Jake," Luther Ironside said.

"You surprise me, Luther. I didn't know you cared," Patrick said.

"Hell, he was a dude, but he had bark on him," Ironside said. "I like that in a man."

"I don't feel like reading the whole letter, Luther, but the gist of it is that the army was delighted to get its money back. One of their cavalry patrols found Silas Shaw's body in the desert. The man had shot himself. On a happier note, the Pinkertons sent Dallas, under the supervision of a doctor I might add, to Denver to recuperate from his wound." Jacob smiled. "It seems he met a young lady on his return and she's caring for him very well."

Ironside nodded. "Better her than a"—he caught Shamus's glare and grabbed for a lifeline—"sawbones in Silver City."

"I agree with that," Shawn said, grinning. "Almost stepped in it again, didn't you, Luther?"

Shamus let his glower scorch Ironside for a few moments then said, "Jacob, will you remain at Dromore for Christmas?"

Jacob nodded. "I'd love to, Colonel."

"I plan to invite the neighboring ranchers," Shamus said. "We'll have a big soiree this year and entertainers if such can be found."

"If not, I can read Mr. Dickens' novel, *A Christmas Carol,* to the assembled company," Patrick said, his face eager. He pushed his glasses higher on his nose. "I imagine it will be very well received."

"Yes . . . yes of course," Shamus said. "But I'm sure we can find some musicians in Santa Fe who'd be willing to make the trip."

Ironside said, "Hey, Colonel, there's a feller u

there they call Yodeling Bill Yaxley. He sings and dances and plays the banjo. I could get ol' Bill to come down."

"Not quite the kind of musician I had in mind, Luther," Shamus said. "But I'll take it into consideration."

Ironside warmed to his subject. "Bill brings a plump little gal with him who does a dance called the seven veils or some such. Now what's her name . . . Sophie? . . . nah, it's not that."

"Salome?" Patrick suggested.

Ironside's face brightened. "Yeah, that's it, Pat, Salome. Man, she strips to the—"

"I rather fancy," Lorena said, "that a plump little gal named Salome and her seven veils would be the hit of the Christmas party."

"Damn right," Ironside said.

As the O'Brien brothers fought to hide grins, Shamus coughed, then said, "As I told you, Luther, I'll take your suggestion into consideration."

"Don't wait too long, Colonel. Bill and Salome are a popular act," Ironside said.

"Indeed," Shamus said, the tone of his voice indicating that the discussion was closed.

The parlor door opened and the butler stepped inside. "Begging your pardon, but there's a gentleman in the foyer who wishes to speak to Mr. Jacob. He says his name is Dr. John Henry Holliday."

Shawn looked at his brother. "Jake, is that the one and only Doc Holliday?"

"Judging by the sinking feeling I've got in my belly, it can be no other," Jacob said.

"Hadn't you better go talk to him, Jacob?" Shamus said. "And remember, we offer the hospitality of Dromore to any honest traveler."

Jacob rose to his feet. "Doc is a traveler all right, but no one ever called him honest." He headed to the foyer.

Wearing a long black coat with a velvet collar and a plug hat, Doc Holliday stood in the drafty foyer, a carpetbag at his feet. Thin and frail, the gray shadows of death in his face, he looked like a walking cadaver.

"How are you, Doc?" Jacob said. He did not extend his hand.

"I need your help, Jake," Doc said, his voice a faint whisper. "I'm in big trouble."

At that moment, Jacob O'Brien knew so was he.

TURN THE PAGE
FOR AN EXCITING PREVIEW

Welcome to the peaceful little town of Doubtful, Wyoming, which has more than its fair share of kill-crazy gunslicks, back-shooters, and flat-out dirty desperadoes. It also has a sheriff named Cotton Pickens, who tries his best to keep law and order without getting his head blown off before breakfast.

DOUBTFUL'S GOT A NEW DEPUTY . . .
FOR THE MOMENT

Cotton Pickens got where he is by virtue of a quick draw and slow wit. He knows the difference between lawbreakers you have to lock up . . . and the kind you might as well just let go. Deputy Rusty Irons, though, ain't the sharpest tool in the shed. Someone kidnapped his mail-order brides. They were probably doing him a favor, but a deputy in love is blind.

As for the various carny barkers, medicine show con artists, and revival-meeting fly-by-nighters who pass through Doubtful, Cotton just tries to keep the peace and keep the traveling hucksters moving on. But in one terrible moment, it all goes straight to hell as the town explodes in a frenzy of killing and bloodshed. That's when a lawman like Cotton earns his pay, saves his soul, or loses his life by looking evil straight in the eye. Of course, there's also the matter of keeping his new deputy alive and in one piece.

SUPPORT YOUR LOCAL DEPUTY
A Cotton Pickens Western

by William W. Johnstone
with J. A. Johnstone

Coming in March 2013
wherever Pinnacle Books are sold.

Chapter One

My deputy, Rusty Irons, was as itchy as a man ever gets. We were at the Laramie and Overland stage station waiting for the maroon enameled Concord stage to roll in. He couldn't come up with proper bouquets, not in the barely settled cow town of Doubtful, Wyoming, but he managed some daisies and sagebrush he'd collected out on the range.

Rusty was waiting for his mail order brides. That's right, Siamese twins from the Ukraine, joined at the hip. He'd ordered just one, but they sent him the pair. He'd gotten the hundred-fifty-dollar reward offered for Huckster Bob, wanted dead or alive. Rusty got him alive, collected his reward, and applied the money to getting himself a wife.

So there we were, waiting for the stage to roll in. It was an hour late, maybe more.

Well, my ma always said there's nothing worse than a sweating bridegroom, and Rusty filled the bill. He had sweat running down his sides. His armpits had turned into gushers.

"Well . . . you get to be best man," Rusty sputtered.

"If I don't arrest you first for bigamy," I countered.

"I looked it up; there's no law in Wyoming Territory against it."

"Well, I'll arrest you for something or other," I said. "You found a preacher who'll tie the knot?"

"No, but I'm going to argue that all he has to do is marry me to one of 'em."

"What'll you do with the other?"

"I can't auction her off, so she gets to be the spectator."

"They speak English?"

"Not a word. They're from Lvov, Ukraine."

"Well, that's a good start. You won't get into arguments." I pointed out. "My ma always said the best part of her marriage was when my pa was snoring."

Rusty grinned. "You're the result."

I wasn't sure how to take that, but thought I'd let it pass without a fistfight. His armpits were leaking worse than ever and I didn't want his sweat all over my sheriff suit and pants.

"You figure they're joined facing the same way?" I asked.

"I wouldn't marry them if one was facing backwards. Here." He pulled out a tintype.

The image of two beautiful blondes leaped out at me. It looked like they were side by side, except they had a single dark skirt.

Rusty pointed to one of the women. "This one here's Natasha, and the other is Anna."

"You know which one you'll hitch up with?"

"We'll toss a coin. Or maybe they've got it worked out."

"What if one wants you and the other doesn't? Or you want one and not the other?"

Rusty, he just grinned. "Life sure is interesting."

Word had gotten out, and a small crowd had collected at the wooden stage office on Main Street. Some of the women squinted at Rusty as if he was a criminal, which maybe he was. But mostly they were wondering what sort of twisted beast would want to marry Siamese twins. Fifty of the good citizens of Doubtful stood in clumps, whispering and pointing at Rusty as if he belonged in the bottom layer of hell.

Rusty, he just smiled. "I'm glad you got me that raise."

"You'll need it," I replied.

I'd gone to the Puma County supervisors and talked them into raising Rusty's wage by five dollars, because of his impending wedlock and his faithful service as my best and most useful deputy. That put him up just two dollars below my forty-seven a month sheriff salary, but I didn't mind.

I saw Delphinium Sanders, the banker's wife, glaring as hard as she could manage at both of us. And George Waller, the mayor, was studying us as if we belonged in a zoo—which maybe we did. I sure didn't know how things would play out, or who'd marry whom, but it made a late spring day real entertaining in the cow town of Doubtful.

Hanging Judge Earwig was there too, and thought maybe he'd do the marrying if no one else would. Judge Earwig was broadminded, and didn't mind it if people thought ill of him. He might even marry both the twins to Rusty, seeing as how there wasn't any law against it. That'd come later, when the next legislature got moralistic. Or maybe Rusty could take his gals to Utah and find a Mormon cleric to fix him up, but I didn't put much stock in it. Utah had outlawed that sort of entertainment.

* * *

That stagecoach sure was late. Dry road, too. The dry spring meant no potholes or mud puddles. The waiting was hard on Rusty.

"Hey, Rusty, you got a two-holer, or are they gonna take turns?" some brat yelled.

I went after the freckled punk, got an ear and twisted it. "Cut that out or I'll throw you down a hole and you'll stink for a week."

"Aw, sheriff, this is the best thing to hit Doubtful in a long time."

"You're Willie Dickens, and your ma didn't raise you right. I let go of your ear, you promise to respect people?"

"Anything you say." Willie yanked loose, smirking.

I let him go. The whole thing was turning into an ordeal for my deputy sheriff, instead of a moment of joy. It wasn't hard to tell what all them good folks of Doubtful were thinking. The marriage would have a threesome in the bedroom.

And still no coach.

Then, about the time I was ready to head back to the sheriff office and look over the mail, we spotted the coach rounding the hill south of Doubtful. It was coming along at a smart clip, maybe faster than usual because them drays looked pretty lathered.

"Well, Rusty, here it comes," I said.

Jonas Quill, the jehu, pulled back the lines slightly, and the sweated horses gladly quit on him, while the coach rocked gently. He yelled down at me. "We got held up, man."

"Held up?"

"Four armed men, masked."

By then, the maroon door of the coach had swung open. Six passengers emerged; four rumpled males, mostly whiskey drummers, and two frightened women in bonnets, both gray-haired.

No Ukrainian Siamese identical female twins.

Rusty seemed to leak gas.

"Clear away from here," I yelled at the mob. "We got trouble."

"Where are they?" Rusty asked.

"Don't know, but we got business. Sheriff business." I looked at the six who had just gotten off the stagecoach. "You passengers, stick close here. I'll want statements from all of you."

One woman looked annoyed and started off.

"You, too, Mrs. Throckmorton."

"I surrender to my fate," she said, and kept on going.

Rusty looked shell-shocked, so it was up to me. "Quill, tell me. What happened and what got took?"

"Nothing got took. Just the twins."

"My mind isn't quite biting this cookie, Quill."

"Three masked men on saddle horses, another in a chariot."

"A what?"

"A two-wheel chariot hung on two trotters. Man driving it was masked, too."

"A chariot like them gladiators used?"

"A two-wheel stand-up cart, with a lot of gold gilt and enameled red on it. They stop my coach, one has a scattergun aimed at me. They open the door, point it at the twins, and say "ladies get out," but the twins, they don't speak a word of English, so the masked men prod the ladies out with their revolvers. That takes some doing, four legs, one skirt, but they get the Siamese twins out, get them into the chariot, and the man with the whip smacks the butts of those trotters and away they go, the three of them standing in that chariot."

"That's it?"

"The others want the twins' luggage, and they load it on a packhorse."

"And you didn't fight it?"

"They made us drop our weapons," one of the drummers said.

"What else did they take? The mail? Anything in the lockbox?"

"Nope," said Quill. "The foreign women and their bags, is all."

"Did they give any reasons?"

"They said not to shoot 'cause we'd hit the women, and that was true. They headed due west, over some off-road route."

"Good, we'll have some tracks to follow," I said.

"Them were my brides," Rusty complained.

"Real purty, they were. But sure hobbled up." Quill frowned. "I can see the direction your steamy little brain's taking, Irons."

It was getting a little out of hand.

"Rusty, you interview the male passengers, and I'll interview these women. Meanwhile, you people, clear out of here." I waved my arms to shoo them out.

But no one moved. Half the town, it seemed, had flooded in.

Rusty and I got what we could from the passengers. Nothing was taken except the Ukrainians. No one was forced to empty pockets. No valuables ended up in bandit pockets. The kidnappers were young, well masked, rode easily, wore wide-brimmed hats and jeans and dirty boots. They were polite with no apparent accents and offered no reasons. Treated courteously by the bandits, the Ukrainian twins went peaceably, not understanding a bit. They were even smiling.

"Were they hostages? Will they be returned for a reward?" Rusty asked the drummers.

"Nope, no sign of it," said one in a black bowler.

"Who'd want female Siamese twins?" Rusty asked.

"They were real lookers," another salesman ventured.

Rusty whipped out his tintype. "These the ones?"

They studied the black and white a while. "Not sure, but seems so," one said.

"Did these women seem in distress?"

"Nope, they thought it was all pretty merry."

The passengers had been detained long enough, so me and Rusty cut them loose, cut the jehu loose, and headed for Turk's Livery Barn. We had some hard riding in front of us.

Chapter Two

Rusty, he wanted a posse. He was plumb irate. Them was his brides got stolen, and he was rooting around, looking for ways to hang the wife-rustlers at the nearest cottonwood tree.

"Hey, cool off," I said. "Go saddle up and take some fixings. I'll get Critter, and we'll get this deal shut down in no time."

"Who'll run the office?'

"I'll send Burtell," I said, referring to a part-time deputy.

"I want a posse. That was Anna and Natasha got took. I want plenty of armed men."

"This'll be the easiest kidnapping we ever solved. Where can they hide? We got some dudes in a red and gold chariot, kidnapping beautiful Siamese twins in one skirt, and they speak Ukraine, whatever the tongue is. We got 'em cold, Rusty."

He didn't want to believe it, and I didn't blame him. He got robbed out of two real pretty gals, and a lot of real fine nights once he got hitched to one or the other . . . or both.

But my ma, she used to say twins were double the trouble. She'd settle for twin cocker spaniels, but not any pair that would put her out some. In truth, if we got them joined-up twins back, I wasn't sure Rusty could handle the deal.

He turned toward the office where he'd left his horse and I turned toward Turk's Livery Barn, fixing to saddle up Critter the Second. The first got his throat slit, and I looked hard before I found the Second, who was meaner than the first, so it worked out all right. I don't know what I'd do with a gentle horse. Horses are like women. If they don't buck when you're riding them, they're no good.

Critter was out in the yard, which wasn't good. He kicked down any stall he got put into, so Turk often put him outside. I got the bridle and went after him, and sure enough, he headed for a corner in the fence and waited for me, his rear hoofs itchy to land on me. I tried moving along one rail and he switched that way, so I tried the other rail, and he switched that way.

"Critter, dammit, we're going to look for some women. Or one woman. I don't have it straight. So shape up," I yelled.

He turned and eyed me, and settled down. I bridled, and brushed, and saddled him without trouble. Critter was a philosopher.

"Dog food," called Rusty as he led his horse toward the barn. "He needs to be turned into dog food."

"I won't argue with it," I called back.

"Shouldn't we have a buggy or a cart?" Rusty asked. He was thinking about how to transport the Ukrainian ladies. You can't expect Siamese twins to climb up on a horse, but maybe a pair of horses would work if they crowded close.

He was armed to the teeth, with a saddle gun and a pair of mean-looking Peacemakers hanging from his skinny hips. He was gonna get his women back, even if he burned some powder. "You got any idea why them gals got took?"

"It sure is interesting," I replied.

* * *

Turk spotted us. "You going after them stage robbers?"

Rusty nodded. "That's my women they took."

"Double the feedbags," Turk pointed out. "You sure got odd tastes."

That was my private opinion, but I wasn't voicing it. Rusty was the best deputy I had, and I didn't want to rile him up.

Word spread through town like melted butter, and they were all watching as we rode out. Mostly watching Rusty, not me. The women stood along Main Street with pursed lips, and I could read their every thought.

Soon we were trotting down the Laramie Road, heading for the ambush spot, so I could see what was to be seen, and we could see what the chariot wheels did to the turf. It should be easy enough to follow that cart, and with a little luck I'd have the bandits in manacles and heading for my lockup in a day or two.

Rusty, he sure was silent.

"What are you thinking, Rusty?"

"Maybe I won't marry after all. They'll be plumb ruined. I was marrying double virgins, and now look at it. It's a mess."

"You sure got big appetites, Rusty. Double everything—double marriage, double honeymoon, double household, double mouths to feed."

"Yeah, that's me," he said, a little smirky. Somehow he was seeing that he was double the rest of us. He looked over at me. "What if they both expect babies at the same time, eh?"

I didn't push it. Life sure was going to be interesting.

Critter loved to get out, and he was pretty near popping along. Rusty's nag had to trot now and then to catch up. We were riding through empty country, nothing but hills and sagebrush, and not worth anything except to a coyote. But that was Wyoming for you. Ninety percent worthless, ten percent pretty fine.

It took us about three hours to reach the ambush place, well chosen to hide the ambushers behind a curve in the road. The jehu had given me a pretty good idea of it. There were signs around there, all right—some iron tire tracks, some hoofprints, some handkerchiefs, and plenty of boot-heel dimples in the dun clay.

And sure enough, the iron-tire tracks led straight west, off the road and over open prairie, so we followed them.

"We'll nail 'em, Rusty. How can we lose? Look at them tracks, smooth and hard."

But the tracks gradually turned and finally came entirely around and headed for the Laramie

Road, maybe a mile south of where the ambush happened. And there they disappeared. Those clean iron-tire tracks vanished. We messed around there a while, widening out, looking for the tracks, but it was as if that chariot had taken off from the earth and rolled on up into heaven.

Rusty was having the same sweats as me. That just couldn't be. Big red and gold chariots didn't just vanish—unless through the Pearly Gates. I wondered about that for a while. Were them Ukrainian ladies taken on up?

The road had plenty of traffic showing on it, and we scouted it one way and then the other, checking hoof prints, poking at ruts, and kicking horse turds, but the fact was, the kidnappers had ridden off into the sky, and were rolling across cumulus, or maybe thunderheads, to some place or other.

"You got any fancy theories, Cotton?" Rusty sure looked gloomy. Like he had been deprived of a night with two of the prettiest gals ever born.

"We could ride on down to Laramie and see what's what," I said.

"Who'd want 'em?" Rusty asked.

"Some horny old rancher, I imagine."

"Well, there's no man on earth hornier then me." It was dawning on Rusty that he'd lost his mail order bride—or brides, I never could get that straight—and he was sinking into a sort of darkness. I thought it was best to leave him alone. "I'll get ahold of the sheriff, Milt Boggs, and tell him what's missing, and for him to let us know if we got a red chariot and two hipshot blondes floating around southern Wyoming."

"We catch them, what are you going to charge them with?" Rusty wanted to know.

"Now that's an interesting question," I said. "My ma used to say people confess if you give them the chance."

"Well, she inherited all the brains in your family," Rusty said, just to be mean.

Truth to tell, my mind was on what might happen when we got back to Doubtful without two hip-tied blondes and a red chariot and a mess of crooks trudging along in front of my shotgun. Townspeople'd be telling me to quit, or maybe trying to fire me again. Seems every time I didn't catch the crook or stop the killer, they wanted to fire me. I've spent more time in front of the county supervisors trying to save my sheriff job than I've spent running my office.

About dusk, we got back in town, and all we raised were a few smirks. Like no one thought that kidnapping Siamese twins from the Ukraine was worth getting lathered up about. Especially when it was all Rusty's problem. He's the only one got shut out of some entertainment. So we rode in by our lonesome selves without a parade of bandits and bad men parading in front, and without those brides. People sort of smiled smartly, and planned to make some jokes, and maybe petition the supervisors to get rid of me, and that was that.

Me, I felt the same way. If Rusty hadn't mail-ordered the most exotic womanhood this side of Morocco, it never would've happened.

Turk showed up out of the gloom soon as we rode into his livery barn. "Told you so."

"Told us what?"

"That you'd botch another job again."

I was feeling a little put out with him, and if there were any other livery barns in town, I would have moved Critter then and there. My horse chewed on any wood he could get his big buck teeth around, and sometimes Turk sent me a bill for repairs, but I could hardly blame Turk for that.

Rusty unsaddled, turned out his nag, and disappeared. He was feeling real blue, and I didn't blame him.

"Hey," Turk said, "while you gents were out the

Laramie Road, chasing Ukrainian women, a medicine show came up the Cheyenne Road and set up outside of town."

"Medicine show?"

"None other. Doctor Zoroaster Zimmer's Three Way Tonic for digestion, thick hair, and virility. Three dollars the six-ounce bottle, thirty-five dollars a dozen. And you get to watch a juggler, belly dancer, an accordion player, and a dog and pony act, and then lay out cash for the medicine."

"Zimmer? Seems to me he's on a wanted dodger in my office. Whenever he hits town, jewelry and gold coins start vanishing, and dogs howl in the night. I think his tonic's mostly opium, peppermint and creek water, but I'll find out."

"Yeah, Sheriff, and guess what? I wandered over there to have a gander. He's driving a big red-enameled outfit with gold trim. But there's no chariots or Ukrainian blondes in sight."

Chapter Three

Doubtful, it had growed some, and was fixed in the middle of some of the best Wyoming ranch country around. So there were plenty of people in the Puma County seat, and also plenty more out herding cows and growing hogs and collecting eggs from chickens. There were even some horse breeders around town, most of them raising remounts for the cavalry.

The town was half civilized. I knew the rough times were over when some gal named Matilda opened up a hattery. I don't know the proper name of a hat shop, but it don't matter. Hattery is what she operated, and she did nothing but sell bonnets and straw hats full of fake fruit to the town's ladies. And gossip, too. All the local gals went in there to gossip about the rest of us. Sometimes I got a little itchy about sheriffing in a halfway-civilized town and thought I should pack up and head for the tropics.

But my ma, she always said don't shoot a gift horse between the eyes, and that's how I looked at my job.

That eve, Rusty quit early on me, and headed off to his cabin to nurse his disappointment. He had his heart set on marrying the Ukrainian beauties, and never having to have a conversation with his women because he wouldn't understand a word they said. I thought it was a fool's dream, myself. What if they was saying mean things about him, in their own tongue, maybe even at night with the pair of them lying beside him?

The town was drawing everything from whiskey drummers to medicine shows these days, and I intended to get out to the east side to have a close look. Half the shows rolling through the country roads of the West were nothing but gyppo outfits, looking to con cash out of the local folks, while swiping everything that wasn't nailed down tight. And if they could get a few girls in trouble while robbing citizens and peddling worthless stuff, they did that, too, and smiled all the way to the next berg.

I'd wander over there. But first I'd patrol Doubtful, as I did every evening—wearing my badge, walking from place to place, rattling doors to see if they were locked, and studying saloons closely to see if there was trouble. Sometimes there was, and the barkeeps would be glad I wandered in at a moment when some drunken cowboy, armed to the teeth, was picking a fight.

So I did my rounds, seeing that all was quiet at Maxwell's Funeral Parlor, and no one was busting the doors at Hubert Sanders' Merchant Bank. I peered into Barney's Beanery, and saw that it was winding down for the eve, and peered into the dark confines of Leonard Silver's Emporium. I checked the office of Lawyer Stokes, and saw no one rifling his file cabinets. McGivers' Saloon was quiet, and so was the Last Chance, where I saw Sammy Upward yawning, his elbows on the bar, looking ready to close early.

There were a few posters promoting Dr. Zoroaster Zimmer's show. The man had a string of initials behind his name, but I never could figure out what all they meant, but the PhD meant he was a doctor of philandery or something like that. The KGB puzzled me, but someone told me it was British and had to do with garters and bathtubs. You never know what gets into foreigners. At any rate, Professor Zimmer had them all, and they followed his name like a line of railroad cars.

I thought I'd like to meet the gent.

Denver Sally's place, back behind saloon row, looked quiet, the evening breezes rocking the red lantern beside her door. Most of her business came on weekends. The Gates of Heaven, next door, looked as mean as ever. Who knows all the ways a feller wants to get rid of his cash?

Doubtful was peaceful enough, that spring evening. So it was time to drift out beyond saloon row, east of town and take a gander at this here medicine-man show. A mess of those shows were wandering through the whole country, setting up in dark corners of little towns, and running an act or two across a stage set up on a wagon. The medicine man would step out and peddle his stuff, and when he gauged he'd done all the selling he could, he'd pull up stakes and head for the next little town and do it all over again.

Sure enough, east of town on an alkali flat, a couple of torches were going.

I moseyed closer and saw two fancy red and gilt wagons—one with a lamplit stage—and a makeshift rope corral with some moth-eaten drays in it. Maybe twelve, fifteen suckers were watching a jet-haired woman in a grass skirt wiggle her butt and make her bosom heave. I'd never seen that, and it seemed entertaining, but I had sheriff business to do, namely, look for a red and gilt chariot, and two blond Ukrainian women joined at the hip.

It took a quick prowl around the rear of the place, and into the other wagon, to satisfy myself no one was hiding a chariot or Siamese twins, blond or any other color. Whoever kidnapped the ladies, it wasn't that miserable outfit.

I spotted a gent smoking a cigar back there, and thought he might have some answers. He saw the glint of my badge even before we spoke. He sucked on his gummy cheroot, and knocked off the ash.

"You looking for something, Sheriff?"

"Just keeping an eye on things. How many people you got in this outfit?"

"Six and the professor."

"Any women?"

He stared at me as if I were an idiot. "That's Elvira Smoothpepper out there. And we got Elsie Sanchez, the Argentine firecracker."

"No Ukrainian blondes?"

"You got eyes, don'tcha?"

"Who else's in the show?"

"Sheriff, there ain't anyone with a wanted poster on him. There's me and another teamster. He's the accordionist, and there's a tap dancer named Fogarty, and the professor."

"What does the professor sell? What's his medicine?"

The gent smiled. "Try it sometime and come back and tell me."

"Any chariots around here?"

"Any what?"

"Oh, never mind."

"You all right, Sheriff? Want to lie down? That second wagon, it's got bunks. Had a little too much?"

"Who's the professor?"

"He's whatever he is at any moment. Right now, he's a medicine man, and he's working the rubes for a few bucks."

"Yeah, well I'll go watch the show," I said.

"It beats pissing on a fence post."

Half of the crowd was cowboys, out from the saloons. I recognized a few, most of them that hung out at Mrs. Gladstone's Sampling Room. They were tied up with the Admiral Ranch, other side of the county. But there were some locals too, including the mayor, George Waller, who looked embarrassed when he saw me.

"I just came to view the competition." Waller was a merchant, and any outfit that sold anything was competition, as far as he was concerned. "Maybe you should arrest the whole lot."

"What for?"

"They're all crooks."

"Well, that's progress. You show me one act of crookery, and I'll pinch the person straight off."

Elvira Smoothpepper was making her belly roll and the grass skirts sway, and that was pretty entertaining. The accordionist got to wheezing away, and pretty soon the act creaked to a stop.

and out came Professor Zoroaster Zimmer, in black silk top hat, tux and tails, and a grimy white vest that looked a little worse for wear.

I'd never seen the like.

He spotted me at once, and welcomed me. "Ladies and gents, here's the sheriff of, ah, Puma County, Wyoming. Come to see our little show, and maybe endorse my product, namely, the Zimmer Miracle Tonic, guaranteed to cure piles, insomnia, gout, St. Vitus Dance, and all bowel troubles. Welcome, Mr. Sheriff.

"Now, esteemed friends, I want to tell you about a product that should need no introducing, since it sells itself. You need only ask your neighbor, who has the remedy on his shelf, ready to use, and you'll see how effective is. Mr. Sheriff, please come up."

"Me?"

"Of course, you. Step right up, my friend."

"I haven't got anything ailing me, Doc."

"Oh, my friend, do you have restless nights? Toss and turn nights?"

"Naw, I sleep like a log."

"Do you ache after a long day on your horse?"

"Now, you're talking about Critter, the orneriest critter on four legs. Yes, I'll allow that I ache some after a long ride on that beast."

"Were you out on him today, Sheriff?"

"Pretty near the whole blasted day, Professor."

"Then you must feel weary, right down to the bone."

"Well, we were out looking for some blond Ukrainian women who are attached at the hip. They plain disappeared."

The crowd got mostly dead silent, and a couple of snickers came from some of them cowboys.

"I think you are very weary, sir, after a day of searching for blond Ukrainian women. Are you a bit worn?"

"I am done in."

"Well, perfect. I would truly like to have you sample Doctor Zimmer's Tonic and report the results to all these fine folks."

"My ma, she used to say, one drink is enough."

"Oh, this is not drink, sir. This is an elixir to balm the soul, elevate mood, celebrate life, and rejoice in your own splendid body. Now how old are you?"

"I forget; past thirty, anyway."

"Ah, the shady side of thirty. Let me tell you, my friend, that is when Doctor Zoroaster Zimmer's Tonic works wonders the fastest. It works wonders at any age, sir, but especially after thirty."

The maestro of this here event reached for a bottle of the stuff, which was sitting on a little shelf with a gold halo around it, so the bottle looked like a saint.

He sure was smiling. He grabbed that stuff, and pulled the cork, and poured a little into a tumbler, and handed it to me, while all them cowboys and Mayor George Waller watched.

I remembered what my ma used to say, no guts, no glory, and I downed the stuff in one gulp.

Well, it took a moment to work through me, like a glow of a lot of fireflies, and then I plumb keeled over. The accordionist caught me going down.